KU-865-023

ANGELA DRACUP

A KIND
OF JUSTICE

Complete and Unabridged

ULVERSCROFT
Leicester

First published in Great Britain in 2005 by
Robert Hale Limited
London

First Large Print Edition
published 2006
by arrangement with
Robert Hale Limited
London

The moral right of the author has been asserted

Copyright © 2005 by Angela Dracup
All rights reserved

British Library CIP Data

Dracup, Angela
    A kind of justice.—Large print ed.—
    Ulverscroft large print series: crime
    1. Amnesia—Fiction 2. Recovered memory—Fiction
    3. Detective and mystery stories 4. Large type books
    I. Title
    823.9′14 [F]

    ISBN 1–84617–134–2

Gloucestershire County
Council Library

992939479 6

SPECIAL MESSAGE TO READERS

This book is published under the auspices of

THE ULVERSCROFT FOUNDATION

(registered charity No. 264873 UK)

Established in 1972 to provide funds for research, diagnosis and treatment of eye diseases. Examples of contributions made are: —

A Children's Assessment Unit at Moorfield's Hospital, London.

•

Twin operating theatres at the Western Ophthalmic Hospital, London.

•

A Chair of Ophthalmology at the Royal Australian College of Ophthalmologists.

•

The Ulverscroft Children's Eye Unit at the Great Ormond Street Hospital For Sick Children, London.

You can help further the work of the Foundation by making a donation or leaving a legacy. Every contribution, no matter how small, is received with gratitude. Please write for details to:

THE ULVERSCROFT FOUNDATION, The Green, Bradgate Road, Anstey, Leicester LE7 7FU, England. Telephone: (0116) 236 4325

In Australia write to:
THE ULVERSCROFT FOUNDATION, c/o The Royal Australian and New Zealand College of Ophthalmologists, 94-98 Chalmers Street, Surry Hills, N.S.W. 2010, Australia

Angela Dracup was born and educated in Bradford and read psychology at Sheffield and Manchester Universities. She is a chartered psychologist and works with education authorities to assess the needs of children with learning and behavioural problems. She is married with one daughter and lives in Harrogate, North Yorkshire.

A KIND OF JUSTICE

Josie Parker is found drowned in the bath on her wedding night. The circumstances indicate murder and DCI Ed Swift is forced to regard the distraught bride-groom, Jamie, as chief suspect. But Jamie claims to have lost all recall of the time leading up to his bride's death. When Swift investigates the family dynamics of the newlyweds he uncovers a shocking trail of deceit and treachery. Then Swift takes Jamie back to the scene of the crime and the young widower recaptures his buried memories. Swift must reveal the truth behind Josie's killing if justice is, finally, to be done.

Books by Angela Dracup
Published by The House of Ulverscroft:

THE ULTIMATE GIFT
AN INDEPENDENT SPIRIT
A TENDER AMBITION

*To Frank, with thanks
for all his love and support*

Prologue

Momentous thoughts passed through Josephine Haygarth's mind as she walked up the aisle to join her bridegroom. The tension in his face relaxed as she smiled at him. She knew he was nervous; his whole being yearning to please her, to match what he saw as her perfection, both for today and for the rest of his life. She was his woman, his own unique person, his lover, his idol. Adoration spilled from his eyes as she moved to stand beside him. She recognized the power she had over him and her heart banged in warning against her ribs. She projected herself into the future, as she had done so many times in the past weeks. She knew she had made the right decision. And yet there was still conflict, a lingering uncertainty she had schooled herself to hide. She was aware of living feverishly in the moment and thrilling at the prospect of what lay ahead. But there was dread too.

The one thought which did not trouble her at all was that of death. Death was an infinity away. She was a creature of youth and life. But as she began to recite her marriage vows,

Josephine had, in fact, six hours of life left to her. Murderers don't make a habit of giving their victims warning. Frequently they themselves have no prior knowledge of the evil they are about to perpetrate.

1

It was just before eleven p.m. as Sue Sallis turned her car into the gateway of the Moorlands Hotel. Lights blazed from the long windows along the frontage, and beyond the heavy glass entry doors she could see a cluster of figures awaiting her arrival. Easing herself from the air-conditioned cool of the car into the August evening she felt the heat surround her like a warm veil. The sun had been shining with deadly persistence for the past three weeks, parching plants and lawns and draining the reservoirs of the Washburn Valley. Summer flu was running through Yorkshire; a silent, invisible invader against which there seemed little defence. Schools, hospitals and workplaces were running on skeleton staffs and elderly people were dying in worrying numbers.

Sue held out her warrant card as she passed between the open glass entrance doors and stepped into the foyer. A navy-suited man in his thirties separated himself from the group and came forward, his face a mask of grim solemnity.

3

'John Ford, hotel manager,' he said formally.

'Detective Sergeant Susan Sallis,' she told him. 'The doctor contacted us.'

'Yes. I'm afraid there's been a terrible . . . accident.'

The hushed, shocked group behind him shifted their stance, fastening their eyes on the young officer as though seeking some sort of guidance.

She nodded briefly to the manager. 'Will you show me where to go?'

He led her to the lifts. 'Could you fill me in?' she said crisply, as the doors slid shut. 'I've simply been informed that one of your guests has been found dead. We're rather thin on the ground at headquarters, several officers down with flu. Communications are similarly thin, unfortunately.'

'It's same for us,' he agreed. 'We've had a wedding party in today. A hundred guests and a third of the staff off sick. Somehow we've managed to get them all fed and watered. And now . . . this.' His sigh conveyed regret with a faint dash of irritation. 'I have to say,' he added stiffly, 'despite all due respect to the distress of those bereaved, that I hope the body can be moved as soon and as unobtrusively as possible.'

Sue noticed that he was holding himself

rigid, his face now white with anxiety and foreboding. 'I had thought the doctor would have no concerns about what to record on the death certificate,' he ventured with faint disapproval, 'but he was insistent that the police must be informed.'

Sue nodded acknowledgement. She waited for a moment, but Ford kept silent. 'And what is your view, sir?'

'I'm sure this death was an accident,' Ford informed her, although his obvious anxiety seemed to belie his words.

'What makes you say that?' Sue had been completely frank about her scanty knowledge of the circumstances of this death. It would be interesting to hear Ford's account at this early stage, especially in the privacy of the lift where a manager's professional discretion would perhaps be less guarded than in a public arena. She waited for a brief description of the events.

'It would be appalling enough if this had been an accident, but if it were to emerge that there's been a killing — well that would be a total tragedy. For such a thing to happen on this day.' He stopped. The lift shuddered to a halt. She saw that the manager's hand was trembling as he reached out for the button to release the lift doors.

Swiftly Sue reached up and pressed the

close button. 'Could you elaborate on that, sir?'

He took in a breath. 'The dead woman is the bride,' he said.

★   ★   ★

Stepping out of the lift into a thickly carpeted corridor lit with dimmed overhead spotlights, Sue saw a small clump of people huddled outside a door a few yards to her left. One of the men detached himself from the group and came up to her. 'Are you from the police?' he asked. He was a thin, smallish man of around sixty, his face lined and wolflike, yet filled with unmistakable authority. This was a man used to taking the lead, taking charge, even in the most desperate of circumstances.

'Detective Sergeant Sallis,' she told him. 'And you are?'

'Clive Parker,' he fired back at her. 'The father of the bridegroom.' His gaze was glinting and fierce, putting Sue on her mettle.

'Is the doctor still here?' she asked.

Parker nodded. 'One or two of the guests were showing signs of hysteria, so he's been offering advice. But I should imagine he's anxious to be on his way. The man's already told me there's no more he can do.'

'Right. I'll speak to him now,' Sue said,

6

curiously impressed by this man's unshake-able composure. The tightness of his features betrayed his shock and distress, yet his command of himself was enviable. Especially, she reminded herself, if he had had anything to do with the girl's death. Sue was experienced enough to know the importance of regarding even the most harmless seeming witnesses as being in the frame at the start of the investigation.

Parker was standing very still, his sharp, astute gaze fastened on Sue's face. For a moment she braced herself for his possible request that she listened to his version of events before seeing the doctor and the scene of the crime. As a young female officer she had been subjected to one or two such demands from powerful older men. But Parker simply turned his gaze to the waiting silent group beside the door, saying quietly, 'The doctor's in there. With my son.'

As Sue walked forward the group parted to let her pass, their faces stony and tragic. The room was furnished in dark, dramatic colours; bronze paper on the walls and heavy burgundy drapes at the windows and on the bed. The only light came from a single table lamp on the mahogany dressing-table by the window.

Inwardly Sue braced herself, preparing for

that moment when the full horror of sudden death kicks in with its shivery currents of shock — a sensation which did not diminish however many times one had experienced it before. This evening, as her eyes assessed the scenario, she felt the hairs on her neck lift. A young man dressed in black trousers and a white shirt was half sitting, half lying on the huge four poster bed which dominated the room. Cradled in his arms was a young woman wrapped in a white bath sheet. Her dark hair was loose, falling around her shoulders in thick waves. The pale skin of her arms gleamed in the dull glow of the lamp. She was wearing full make-up, bronze eye-shadow, blusher, rose pink lipstick. Film star beautiful. The two of them looked as though they had taken in a long breath and then frozen. The man gave no indication of having registered Sue's arrival. In fact, although she could see the insistent flicker of a pulse in his temple, he seemed to be in some kind of trance.

Looking down at the two of them Sue had a sudden memory of the story of the sleeping beauty, the princess's hundred year sleep and her eventual awakening by her prince's kiss. But this wretched couple were not going to have anything like the happy ending that crowned the fairy story. Some evil wizard of fate, or of flesh and blood, had already stolen all their happiness and good luck away.

The doctor, who had been sitting quietly in a corner of the room got up and stepped forward to introduce himself. Sue recognized the gaunt, silver-haired doctor as a retired partner from one of the local practices. She presumed he'd been called on to do locum work given the current strain on medical personnel since the epidemic took a grip.

'I can't stay much longer,' he told Sue with brisk apology. 'I'm trying to cover for twice as many practices as normal — and there's nothing much more I can do for either of them.'

'Fair enough,' Sue agreed. 'Cause of death?'

'I can't really say. The circumstances are somewhat confused. But, for what it's worth, my examination suggested the dead woman was fit and healthy just before she died. I've also been in touch with her family doctor who's a former colleague. There's no known history of any condition such as epilepsy or cardiac disease that might be linked to the cause of death. Oh, and she went down with the flu two weeks ago and made a swift recovery. So that's another thing to rule out.'

There was a silence. Sue was conscious of a current of dark sensation crawling over her scalp. It looked as though she was at the scene of a suspicious death which could well turn out to be a murder. The doctor had no need to spell things out.

'Her name is Josephine Haygarth,' he told Sue. 'Well, I suppose her name is now Josephine Parker,' he amended. 'The marriage was at three o'clock this afternoon.'

Sue stepped forward and placed her fingers on the woman's white neck, trying not to look into the watery stare of her dark blue eyes. The soft flesh was free from any pulse or twitch of life and the warmth was beginning to drain from it. This particular princess would never wake up. Sue felt her nerves jump as the man holding the body suddenly shot out a protective hand, warding Sue off as though she were a trouble-some insect.

'She is dead,' the doctor said quietly. 'There's no chance of revival procedures being any use.'

Sue inclined her head. 'How long?'

'Around two hours, in my opinion. That fits with what the manager told me as regards the time the incident was reported to him.'

Sue looked at her watch. 'About nine then?'

'Yes.'

'And the man with her is the bridegroom?'

'Yes. Poor chap. What a wedding night.'

'And the 'circumstances'?'

'Apparently Josephine's husband found her collapsed in the bath. He pulled her out.'

Sue's forehead puckered as the information kicked in and she began to picture the grim scene. 'Could this be a simple accident?' she wondered. 'Presumably she'd be exhausted after a big emotional day and she'd most likely have been drinking.'

'It's possible, although in my experience it's unusual for a healthy person to drown by accident in a domestic bath. We can't rule out natural causes, of course. An embolism of some kind for example, or a fit even though she has no history. Or some other type of lapse of consciousness.' His tone made it clear that he was not at all convinced by the natural death theory.

'Or it could be a deliberate drowning?' Sue was talking more to herself than to the medic.

'That's also a possibility.' The doctor glanced at his watch. 'We'll need a full autopsy report before we can be more specific.'

'Right.' She began to run through what would need to be done next. Inform the coroner. Get the forensic team to examine the room. Talk to the guests still present. She was going to need help.

Noticing that the doctor had begin to shrug

himself into a linen jacket she glanced back at the pathetic yet macabre tableau on the bed. The young groom seemed as waxen and dead as his new wife. 'What's his Christian name?' she mouthed to the doctor.

'James. Known as Jamie apparently.'

'Is he OK to answer questions?'

'There's no medical problem as far as I can see. He's simply in shock.'

Sue gave a grimace. 'He looks completely out of it to me.' She reached out and touched the young man's arm. 'Jamie!' she said. Then more urgently, 'Jamie, I'd like to ask you a few questions.' As she increased the pressure of her fingers, the young man turned his head away, flinching irritably at her touch.

'Has he spoken at all?' she enquired of the doctor in low tones.

'Oh, yes. He was able to tell me that he was the person who had found her, and to give the name of her doctor. That was about it. Look, I really do have to go. Just call the emergency medical services if there are any serious problems.'

'OK.' Sue saw that she was going to have to deal with this on her own until she could get some back up from the station. That is if there was anyone left who was still upright and functioning.

The doctor turned at the door and offered

a grim smile. 'Right then, I'll leave you to it.'

'Thanks.' Sue pulled a wry face as the door closed behind him. More in hope than expectation she perched on the edge of the bed and made a further attempt to engage the attention of the groom, but there was no flicker of response. The room seemed unbearably warm. Sweat was dampening the fabric of her short-sleeved blue shirt and her trousers felt as though they had stuck to her thighs. She waved her hands in front of her face to create a draught, but she might as well have switched on a hair dryer.

Rising from the bed, she located the control switch for the air-conditioning. It was tempting to switch the control to its highest setting, but she remembered that in doing so she could play havoc with the pathologist's findings. She would just have to fry. Glancing swiftly around the room, she saw that a slender dress, in ivory silk, presumably the bridal gown, was laid over the *chaise-longue* under the window. Resting on top of the gown were items of gossamer light under-wear, silky bra and thong, stockings with creamy lace tops. They had the appearance of having been thrown down casually. Did that mean that the wearer had intended to put them on again fairly soon, or that they had been discarded in haste? Or maybe both. Sue recalled her own wedding celebrations three years before. In her view a bride and groom had every right to have a quick shag during the post-nuptial proceedings. If you were going to hire a boudoir like this and a whacking four-poster bed, why not make the most of it?

She looked again at the bed. The grieving groom was whispering into his dead-bride's hair. 'Josie,' he moaned, over and over, letting the words spill across his lips and sink into the dark strands.

Sue swore softly. Somehow she was going to have to prise the body from the desperate grasp of the bereaved man. Not just for procedural reasons, but because the doom-laden vignette was beginning to get to her.

'Jamie,' she said with quiet authority, stepping up close once again. 'Jamie. We need to lay Josephine down, and then seal off the room so that my colleagues can make a full investigation.' And we need to get her out of your clutches and prevent any more contamination of possible vital evidence, she added silently.

Jamie let out a low moan. He sounded like an animal in pain. His clasp on his lost love tightened, as though Sue were about to snatch her away from him. God! What should she do now? She remembered dictums from

14

her induction period as a uniformed PC: maintain a calm front, remember that the public are relying on you to take the lead. 'Jamie, you have to let her go. Come on!' She spoke with quiet authority, reaching out and making a gentle effort to pull his arms free from their claw-like grasp around the girl.

He moaned again, nudging her off. 'No, no!'

Well, at least he was talking. 'Jamie! She's already gone. She's dead. You can't hold on to her for ever.' Sue flinched at the sound of her voice, stern and cold in the face of his sorrow. 'Look, why don't I get one of your friends, or your family to come and be with you whilst we lay Josephine down?'

No response.

'What about Josephine's family? I could get them.'

Suddenly he came to life. 'Don't! Don't you do that. *I'm* Josie's next of kin now. I'm her family, not them. She's mine.' His eyes blazed at Sue, and she found herself involuntarily starting back from him.

She seized the moment. 'OK. Fair enough. Then are you ready to talk to me about your wife? Answer some questions?' He stared at her, helpless and horrified and she felt like someone kicking a child who has been turned out on the streets, terrified and bewildered.

'Jamie?' she pressed.

His spine sagged. He nodded.

'Can you tell me what happened when you found Josie?' Sue encouraged. 'Very simply, just how it was?'

Seconds crawled by. 'I couldn't find her,' he said eventually, his voice dreamlike and barely audible. 'I couldn't find her.' His eyes sought Sue's, filled with miserable bewilderment as though she might be able to offer him some explanation for this problem of loss.

'When couldn't you find her?'

He was silent for a while as though Sue's words had been delayed on some inadequate satellite link. 'At the party,' he said at last. 'They were dancing. She'd gone. I looked all over.'

A trip to the women's cloakroom, Sue wondered. A freshen up. Not so unusual surely. Why would he have been so worried?

'Did you tell anyone else about this? That you were worried where Josie was?'

She waited for her words to be transmitted across whatever neurological barrier was delaying them. 'No,' he said, dropping his head down. 'I came in here to find her and she was in the bath.' He straightened up slowly, unhooked one of his hands from around the dead girl's shoulders and stared

16

down into her face. His face crumpled, the skin of his jaw trembling. In a sudden single movement he released his dead bride and shot into the bathroom. Sue heard terrible sounds of wretching and then the splash of vomit.

The body had come to rest in an awkward curl on the bed. As Sue looked down at it, resisting the urge to arrange it into a neat line, she heard an urgent tapping on the door. Almost instantly it opened and Clive Parker's erect form began to walk through.

Sue sprinted forward. 'No! Stop there, sir!' she told him sharply, noting the flicker of anger on his features as he halted in his tracks. 'I'm going to have to seal the room off. No one is to come in and contaminate it.'

'Good grief! That's a bit over the top, isn't it?'

He had the grace to step back, allowing Sue to slide herself through the door and out into the corridor. 'I'm sorry to tell you,' she told him, looking around and raising her voice for the benefit of all those still waiting in the corridor, 'that I'm going to have to contact the coroner. The doctor wasn't able to establish the cause of death.'

A murmur of horror rippled around the waiting group.

'Oh dear,' Clive Parker said softly. 'I'd

17

hoped we could avoid this.'

Sue gave an inward sigh of relief, having prepared herself for Parker to challenge her decision.

A woman in her fifties, her figure wrapped in folds of peach silk, her hair swathed in a 1930s-style turban with plumes, hurried forward to speak to Sue. 'Cassie Parker,' she said tersely. 'I'm concerned about my son. I'd like to see him.' She made a move towards the door of the bridal suite, put her fingers around the door handle.

'I'm sorry,' Sue said, finding herself with no option but to bar the woman's way by placing her own back against the door, 'I can't let you go in there.'

'Oh surely I'm not going to *contaminate* anything.' Her eyes flashed out anger at the young officer. 'I just need to see my son.' Like her husband she seemed to be a woman who was used to getting her own way. Sue wondered which of them came out on top when there was a serious diversion of opinion.

'If you'll just wait there, I'll get him to come out to you,' Sue said, speaking more in hope than expectation.

Jamie was standing by the window. He turned as he heard Sue's entry. His lips were purple-tinged and his eyes glittery with pent up feeling. 'I'm all right, now,' he said, his voice heavy with resignation and weariness. 'Do you think you could get them to give me another room? I just need somewhere to be on my own.' His eyes flickered to the corpse on the bed and instantly shot away to the furthest corner of the room.

Sue looked at him with concern. 'I'm sure that could be arranged. And I think it might be an idea to have someone sit with you.'

He made a dry sound in his throat. 'I'm not going to do anything crazy. You've no need to keep me on suicide watch.'

Which could mean exactly the opposite, Sue thought. Moreover if this death was a murder, then Jamie Parker was a suspect and she had better make damn sure he had someone keeping a watch on him every inch of the way. Preferably a police officer.

'Your mother would like to speak to you,' Sue told him. 'She's just outside.'

Jamie's stare was blank, his eyes shining like dark holes in a whitened landscape. He gave a little jerk of his head as though to pull himself back to the here and now. His thick dark hair flopped on to his forehead and the light from the table lamp outlined the delicate arch of his cheekbones making Sue aware that he was clearly his father's son, but without the hawkishness. 'Whatever,' he said wearily, lifting his shoulders in a gesture of indifference.

Having steered Jamie outside into the corridor and into the embrace of his redoubtable mother, Sue found herself button-holed by the equally formidable father. As he leaned forward to claim her attention she noticed that the other members of the group who had been waiting in the corridor had dispersed. There was a sudden sensation of horror at having allowed a group of possible prime suspects to walk off into the night and never be seen again.

Damn! She stamped down the leaping tongue of panic. No one could have been expected to do more than she had so far achieved, given the circumstances. However she was painfully conscious that it was only weeks since she had gained the rank of sergeant, and the honour and responsibility of it still felt like a glorious mantle around her shoulders. There was much to be proud of, but much more to prove. She was, after all still a novice, not to mention the youngest serving sergeant in the division. She must get this right.

'If this isn't a straightforward business,' Clive Parker informed her, 'then I think it's time some rigorous investigative procedures were put in place. None of us are in the mood for being kept hanging around like this, as I'm sure you'll appreciate, Sergeant.' He shot Sue a look that instantly catapulted her back to the time when she was leggy schoolgirl in knee socks and all the reins of power were held by invincible adults.

Forget that, she instructed herself. And remember, neither apologize nor explain regarding the observance of the law.

'I can confirm, sir, that this is not a straightforward case of death from natural causes,' she told Parker. 'I shall be requesting back up from my team as soon as possible, and in the meantime I would appreciate it if you and your family would stay on at the hotel to talk to us later on.'

'As we have suites booked here for the night, I had not been intending that any of us should leave,' he countered, his gaze on Sue's face as steady as a rock.

'Good.' Having spotted Ford hovering at the far end of the corridor, Sue gave Parker a brief nod and began to put some distance between herself and him. She could feel his eyes on her departing back.

'Could you give me any indication as to how many guests are still in the hotel?' she asked Ford.

'We only had the wedding party booked in,' he told her.

'Right. So how many are still here?'

'Well, er, around fifteen as far as I'm aware.'

'I thought you said there had been a hundred guests?'

'That's right. But most of them were not booked to stay the night.'

'I see. So these fifteen or so people — are they mainly family members of the bride and groom?'

'I believe so. And also the best man and one or two of the bridesmaids.'

So eighty odd guests — possible suspects — had disappeared to goodness knows where. Had they all fled, Sue wondered, like passengers abandoning a sinking ship when the tragic news had been announced.

'Mr Parker gathered everyone together and suggested it would be best for those guests not close to the bride's family to disperse,' the manager offered in impartial tones.

'I see.' Such cool in a crisis! Mr Clive Parker was beginning to interest Sue. 'And about what time was that?'

Ford considered. 'Shortly after the doctor had pronounced that the . . . young lady was dead. Around ten o'clock.'

'And where are the dead girl's parents?' she asked, curious that she had not yet encountered them.

'I would assume they're in their suite. It's the Wharfedale, on the floor above this one.' A pause. 'Er, I was wondering when we would be able to remove the body,' he asked, as he had earlier.

'I can't give an exact indication,' she responded crisply. 'As soon as all the necessary procedures have been completed.' She knew she sounded like a hard bitch, but sometimes it was the only way. 'In the meantime I wonder if you could find Jamie Parker a new room where he can be on his own,' she told him, and before Ford could raise any further issues she made swiftly for the lift and went in search of the bereaved parents.

En route she called the station and requested urgent staff support. The duty sergeant sounded both doubtful and exhausted. 'Just send anyone available,' she told him tersely. 'If they can stand and utter speech, they'll do.'

There was no reply to her knock on the door of the Wharfedale Suite, which was very slightly ajar. She walked in. The rooms beyond were deserted. Items of wedding finery had been thrown down on the bed: a man's black jacket with a wilting carnation pinned to the lapel, a woman's turquoise suit and strappy high heeled sandals. The half empty state of the cases on the luggage stools suggested that the occupants of the room intended to return. But even so, it concerned Sue that they had temporarily gone missing. Having searched the ground floor reception rooms and found those also deserted, she came to a standstill, suddenly painfully conscious of the impossibility of being able to deal with all that needed to be done in this complex scenario.

She brought up the home number of her team leader from her phone's memory, then paused frowning. DCI Ed Swift had reluctantly retired home two days before with a particularly bad dose of flu. Nevertheless, as he left the station, white, hunched and grim he had told Sue to get in touch if there were any urgent problems.

'Right,' she muttered, pushing her finger on the OK button, and holding her breath.

'Yes!' The answering voice was female with a definite hint of steel. This must be Ed Swift's daughter, Sue decided. She had met her once at a retirement party. A girl around seventeen with challenging, noticing eyes and a mind and a half of her own. Sue introduced herself and asked to speak to DCI Swift.

'He's on sick leave,' the girl said, in a tone which suggested that she knew exactly what Sue was after and would probably go to some lengths to ensure she didn't get it.

Sue felt her backbone tighten. 'I do appreciate that. It would be most helpful if I could talk to him to gain advice.' She heard a noise in the background, than a muttered, 'Dad, you're supposed to be in bed.' After that it was clear that a hand had been clamped over the mouthpiece. Little madam! Sue sensed tension building inside her. And then she heard Swift's voice; low, measured, quietly authoritative. 'What's the problem, Sergeant?'

'Thank God!' Sue heard herself exclaim before she could stop herself.

2

Having collected three sets of protective clothing and a newly appointed young detective constable from the station, Ed Swift took the main road running alongside the River Wharfe before turning up the steep B road which turned back on itself in a southerly direction, leading eventually to the huge crag of rock which crowned the summit and attracted thousands of climbers and sightseers every year. The Moorlands Hotel was situated around halfway up the flank of the hill. The moist heat of the night had created a faint haze in the atmosphere and the lamps guarding the entrance to the main gates were faint and smudgy.

Swift was conscious of an echo of that smudginess in his own head. The virus which had cut him down three days ago had only recently slackened its grip. The high temperature and drowsiness had left him, but there was a residual sensation of diminished physical strength and a slight distancing from reality. The immediate effect of the call from Sue Sallis had kick-started his motivation to be at work again but, as his eyes strained to make out the curve of the drive in the darkness between the thick banks of rhododendron bushes, he wondered if he had been over-optimistic in considering himself fully fit for the resumption of duty.

Sensing, rather than seeing, two shadows move across the lawn beyond the bushes, Swift brought the car to a halt. The shadows became sharper now, clearly two human forms: a tall, heavy man leaning on a much less substantial woman. The man seemed to be having difficulty taking each step, the woman taking a good deal of his weight. 'She looks as though she needs some help,' he told the constable. 'And if they're part of the wedding party, we'll need to question them.'

'Shall I go and get them, sir?' The constable, by the name of Pete Fox, a lanky, athletic man in his twenties, was already swinging himself from the car, his expression eager and purposeful.

'See what you can do. But go easy, they could be bereaved members of the family. Persuasion might be the best approach. I'll go on up to the hotel to join Sergeant Sallis.'

'Will do, sir.'

Sue was waiting to report to him as he parked his car outside the front entrance and gathered up the sets of white overalls. 'Are you feeling OK, sir?' she asked, although her first instinct had been to exclaim how dreadful he looked. Ashen, strained, ill. 'I'm really sorry to have dragged you out.'

He gave a wry smile and shrugged. 'Who's here? Still just you?'

'I've been assured a forensic team is on their way — that's if the division can cobble together a bunch who haven't been struck down with flu.' She glanced up at Swift, wincing at her clumsiness. 'Sorry, sir, no disrespect meant! Anyway it looks like we're on our own for the moment.'

'I've brought the new DC with me. He's rounding up a couple of stragglers in the garden. So what have you discovered so far?'

Sue flipped open her notebook and gave a rapid précis, starting with the doctor's report and moving forward.

'What about the family?' he asked, glancing into the brightly lit, apparently empty foyer.

'The groom's family are in their suite. I haven't tracked down the dead girl's parents yet. And I'm afraid I haven't been able to make a proper appraisal of the death scene either, sir.'

'There's only so much one person can do on their own,' Swift responded evenly. He glanced back to the gardens. Dark shapes were moving slowly in the direction of the entrance. 'Maybe those two are the ones you've been looking for.'

Sue followed his gaze. 'The guy doesn't look too steady, does he?'

'I think you'd better give the DC a hand, Sue. If the parents seem up to it, start some questioning. I'll take a quick look at the death scene. I'm assuming it's not been disturbed?'

'Not since I arrived, sir. I can't say for earlier on. If the suite wasn't locked, then I suppose anyone could have been in. I've got a set of keys,' she said, handing them to him.

'Anything else?' he asked.

'The groom's parents seem quite pushy,' Sue told him. 'And there's a lot of anxiety about getting the body moved.'

'That's understandable.' Already the faint fog in his head was clearing. The sharp tingle of expectancy at the beginning of an investigation began to run through his veins like an injection of amphetamine.

Having calmed the manager with a careful reiteration of the procedures to be currently observed, and those likely to follow, Swift slipped into one of the protective boiler suits, pulled on gloves and entered the room where the corpse lay. Closing the door behind him, he stood for a moment letting his eyes move slowly over the scene. The gloom seemed intense, the single lamp giving very little away. He flicked the switches at the side of the door. Under the small, powerful spot-lights let into the ceiling the scene took on a shadowless hard-edged appearance.

Automatically he began to make an inventory of the contents of the room. The dicarded clothes and personal items on the dressing table claimed his attention first, and after that the individual items of furniture and their positions. And then, because this death had the possibility of being the result of a murder, the absence of any signs of violence.

He noticed that the door to the bathroom was closed. Opening it he found that the window had been thrown wide open, letting in the sultry heat of the August night and the scent of garden roses. The bath had been drained, but streaks of water glistened in its base. There were wet towels on the floor and the usual array of male and female toiletries on the shelf above the handbasin. A chunky hair-dryer lay on the floor, its extra-long flex snaking across the tiled floor, the plug inserted into a socket just outside the door of the bathroom. Bending down he noted a few drops of water on the end of the nozzle, both on the outer and inner surfaces. But, once again, nowhere in the room were there any signs of a struggle.

He went back into the bedroom and moved

slowly to stand over the body. Squaring up to the girl's beautiful dead face and her blankly staring eyes, he allowed himself to think first of his dead wife and then of his daughter, the latter very much a creature of the here and now, living life to the full. It was a ritual he always observed when faced with the physical reality of death — a tranquil acceptance that Kate had gone and a heartfelt gratitude that Naomi lived and thrived. He supposed it was a form of superstition. If he confronted the demons of mortality head on then somehow Naomi would remain safe. It was a fallacy he kept entirely to himself.

He noted the way the body had come to rest, slightly curved, the head turned towards the door as though watching her attacker leave. Her possible attacker, he reminded himself? But where were the signs of attack? He had already privately rejected the likelihood of an accidental death. The human body had a number of physiological alert mechanisms which made it unlikely for robust, healthy adults to remain long enough under shallow amounts of warm water in order to perish. He had learned from a former medical colleague that the reflex action against over lengthy submersion kicked in effectively even when bathers were fatigued or had consumed alcohol. On the other hand the dead woman could have had some underlying medical condition that might explain the sudden death. But even as the thought entered his mind, some instinctive gut reaction prompted him to put that particular theory on the back burner. Suicide he also relegated to low priority status, for broadly the same reason. Electrocution then, from the introduction of the connected hairdryer into her bath? Or drowning by being forced under the water? He looked at the slender calves protruding from the bath sheet. For a moment it seemed that there could be faint pinkish marks of pressure on the ankles. He bent closer. At first he had been convinced, but the more he looked, the harder it was to determine anything of substance.

He straightened up. Well, he would simply have to wait for the findings of the autopsy for those queries to be answered. But in the meantime he was keen that a pathologist should make an examination of the scene before the body was removed. Two years ago he had worked on a case where a teenage student had been discovered dead in the bath by his landlord. The process of determining the cause of death had been complex and problematic, prolonged and compounded by the landlord's having removed the body to the hospital in his car, as a result of which the pathologist had not had as full information as he needed in order to reach a ready conclusion. The resultant distress to the family and the delay in making progress with the investigations had been significant. All of which had been a gift to the prurient, blame-seeking arm of the tabloid press.

Swift took out his mobile and thumbed through the stored numbers.

Minutes later, as he peeled off his protective clothing in the eerily lit corridor, he heard the lift glide to a soft halt and the doors open. A woman, tall and svelte, stepped out, instantly registered his presence and began walking towards him. Or perhaps bearing down on him would have been a better description. In her four inch heels she was almost his height. Her eyes connected with his, the expression in them steady and challenging. 'Are you the sergeant's senior officer?' she asked.

'Chief Inspector Swift,' he told her.

'I'm Cassandra Parker,' she announced, cutting him off as he was about to ask. 'The mother of the bridegroom.' She hesitated, and for a second he thought she was about to lose her steadfast resolve like an experienced skier faltering because of a moment of lost concentration. He saw her chin rise, heard the slow, considered drawing in of a breath as she steered herself back on course. Given the tragedy which had just occurred and her close involvement with the deceased he guessed that she must be exerting an almost inhuman effort. 'My poor son,' she said. 'I can't imagine what he must be feeling.' A muscle in her cheek flickered. 'No, that's not true at all. Of course I can! I'm his mother.'

Swift inclined his head in sympathy. 'Indeed. His feeling of loss must be terrible.'

The tense suspicion in her face eased slightly. He had the impression that the sympathy in his voice was the opposite of what she had been expecting, and that he might be an ally rather than an enemy. She said, 'That's why I need to impress on you the urgency of moving Josie's body as soon as possible. How can the poor boy get any rest when he's thinking of her lying there?' She closed her eyes. 'Dear God, it's all so terrible.'

'Your daughter-in-law will be moved as soon as the necessary procedures have been completed,' he told her.

'Procedures! For heaven's sake, can't you let the poor girl have a shred of dignity? She may be dead, but to be lying around in a hotel room, half naked or whatever — how grotesque is that?' Cassandra's eyes flashed with hostility and frustration.

'I'm very sorry about any delay and further distress,' Swift told her, making it clear that in this matter his decision was not up for dispute.

'You've seen Josephine, haven't you?' she persisted. 'You've looked in the room where she died. Is there anything you can tell us? My husband will be very anxious to have some information as soon as possible. We have been hanging around waiting for nearly three hours,' she reminded him accusingly.

'I'm afraid that's likely to be one of the first of a number of inconveniences,' he said. 'I'll need to talk to your son and to Josephine's parents before I can tell you anything further.'

'You're thinking about questioning my son! At such a time. How can you even consider it? It's not only cruel, but crass!'

In the early days of his career Swift would have felt the reproach keenly, and been in basic agreement with it. As a stranger, even though he was involved professionally, he had never felt comfortable about speaking the banal words of condolence necessary at a death, or the unavoidable sense of somehow pretending some feeling of personal loss. But after Kate's sudden, violent death and the shock he had suffered on being told how she had been crushed to death in a railway collision, he had found it less difficult to confront the bereaved. From that time on he had become one of them. 'If he doesn't want to speak to me tonight, then, of course, I'll respect his wishes,' he said quietly.

Cassandra regarded him with loathing and a growing fear. 'Why are you here?' she demanded. 'You wouldn't be here, would you, if you didn't think something ghastly had been going on? Foul play — isn't that what they call it? Or is there some more up-to-date term these days?'

'I can't say anything further until I've spoken to your son and the other next of kin,' he said.

Her gaze ripped into him. 'God! I can't believe it. You're saying she's been murdered, aren't you? You think someone killed her. Someone here, at the wedding.' Horror and fury jostled for dominance in her sharply defined features. *How dare you?* she seemed to be saying. 'My husband will be up in arms when he hears what's going on.'

'I can't say any more at present,' Swift said, meeting her mounting hysteria with calm. 'Where is your husband, by the way?'

'He went out to get a breath of air. I think it had suddenly hit him, what's happened. He was very fond of Josie, and so proud of them both today. They looked so happy; they were made for each other.' She threw him a look of appeal. Suddenly her face crumpled, tears burst from her eyes and the lines of her face became those of a defeated old woman.

Swift guided her to the lift. 'I think, for now, it would best for you to rejoin your husband,' he told her, speaking very softly.

She dabbed at her eyes and nostrils. And as she did so, she was miraculously gathering up her composure. 'I think I should be there,' she said, 'when you speak to my son.'

Swift gave a slight nod in acknowledgement of her words, but made no comment. He wondered if she had any idea yet of how the day's events would have altered the relationship she had previously had with her son. How it could never be the same again.

*   ★   ★

Swift found Sue Sallis in the foyer, glancing through the jottings in her notebook. On seeing him she jerked her head towards a door adjacent to the reception desk. 'The manager's in there, prowling and waiting to pounce,' she murmured with a lift of her eyebrows. 'I've told him he'll get information about moving the body as soon as we can give it.'

'And the couple in the garden?' he asked.

'The dead girl's parents. Jack and Melanie

37

Haygarth. He's not feeling well. He's gone back to his suite and Pete's keeping an eye on him. His wife says she doesn't think he needs a doctor, just a chance to rest. He certainly wasn't up to answering any questions.'

'And where is his wife?'

'She went to the Ladies cloakroom.' She glanced over his shoulder. 'Ah, here she is now.'

Swift turned. The woman coming towards him would be in her mid-forties, he guessed. Her wedding finery had been jettisoned for navy cotton trousers and a white T shirt. She was small, her figure slender and girlish, her face fine-featured and intelligent. Her short dark hair fell in feathery strands over her cheeks and forehead, making her dark eyes seem huge against the moon-like paleness of her skin. Although she showed no signs of having been weeping, the pain of the last few hours was etched in every line and curve of her face, a wounding of the spirit which was pitiful to observe. He could tell that she was tensed like a wire, bracing herself with a huge act of will to contain the grief which threatened to burst out of her at any moment.

'Are you Chief Inspector Swift?' she asked, with a sad ghost of a smile, presumably prompted by some astounding reflex mechanism of courtesy. 'I'm quite prepared to talk to you and help in any way I can.'

'Thank you,' he said gently, his concern and curiosity aroused. 'Have you set up somewhere we can talk in private?' he asked Sue.

She nodded, then led him and Melanie Haygarth past the manager's room to a tiny office at the far side of the foyer. It was lined with filing cabinets, leaving just enough room for a desk and two small armchairs upholstered in grey tweed. Melanie Haygarth sank into one of them and laid her arms along those of the chair in a gesture of exhaustion and silent misery.

Sue threw Swift a questioning look. *Do you want me to stay?*

He glanced back at the shattered woman in the armchair, and mouthed a negative to Sue. 'Go and see if you can get any more information from the groom,' he asked her quietly. Before he could offer the usual words of condolence, Melanie Haygarth began to speak.

'What do you need to know?' she asked, her voice fragile yet still conveying conviction. 'I suppose you wouldn't be here if you didn't think this was . . . ' She stopped. 'Are you thinking this could be a murder?' she said, her voice dying away as she framed the question.

Swift was surprised at her leaps of conjecture. Many next of kin resisted the whole notion of murder unless the circumstances were beyond doubt, and even when the evidence was overwhelming some were still unable to face the horrible truth. 'From what I've seen and heard so far, I'm treating this as a suspicious death,' he said carefully.

'Yes,' she said. *And so am I* seemed to echo through the room in her low despairing voice.

'Do you have any reason for thinking your daughter could have been murdered?' he asked.

Shd did not respond immediately. Her fingers on the arm of the chair twitched. 'No.'

Swift judged her hesitation had been long enough to make the negative response suspect. He filed the information mentally, then waited.

'I suppose,' she said slowly, 'I'm forcing myself to face up to the worst-case scenario. That my darling beloved Josephine could have been murdered. On her wedding day. Her wonderful, special day. I do that sometimes when things are bad. I imagine the worst possible reasons or outcomes. I suppose it's to protect myself. If I look ahead and forsee the bleakest picture, then what will happen in reality can only be better.' She gave a swift, vicious jerk of her head. 'Dear God!

How pathetic is that? How could anything ever be bleaker than this? To have my daughter die on the day we've all been looking forward to for months? To have her die at all, when it should me and her father who died first. A parent doesn't want to outlive their child. The world isn't a good place for them to be in any more.'

'No,' he agreed.

'I don't want to break down,' she said. 'Not yet. I think the grief might sweep me away into some kind of insanity or collapse. I'll answer your questions, as well as I'm able. I'd rather do that than be left on my own.' She looked up at him. 'I mean it.' Her gaze was intense and full of appeal.

'Can you tell me when you last saw Josephine?' he asked gently.

'I've been thinking about that,' she said. 'Desperately trying to remember, just for myself, you see. The day has been so extraordinary. So many people to greet and speak to. New people I'd never met before: friends of Jamie and Josie's. Members of Jamie's family. Friends of Clive and Cassie's. People coming up to me and then melting away. Everyone so happy and positive about what was happening. Making comments on what wonderful young people Jamie and Josie are.' She winced at the use of the present tense. 'What a wonderful couple they made. What a wonderful shining future lay ahead of them. I remember after the service trying to keep track of them both, savouring the pleasure of seeing them, so vibrant and happy together, looking so beautiful in their wedding clothes. The photographer had them all over the place, posing in the house and in the garden.' She paused and let out a small groan. Her face suddenly crumpled in bewilderment. 'I still can't quite remember when I last saw her after the reception. There was dancing and general mingling . . . '

'Do you remember when you last spoke to her?' Swift interposed softly.

She moved her hands into her lap. As she clenched them together the knuckles shone like small white marbles. 'I think it was before the ceremony. The photographer wanted me and Jack to have our picture taken with her. When I saw her in her wedding dress I felt suddenly choked up. She'd laughed and said it wasn't like me to be weepy.' She drew in a long, regretful breath. 'That was it, really. That was our goodbye. The bride's mother doesn't get to sit with her daughter at the wedding breakfast, so I didn't speak to her then.' She sank into silence. 'I keep thinking that I'll never hear her voice again,' she exclaimed, her own voice edged with panic. 'I keep trying to remember it, to hear her voice in my head. And to remember the way her skin glowed with health and life. And the sheen of her hair.'

Swift listened in silence, respecting the mother's grief.

'I think the last time I saw her was after the band played the 'Waltz of the Flowers',' she said with sudden recall. 'Over the last year or so Josie had begun to get interested in classical music. She especially liked Tchaikovsky's ballet music. She wanted some of it played during the dancing. She and Jamie danced together.' She closed her eyes for a moment and wrapped her arms tightly around her chest as though trying to hold her feelings in check by physical force. 'I was chatting to an old friend of mine and we kept looking across at Josie and Jamie. And my friend said, 'You must be so happy for them'. And I remember a wave of well-being flowing through me. And then Jack came to take me away to the bar to talk to some old friends of his . . . And after that I didn't see Josie again.'

She had been so much in control, but now, suddenly, tears welled up in her eyes. She stood up and tried to make for the door. But the storm of feeling had taken her by surprise and she was blundering about like a stunned animal, weeping and moaning. Swift got up and put a steadying arm around her.

'I'm sorry,' she said after a time. 'Your job must be awful sometimes.'

'Grief is a like a disease,' he said. 'You have to submit to it. And I'm sorry that I haven't any real comfort to offer. Do you have other children?'

'We have Ludo,' she said. 'He's nineteen. Very involved with the girlfriend of the moment.'

'I think you should try to get some rest,' Swift suggested. 'We can talk again in the morning.'

'Yes.' She rose from her chair, ponderous and stiff like a person afflicted by some disabling condition.

'Shall I get Sergeant Sallis to go with you to your suite?' he asked.

'No, I'll be all right.' At the door she turned. 'Thank you for listening to all that. I'm sure I haven't told you anything helpful at all.'

Swift walked with her to the lift, his mind already reviewing the information she had offered and picking out items to retain. As the doors rolled closed he was aware of a red light flashing above the main entrance. Beyond the locked glass doors he could see a young woman gesturing to be let in. An experimental pressing of the panel of buttons to the side of the entrance soon produced the required result and the door catch clicked open.

'I'm assuming you're our pathologist,' Swift said, blocking the young woman's entry until she had confirmed her status.

'Yep. Dr Tanya Blake. I've got my ID somewhere.' Blake was small and thin with vivid green eyes and a girlish demeanour. She dug about in the pockets of her baggy cotton trousers and pulled out a dog-eared card. 'Sorry, lost the little plastic container. It's been a bit of a rush the last few days.'

'You're standing in for Dr Kabinsky?' Swift's mind brought up an image of the local pathologist, a formidable woman of few words who had the disconcerting air of a high priestess. Blake looked as though she wasn't yet ready to leave school.

'Yep. She's on holiday. Italy I believe. Lucky her. So what have you got for me?'

She dug into a battered Gladstone-style bag, drew out a packet of protective clothing, and began pulling on the trousers. The robing process continued as Swift gave her a briefing whilst they rode in the lift up to the bridal suite.

On entering the room, Blake moved straight to the body, dropping her bag on the floor *en route*. She stood for a moment, simply observing, and there was an air of reverence in her stillness. Without taking her eyes from the body, she pulled on thin examination gloves then reached forward. Her hands moved softly about the neck, gently rotating the head. Then she touched the backs of the hands and the fingers, then lifted the arms. Swift had the instant impression of watching someone confidently at ease in the practice of her chosen profession. Blake's movements were delicate, precise and skilled, yet with all the authority of someone who had been doing the job for years.

She opened the towel, exposing the girl's flawless body. 'No obvious wounds on the chest or abdomen.' She pressed against the rib-cage. 'The lungs seem spongy, most likely from ingested water.' She reached down into her bag, pulled out a small chunky thermometer and inserted it into the corpse's ear. 'I can confirm that she's been dead for about three hours, that's using the measure of a drop in body heat of one and a half degrees Fahrenheit for every hour after death, taken in conjunction with the temperature of the room. Maybe a little less than three hours,' she added, tapping numbers into her calculator. She looked at her watch. 'So, time of death somewhere between eight-fifty and nine o'clock.' Gently, she replaced the towel and began to examine the corpse's legs. She bent close over the ankles, then turned to Swift. 'You said that she was found in the bath by her husband?'

'That was what he told my colleague.'

'And the GP has said there was no significant medical history?'

'The doctor who saw her earlier gave that information.'

'Is there any medication around? Painkillers? Sleeping pills? Contraceptive pills?'

'I haven't found any in the room. But we haven't been through her luggage yet. I did find a hair-dryer lying on the bathroom floor. It wasn't switched on. But there were drops of water on both the inside and outside of the nozzle.'

Blake turned back to the body. She placed her hands around the chin, pulled down the lower lip and examined the tongue. 'Mmm, it's not looking like an electrocution. There are no obvious electrical burn marks on the skin, but I can't be more specific until the full autopsy.' She bent again over the ankles. 'There seems to be possible bruising of the skin here. What do you think?'

'I had the same thought. But I'm no expert.'

'You're probably more knowledgeable than

47

you think, given your job,' Blake commented with a small imp-like smile. 'Is the water still in the bath?'

'No. I would assume the husband emptied it before he pulled her out. I haven't spoken to him yet.'

'No traces of food, vomit or blood in the bath?' she asked.

'None that I noticed.'

'Mmm. It's a pity we weren't able to see her actually in the water, that could have given us quite a few more clues. So,' she commented thoughtfully, 'let's hope the husband proves to be a reliable and truthful witness.' Her imp-like smile reappeared. 'But that's your department, not mine — thank goodness.'

'Yes, indeed.' Swift was amused and impressed by her candour. The nature of Jamie Parker's co-operation and frankness in this investigation had already been going through his mind.

She straightened up and began to pull off her gloves. 'Well, I don't think I can say or do much more for the moment.' She looked back at the corpse and her face became still and sombre. 'Off the record, I suspect this is a drowning. And if the marks around the ankles turn out to be clear signs of bruising then I'd say she was probably deliberately drowned. If the attacker had grasped her around the ankles and given a strong swift pull, dragging her head and face under the water, then her lungs could have filled very quickly. She's quite small and probably no more than a hundred and ten pounds in weight, so it wouldn't have been difficult to kill her using that method.'

'Could a woman have done it?'

'If she was reasonably strong and fit, yes. No problem.'

'And, I would presume in this situation, with a victim in the bath, then if the attacker had taken her by surprise it would have been all the easier?'

'Yes. Definitely.'

Swift was silent for a moment. 'Thank you,' he said.

'I don't think I can give you anything else to go on tonight,' she said. 'I'll try to do the PM first thing tomorrow morning, and let you have a report by early afternoon. Is that OK?' Suddenly she looked vulnerable. A young person starting out and taking her first tentative steps in a frighteningly responsible profession.

'It's more than I'd hoped for given the shortage of staff. And thank you for coming so promptly.'

'I'm glad of the work,' she told him,

stripping off her protective clothing and cramming it back into her bag. 'I've only just qualified and I haven't got a permanent job yet, so any shouts I can get from the call-out register are a bonus. And there's certainly no shortage with this flu epidemic raging through the county.'

'You'll get a permanent contract,' he said.

'Oh, yes. I'm not too worried. But the profession is becoming a bit more crowded now. It must be all those TV dramas!'

'Is that what made you choose forensic pathology?'

'Good grief, no! My father's a haematologist, Mum's a harrassed GP, my brother's a psychiatry registrar. It was always going to be medicine. I just made sure to choose a different branch.'

As they stepped into the lift Swift got a call to say that a SOCO team was just about to arrive. Downstairs in the foyer, the manager was staring out into the drive. Headlights carved a large arc as two cars swept round the final bend leading up to the entrance. As the cars scrunched to a halt, figures sprang out, white-clad and ghostly against the dark banks of rhododendrons.

Ford caught Swift's eye as he and the pathologist moved out of the lift. 'Scene of crime officers are just arriving, Chief

Inspector,' he announced, his voice a model of calm restraint. The expression on his face was also a perfect example of professional impartiality. Swift guessed that what was going on behind the mask told a different story. Ford had a dead body littering his immaculate kingdom, one which showed no signs of removing itself with any haste. He had distraught relatives stumbling around the grounds and the corridors. And now the place was to be invaded by a team of boilersuited police. And most likely, his dining-room was fully booked for Sunday lunch in less than twelve hours' time. His cup of despair must be full to overflowing.

★   ★   ★

It was 4.00 a.m. when Swift arrived home. It was still night but the tiny beginnings of dawn were showing in the eastern sky. A small, Mediterranean-soft breeze was lifting the leaves of the cherry trees lining the drive, and revealing their pale undersides. His flat was the ground floor of a Victorian villa and as he pulled the car to a halt he could see that Naomi had left a light on in the hall. He imagined her sleeping in her room at the back of the house, her features child-like once again, relaxed from the edgy irony she maintained during the daytime.

He moved softly down the hallway. In the kitchen he switched on the kettle and tossed a tea bag into a mug. Noting the hollowness in his stomach he dug around in the biscuit tin, conscious of a pleasurable sensation of hunger he had not experienced since the flu took a hold on him three days before.

'It is very, very late.' Naomi stood leaning against the door-frame, eyes narrowed and one arm upstretched against the wood. 'I had wondered about slotting in the curlers and finding the rolling pin, but there wasn't time.'

'You don't quite fit the stereotype of the woman-in-waiting from the seaside postcard gallery,' he commented.

'No. And, of course, as your daughter, it's not really any of my business if you're staying out all hours feeding your addiction for work. But you have been quite ill.' The last sentence had a definite flavour of reproach.

He broke a biscuit in half and contemplated the results. He said, 'I don't want you to . . . ' He stopped, knowing he had started something he did not want to complete.

'You don't want me to worry about you,' she said helpfully. 'You don't want me to feel responsible for you.'

'More or less,' he agreed.

'We both worry about each other. We can't help it. We were a family of three and then Mum went out one day, got mangled and squashed in a crashed train and never came back. I think we have every right to worry.'

He took a sip of tea. 'I just wish it hadn't happened to you so soon. Having to worry about a parent.'

'Actually,' she said, 'you look quite a lot better than when you set off earlier. Work is clearly the best medicine.'

He smiled and put a piece of biscuit in his mouth.

'What was it that needed your presence so urgently?' she asked. 'Did they really need your expertise to find the latest lost pooch? Or did they finally get a lead on the guy who's been pinching red satin thongs from middle-aged ladies' washing lines and need you to nail him?'

'If only my work was so glamorous,' he told her. 'It was a suspicious death. Looking very like murder. A young woman who leaves a bereft family. And a bridegroom.'

She drew in a wincing breath. 'Sorry,' she said. 'That's serious work.'

'Yes.'

'So when will you be back on duty? Are

you planning to have more than a couple of hours sleep?'

'Maybe three.'

She shook her head in mock despair. 'I'll wake you if you oversleep.'

3

It was 7.30 a.m. when Swift returned to the Moorlands Hotel. He had arranged that Sue Sallis and Pete Fox would meet him in the miniscule office where Swift and Melanie Haygarth had talked a few hours earlier. He wanted to review progress to date and make plans for further intervention in the case.

The office, whilst cramped and airless, had the benefit of privacy. Ford, looking strained and tired, had been gracious in allowing the police officers free use of the room, and had gone so far as to provide a breakfast of toast and coffee. Earlier Josephine Haygarth's body had been discreetly moved from the bridal suite into the waiting mortuary van via the service lift and the hotel's rear exit. Swift judged that the manager's relief at the successful completion of this sensitive manoeuvre had been an important contributory factor to the boost in his willingness to co-operate.

'So what have we got so far? I think it would be helpful to have a brief summing-up.' Gaining nods from both his colleagues, he turned to Sue who, whilst pale and tired-looking, wore her habitual expression of eagerness to get on with the investigation in hand. Swift saw that she had had time to return home. Her hair looked newly washed and the navy cotton trousers and pale blue shirt she had been wearing a few hours before had been swapped for a sleeveless cream dress printed with a design of floating green leaves. 'Would you like to start, Sue?' he said.

Sue replaced her coffee cup on its saucer, flicked over the leaves of her notebook, laid it down on the desk, then began to speak. 'When I first arrived at the hotel yesterday evening the case seemed one where the cause of death was wide open. The dead woman's husband reported that he had found her in the bath. He was holding her dead body on the bed. I presumed he had pulled her out, although that needs clarifying.'

'Had he tried to resuscitate her?' Pete Fox interrupted, leaning forward and fixing his eyes on Sue's face. Swift noted the intensity of his gaze, briefly wondering if it was an affectation, or simply a reflection of his newness to the job and a need to demonstrate his interest and commitment.

'He didn't say, and so far I haven't had the opportunity to ask him,' Sue told him. Her tone was a touch cool. *I know what I'm about and don't butt in until I'm finished.* 'But, for what it's worth, he was in a pretty poor state when I first arrived. He could hardly bring himself to speak and I had quite a struggle to persuade him to let go of the body. It's likely that by his actions, which I must say were understandably impulsive in the circumstances, he's damaged or destroyed evidence which could have been significant. Do you agree, sir?' She looked across to Swift.

'Yes, I do. I'm also interested that in your notes you made the observation that Jamie didn't seem over anxious to talk to his mother or allow him to comfort her. That, again, need not necessarily be regarded as odd or unusual, given the degree of shock he would have been struggling with. But I think we should bear it in mind. So, any early conclusions, Sue?'

Sue leaned back slightly in her chair. 'Given that both the doctor on call and the pathologist seemed of the opinion that accidental drowning was an unlikely option, and given that we can probably rule out natural causes, I think we're dealing with a murder. Obviously the pathologist's findings are crucial here. But I think we've enough to go ahead with our questioning, treating this as a murder.'

Swift nodded. 'Hopefully we'll have the pathologist's report in a few hours' time.'

'What about suicide?' Pete asked.

'What about it?' Sue came back at him.

'Maybe she was having doubts. Maybe she didn't really want the commitment of being married. Maybe she didn't really want to be married. Or maybe she had doubts about Jamie — thought she'd got the wrong man.'

There was a silence.

'There's been no suicide note found,' Sue pointed out, and Swift saw that her face had tightened.

'It could come to light later. Maybe it's at her family home, or even in the post. There was a case recently of a man who mailed the note to his lover before he topped himself,' Pete said.

Whilst Swift recognized that a degree of rivalry could inject a keen edge into an investigation he was having no point scoring. 'It would be premature to rule anything out at this stage,' he said evenly. 'Is there anything else you would like to offer, Pete? You spent some time with Jack Haygarth — did that throw up anything of interest?'

'He's not a well man, as you are probably aware, sir. His wife told me he had heart surgery two years ago. He's on constant medication and he has to watch his lifestyle — diet, alcohol consumption and so on.'

'You got all this information from Mrs Haygarth?'

'Yes, sir. While we were helping Mr Haygarth back from the garden.'

'Did Mr Haygarth say anything whilst you were with him?'

'Not at first. When we got to the suite he lay down on the bed and dozed off for about half an hour. When he woke up he seemed rather confused, asking where he was and what was going on. In the end I had to tell him the bad news over again. He didn't say anything for a while, just sat on the edge of the bed with his head on his chest. His breathing was really rough and noisy. I kept wondering if we should call the ambulance service, but when I mentioned it he said he was all right. Poor old guy, he was absolutely gutted with grief.'

'That's an opinion, not an observation,' Swift cut in quietly.

'Sorry, sir.' A flush crept into Pete's cheeks. He put a hand up to his thick fair hair, rubbing at it distractedly and making it stand up in peaks.

'No need to apologize, that kind of opinion is useful in the context of our conversation here. Just remember when you are giving evidence in court, you'll need to support your opinion with a clear description of the behaviour you observed in order to reach your conclusion. Otherwise you'll get pounced on by the lawyers. You referred to Jack Haygarth as old. Do you know his age?'

'He's sixty-five. He told me off his own bat.' Pete looked down at his notebook, running his fingers down the lines. 'He said: 'I don't think I'm going to get through this. I'll be sixty-six next month and my heart's packing up — in more ways than one. Josie was my lovely darling, my beloved girl. I was forty-three when she was born. She was like a gift from Heaven. I'd had another daughter, with my first wife. That little one died when she was two years old. Some blood infection they couldn't identify soon enough to treat. It was a terrible blow. I don't think my wife ever got over it. Some years later she went off to live in Canada with some man she'd taken a fancy to. I had a bit of a breakdown. And then I met Melanie. We got married as soon as the divorce came through. And soon after we had Josie, and suddenly I felt alive again'.' Pete stopped and cleared his throat. 'He was all choked up then. Couldn't go on.'

There was a small, respectful silence.

'God, what a tragic story!' Sue exclaimed.

'You did well there, Pete. You must be one of those who have the knack of getting people to open up.'

Pete tried not to look hugely gratified, but did not quite succeed. Swift silently thanked God for Sue's instinctive generosity in the face of a new, young rival.

'I tried to write down as much as I could of what he told me,' Pete said. 'Get the main points, certainly. Obviously there could be some important things I've missed.' He paused. 'But I don't think so,' he concluded.

Swift saw Sue's eyebrows lift a tiny fraction. 'If this is a murder, and Jack Haygarth turns out to be our man, then you will eat your hat,' he suggested to the constable with a wry smile.

A flicker of anxiety showed in Pete's eyes. Was his superior sending him up? Looking at the pale, drawn face of the chief inspector beneath his dark auburn hair, Pete didn't think so. 'Yes, sir. I most certainly would.'

'How long did you stay with Haygarth?'

'Until his wife came back to the suite. That was just after three-thirty a.m.'

'I interviewed her between eleven-twenty and eleven-thirty-five yesterday evening,' Swift commented thoughtfully. 'I walked with her to the lift and I'd assumed she would be returning to her suite. But apparently not. At

61

least not until much later. Do you know where she was, Pete?'

'No, sir.' Pete looked uncomfortable. 'I'm sorry. I should have asked. It was all a bit . . . emotional.'

'At certain times our questions seem like a dreadful impertinence,' Swift agreed. 'Don't worry, Pete, we can ask her later. Unless Sue has any information.' He glanced at the sergeant.

Sue said, 'After I left you and Mrs Haygarth, I went up to the new room Jamie had been given on the second floor. He answered the door, but he said he just wanted to be left alone to try and get some sleep. I didn't push it.'

'Fair enough,' Swift said. He made a rapid, silent review of the facts to date. 'Do we know if this hotel has CCTV,' he queried. 'I certainly haven't see any cameras.'

'I asked the manager about that,' Sue said. 'There's newly installed closed circuit TV in the two main conference rooms and in the entrance lobby. But it hasn't yet been extended to the upper corridors.'

Pete shook his head. 'God, it's true what they say about the North!'

'Such as what?' Sue flashed at him.

'Still trying to haul itself into the twenty-first century,' Pete flashed back, a small grin on his face. 'Well, Yorkshire at any rate. I haven't got further than that yet.'

'That's rubbish,' Sue said. 'Where are you from, Pete?'

'Devon,' he said. 'We're well up to speed there on CCTV, and the weather's better.'

'Don't mock the North, Pete,' Swift interposed, basically warning the constable not to wind up Sergeant Sallis. 'And especially Yorkshire. You might find yourself in a freezing tarn at the bottom of a quarry with a sack of limestone tied round your neck.'

'Spoken as a reformed migrant from the cushy South,' Sue commented, smiling at her boss. 'And speaking of security in general, I'm shamed to report, as you've probably noticed, that the bedrooms and private suites in this hotel lock with old-style Chubb keys, not slot-in cards.'

'Which means,' Swift mused, 'that doors can easily be closed without being locked.'

'So,' Pete said, 'our murderer could simply have left the dancing and general socializing on the ground floor, then gone up to Josephine's suite, walked in through the unlocked door and surprised her in her bath. The killer could have done all this without anyone seeing them, and gone quietly back to the partying in the time it would have taken for a trip to the cloakrooms. No one would have noticed their absence. And there's no video evidence to draw on.'

'Surely drowning someone would take longer than the average trip to the loo,' Sue countered.

'Not if the killer knew how to drown somone quickly,' Pete said.

'Oh, you know how to drown someone quickly, do you?' she said acidly.

'As a matter of fact, yes.'

'This is all a matter of speculation,' Swift reminded the two protagonists. 'We don't yet have sufficient information to conclude that Josephine was drowned at the hands of an attacker. However if this does turn out to be a deliberate drowning, then I agree that we would be handicapped by the slim security arrangements at the hotel. But at least we would hope to have video information about outsiders entering the main entrance of the hotel who were not included in the wedding party.'

'But there are rear entrances, and they're not covered with cameras,' Pete pointed out. 'We're still back to anyone, anytime, anywhere for whatever reason. And no record to show for it.'

'That's often what we start with. That's why we're trained and paid to find things out,' Swift pointed out. 'As regards what we have so far, I'm prepared to run with the view there's a strong possibility that this is a murder. So now we need to settle on what needs to be done this morning. As far as we know both the dead bride and the bridegroom's families are here at the hotel, together with the best man, and maybe two bridesmaids. I'd like to know if any of them has anything odd or unusual to report. I'd also like to know if anything atypical was noticed in the mood or behaviour of the dead woman and/or any of the guests present. We need a contact list of all the wedding guests so we can get a team to do some preliminary questioning. I'd also like to know where Melanie Haygarth was between midnight and returning to her suite earlier this morning. And we also need to look at the TV recordings from the main entrance, starting from early yesterday morning. I'll get the manager to give us the tapes.' He glanced at his colleagues. 'OK?'

Sue and Pete nodded agreement.

'Any further comments or suggestions?'

'I managed to have a word with someone in our press liaison department, sir,' Sue said. 'They're giving out a standard preliminary report: details of when and where the death occurred, that the dead woman had only been married for a few hours. That we're treating the death as suspicious.'

'Right. But I'm afraid it's very likely there will already have been informal leaks,' Swift said. 'Around sixty guests left the hotel with the knowledge that the bride had died suddenly and inexplicably. I would be surprised if there were not one or two of them who wouldn't be able to resist sharing a story as dramatic as that.'

'What about talking to the staff, sir?' Pete asked.

'We'll certainly need to do that. But not as a first priority,' Swift said. 'I want us to cover as much ground as quickly as we can with the two families in the next hour or so and try to get a good feel of things. So I suggest that we work individually. Sue, I'd like you to talk to Jamie again and gain as much information as you can about what happened between Josie's disappearance from the wedding proceedings and the call to the doctor. I'd also like you to speak to his sister, and the bridesmaids if possible. Pete, you speak to the best man, then see if you can get anything further from Jack Haygarth. I'll interview Clive and Cassandra Parker and follow up with Melanie Haygarth.'

'If I'm reading you right, you seem to be thinking this could be a family based murder, sir,' Pete queried.

'Statistics and experience suggest that's always the first avenue,' Swift agreed. 'Do you want to put the case for an outsider to have been involved in this death, Pete?'

'Not really, sir. I'm just trying to think around all the possibilities. After all we know that the hotel was open for anyone to enter during the time the death occurred. And given that it was a big gathering, an intruder would probably not have been noticed. Let's face it, at a wedding the guests fall into two camps and if you spot people who are unfamiliar you simply assume — '

'That they belong to the enemy,' Sue broke in with a wry smile. 'I know what you're saying, Pete — I was a bride myself a few years ago. But what would be the motive for an outsider to have done this killing? Not robbery as far as we know. And surely most of the people who had an agenda with Josie were guests anyway.'

'Maybe that was the agenda,' Pete offered. 'Not being invited.'

'Oh, come on. Pique is hardly a motive for murder.' Sue gave the constable a look that carried a degree of benevolent condescension.

Swift said, 'I'm not ruling out a random killing by an intruder or stranger. But in my view this murder — and don't forget we haven't yet got confirmation that it was a murder — has a bizarre and dramatically horrifying quality about it which suggests that it was most likely an unplanned act of rage by someone close to Josie. Someone who is probably now appalled at what they have done. For this to have been done by a stranger to a new bride suggests a sadism and ritualism that would point to someone who has killed in this way before. And killed for some personal gratification, most likely with a sexual content.'

'We could check the national data base for any similar killings,' Pete suggested.

'Brides in the bath,' Sue said with a grimace. 'Wasn't there some famous mur-derer from years back who drowned his wives in the bath?'

'George Joseph Smith,' Pete came back on the button. 'He was a serial bigamist operating in the early 1900s. He drowned three of his wives and collected hefty life insurance payments for each of them before he was caught.'

'You've been browsing the net,' Sue said with a knowing grin.

Pete nodded, unabashed. 'Too right. I'm a very bad sleeper.'

'We should certainly check the national data base for similar recent killings,' Swift said, aiming to draw his colleagues' sparring to a close.

'But on the other hand,' Pete continued, thinking things through, 'if this case is anything like Smith's we should be looking at the bridegroom as a definite suspect.'

Swift gave a wry smile. 'We most certainly should. Moreover, as he and the family are available for us to speak to, that's what we need to get on with right away.' He stood up and his two officers smartly followed suit.

He paused at the door. 'If this case turns out to be a murder,' he said, 'and the killer is one of the family, or a close friend, then given the circumstances and the anonymity of the hotel as the place of death, it's likely that only two people know what happened and why. One of them is the murderer and not giving anything away, and the other is dead.'

4

Jamie had slept for four hours. When he woke he was still trembling. He felt as though there was a lump of something bitter at the base of his throat, something which would erupt violently from his mouth if he should try to move or speak.

How could Josie be dead? She had been his precious one, his only sweetheart, his life, his whole world. He felt as though his soul was exploding with shock and horror. He had always thought of himself as an ordinary kind of person and that was why he had found it unbelievable that she truly loved him. But she *had* loved him. She had chosen him from all the others who had fastened their wanting eyes on her. She had married him: taken vows and become his wife.

And now he couldn't believe that this terrible thing had happened to her. He kept seeing her dead face, the vacant stare of her eyes like polished stones staring into emptiness. She had left him alone to blunder like a wounded, blinded outcast through the cold, cruel days ahead.

Tentatively he pulled himself into a sitting

position. The lump in his throat bobbed and lurched. He just reached the lavatory in time, heaving up hot browns and pinks. He had vomited so often in the past few hours it was hard to believe there was anything left inside him to come back. He splashed water on his face, then wrapped himself in the towelling gown hanging behind the door, pulling the fabric tightly around himself as though for protection. He wandered back into the bedroom, drawn instinctively to the light from the window. The sun was already shining down, the sky a brilliant forget-me-not blue.

His room was at the side of the main hotel building. Standing beside the window his main view was of the guests' car park, which was now mainly empty of cars. Vaguely he noticed two figures making their way to the silver Bentley which dominated the car-park in shining magnificence. His father's car. And yes, the figures were those of his parents. Behind them was a young man carrying cases and long zip-up bags for those clothes too delicate to be folded. He glanced at the clock on the radio beside the bed. It was 7.45, and they were leaving, going back home. He frowned, dimly recalling some kind of argument; his father speaking in his low, cold voice; his mother heated and insistent. They had been angry, making him feel he had done wrong. That kind of admonition had not happened for some years, though their displeasure had been frequently demonstrated when he was a child. He couldn't remember what it had been about last night — or exactly when. It was after he had come to this room, certainly. And after he had taken two of the pills Di had given him. Yes, that must be right because they'd awakened him, just as he was falling off to sleep. But what had the pi-jawing been about? His brain couldn't get itself around any definite agenda, any specific words. There was just some sense that he was guilty of something in their eyes.

Watching the car make a slow reverse half circle, move majestically to the exit of the car park then disappear into the main drive leading to the road, he felt relief. The clarity of the emotion and the sense of release surprised him; he had thought he would never feel anything except a huge, crushing sorrow ever again.

He recalled that after his parents had gone, Melanie had come to him. But the pill had begun to kick in then, he couldn't resist it. Her face had blurred into darkness, there had just been the feel of her arms around him, the scent of woman that held a frail memento of Josie.

He had no idea what he should do next. He went back to the bathroom and switched on the bath taps. In horror at the sight of the gush of water he pulled his hand away, then wrenched the taps to a vicious close. Even the shower was repulsive and he resorted to washing himself at the basin. He washed his hair, then shaved with elaborate care so as not to cut himself. Going back to the bedroom he realized that his only available clothes were his morning suit trousers and the wing-collared white shirt he had worn at the wedding. The grief roared in again like a hurricane. Tears sprang into his eyes and he staggered against the edge of the dressing table, bruising his hip bone.

A soft but brisk knocking on the door brought him up with a start. Suddenly he felt panic, a complete inability to open the door and confront whatever unknown person stood behind it. Through the buzzing in his head and ears he heard a low gentle voice calling to him. 'Jamie, open the door please. It's Sergeant Sallis here. I'd like to speak to you.'

Jamie swallowed. The horror scene of Josie in the bath, and then soft and lifeless in his arms pushed into his mind. He screwed his eyes together, praying that the picture would stop coming.

The voice came again. 'Jamie, are you all right? I just want to have a quiet talk.'

Jamie frowned, trying to force his thoughts into some kind of meaningful configuration. A hazy image of the down-to-earth young woman he had spoken to whilst he was sitting on the bed cradling Josie came into his head. The tension in his body relaxed slightly.

She was smiling as he opened the door. She looked different to the night before: womanly and almost beautiful in her summer frock, with her hair falling around her face. He remembered that last night it had been pulled back in an elastic band. He hung on to that memory. There was so much else he could not retrieve.

He gestured her to sit in one of the small armchairs in the corner of the room, then perched himself on the end of the bed, hurriedly throwing the quilt over the rumpled sheets. He jerked on the cord of the towelling gown, pulling it tight. 'Sorry not to be more respectable,' he told her. 'My clothes are in the room that was mine and Josie's.' Saying those words was like stabbing himself with a knife. He held himself rigid, praying that he wouldn't break down again.

'I'm afraid the forensic team will need some time to look through the luggage and contents in the room,' Sue told him. 'I'm sure

74

we could find you something to wear. Maybe your best man could sort something out.'

'Yes, Adrian'll get something sorted.' Jamie gave a faint smile. 'He's the sorting type. Not like me.' He dropped his head in his hands and felt the warm tears run through his fingers.

She waited for a few moments. 'Jamie, I'm so sorry for what has happened,' she told him. 'I know it sounds false because I didn't know Josie.' She decided to leave it at that. There was no response from him, and for a moment she wondered if her words had registered with him. 'Do you think you're up to answering some more questions?'

He took his hands from his face and wiped his cheeks and eyes with his fingers. 'Yes. I'll answer any questions I can.' He stared at her. The torture in his face was shocking to look on, and Sue fancied she herself could almost feel the grief which was hollowing and scouring his insides. 'I want to,' he said. 'I want to try to get it straight in my head.'

Sue leaned forward. 'What is it you want to get straight, Jamie?'

He put his hands up and made small chopping movements, like someone debating a point and trying to put it across emphatically to their audience. 'Just what happened last night. I can't . . . ' He jerked his head around and stared out of the window. 'There are blanks, like black holes in my head,' he said.

'Can you go back to the point where the first black hole starts?' Sue asked.

He turned back to look at her. 'What? Sorry, what did you say?'

Sue judged he needed the simplest, most direct approach she could manage. 'You told me last night that you and Josie had been dancing at the party. And that after that you began to worry about not being able to find her. Do you remember what time that would have been, Jamie?'

'No.' He shook his head, as though desperately groping for something to tell her. He said, 'It all went so quickly. The whole day. It was like when you were little and you had a birthday. You longed and longed for it, and when it came the hours all ran away from you so fast.'

'I remember it being like that too,' she said. 'Can you remember where you were when you first thought you wanted to find her?'

'In the ballroom.'

'And how long had Josie been gone?'

'I don't know. She was dancing with different people, and so was I.' There was a long, sorrowful silence.

'And you suddenly noticed that she wasn't in the room?'

He frowned. 'I kind of felt it. I always like to be close to her. All the time if I can. I just looked around and she wasn't there.'

'Did you go to look for her straight away?'

'Yes.'

Did this mean she was dealing with someone chronically over-anxious, Sue wondered? Or simply very confused as a result of extreme shock and grief?

'Where did you look, Jamie?'

He frowned, shaking his head. 'I'm not really sure. In all the rooms where there were guests, I suppose.'

'The reception rooms on the ground floor?'

'Yes, I think so. It's hard to be sure; the things I can remember seem to be all jumbled together. Like dreams, I suppose.'

'All right. You have a vague memory of searching for Josie on the ground floor. What is the next thing you can remember?' Sue took a quick glance at her notes from the night previously, wondering if his account would match what he had said then. Which, unfortunately, had been precious little.

He bowed his head, frowning in intense concentration, his hands plucking at the cord of his dressing gown. 'In the bathroom,' he murmured. 'Josie in the bath.'

'Was she sitting up in the bath?' Sue asked.

Jamie's head jerked up. 'I'm not sure.' His eyes stared at her as though he had suddenly recalled something which transfixed him with terror. 'I can't remember,' he said, in panic. 'I don't know. Oh, Josie — I'm so sorry!'

Sue was careful to note down his exact words. It hardly needed her skills as a detective to conclude that Jamie was wondering if he had killed his wife and blanked out the memory. 'Just try to relax, Jamie. Sometimes memory works when you stop trying to force it.'

'I can remember being on the bed, holding her,' he said. 'There was someone else in the room, the doctor, I think. And then you came.'

'Who called the doctor?' Sue asked.

Jamie looked blank. 'I don't know.'

'Was the door of the suite locked when you came up to find Josie?'

'I don't think so.'

'Didn't that worry you — that the door wasn't locked?'

'Josie never bothered about locking doors. She didn't go for all that heavy security stuff and thinking of everyone outside the family and your friends as the enemy. She said you should trust people.'

Sue drew in a soft breath. 'Was the door

open?' she asked. 'I mean ajar?'

'I think it was closed,' Jamie said. 'Yes, I'm almost sure. Closed, but not locked.'

Sue thought this was progress. She recalled a speaker at a conference she had attended recently: a charismatic female psychologist with plum-coloured hair and an interesting line in interview techniques with subjects who appeared to be suffering a degree of memory loss. Maybe with sensitive questioning Sue could now enable Jamie to retrieve further images. 'I want you to imagine yourself pushing the door open and walking through,' she said. 'Tell me what you can see.'

Jamie considered. 'There's the bed on the left, and the dressing table on the other wall. And two chairs.'

Sue was disappointed. He was simply making an inventory of the room, probably from memories earlier on in the day. Or maybe from weeks back when the booking for the wedding was made. 'What could you hear? she asked.

He shook his head. His face was contorted with tension. 'I can't say. I don't remember.'

Sue decided to abandon the psychological approach. 'OK, Jamie, let's just accept that at the moment you're having difficulty remembering exactly what you saw and heard around the time Josie was missing and then found dead. Except you do remember seeing her in the bath.'

'I think so,' he murmured.

Is he faking this? Sue wondered. Was this 'can't remember' response simply a mechanism to avoid saying something he might later regret? A more acceptable way of withholding information than the stubborn 'no comment' strategy? But just as effective.

She noticed that Jamie's body had slumped as they had been speaking. His back was bowed, his whole body-language a testament to despair, his face grey with distress and fatigue. 'Have you had breakfast?' she asked him.

'I don't want anything,'

She found herself on the point of making a dangerously maternal-sounding remark about the necessity to eat so as to keep up his strength, but checked herself in time.

'Have you finished with me?' he asked dully.

'For the moment.' Sue knew she was unlikely to make further progress at this stage, but she nevertheless considered chancing one last question: the old stalwart about whether he'd seen anything unusual around the time of the death. Glancing again at Jamie's ravaged face, she decided against it. She was still concerned about his state of mind.

'I'll get someone to come and sit with you,' she told him. She saw that he was more alert now, watching her watching him. She had seen the same nervy, assessing glances in intelligent dogs and wary horses. It was not solely the awful tragedy of Jamie's situation which moved her, it was his manner and the hints of his inner personality which stirred her sympathy. And yet, at the same time, she knew that he was a more than likely suspect. She reminded herself to keep her distance. Too great a compassion for a suspect was just as damaging to an investigation as antipathy and prejudice. And then, once again, she wondered about the degree of the young man's calculation.

'I'll be all right,' he told her. 'If you can get Adrian to sort me out some clothes I'll get dressed and come downstairs. Face the music,' he added thoughtfully. 'To coin a phrase of my parents. At least that's something I can remember.'

* * *

Clive Parker was well known in the area as a latter-day wool baron. Swift had learned about Parker and his enterprise soon after he had moved to Yorkshire to join the force serving the extensive semi-rural area north-west of Bradford. Parker was highly regarded as a generous supporter of local projects. He was known for being liberal with his money, rather than his time. A somewhat distant man, reserved and private.

Swift had anticipated that the Parkers' house would be a substantial millstone-grit pile built in the later years of Queen Victoria's reign like so many of the grand houses on the north side of the city. In fact, the simple, classical beauty of the house took him by surprise. Like its neighbours, scattered along a discreet millionaire's row nestling beneath the east flank of Addingham Moor, the house was well shielded from the road by a huge formal garden and a long winding drive. But as the building came into view Swift saw that this residence was no dark satanic throwback to the nineteenth century. Built of pale coral brick with tall arched windows and shamelessly showy Doric columns guarding the courtly front door, the house was a monument to neo-classicism. From its pristine perfection Swift guessed it had been designed and built in the 1970s or even later. The bills from the architect and the builders must have been awesome.

This morning the drive was cluttered with

vehicles. Two overalled women were unloading flower displays from a small white van. From a much bigger brown van, proclaiming itself 'Purveyors of Fine Foods and Wines' in gold lettering, staff in white coats were hurrying to and fro with intent expressions on their faces. A gleaming Bentley stood in stately splendour just outside the front door, causing some inconvenience for the working fraternity.

Swift parked his car to the side of the house, then walked through the open front door into the reception hall. Clearly preparations were well in hand for some kind of function later in the day. Huge displays of summer flowers cascaded from white urns placed in columned alcoves. The lightbulbs in the two massive chandeliers on either side of the hallway were blazing, throwing down swords of brilliance on to the blue and cream tiled floor. Swift sensed an air of expectancy about the place, coupled with a strange, muted sadness. Once inside the doorway, the catering staff moved in silence, their pace measured, their faces grave.

Before he had need to make enquiries as to the house-owners' whereabouts, Clive Parker emerged from a door at the back of the hallway which was partly hidden beneath the wide cantilevered staircase. Swift had not met him before in person, but he had seen Parker at civic functions, and his face was also recognizable from frequent photographs in the local press.

He prepared to introduce himself as Parker approached, but the older man got in first. 'Chief Inspector Swift?' he said, extending a hand whilst maintaining a grim and unsmiling expression. 'I recognize you from the way my wife described you to me. I was expecting you might call. This really is not a good time, as you'll no doubt appreciate. But I did actually want to speak to you. So we could have a few minutes in my study, if you'd like to come this way.'

Swift followed where he was led, noting the speed and firmness of Parker's stride. He also noticed that Parker was freshly shaved and dressed in an expertly tailored navy suit. And that for a man of sixty or so, he had a head of enviably thick silver hair.

The study was around twenty-foot square, the light coming from two large windows, one looking out to the west and one to the north. With the walls and floors lined in light oak, and the carpets and furnishing fabrics a uniform creamy white, the room had a welcoming simplicity about it.

Parker sat behind the big oak desk placed in front of the west window, and gestured to

Swift to take one of the armchairs placed opposite him. It was a good way of showing who was in charge, Swift thought. It also struck him that once the sun came around to the west of the house, the person facing the desk would need to shade their eyes.

'I'd like to offer my condolences on the death of your daughter-in-law,' Swift said, speaking before he had settled himself in his chair and preventing Parker from getting in first again, which he had clearly been preparing to do.

Parker raised his hands. 'This is a terrible, terrible business. Unbelievable. Have you got any further in discovering the cause of death?'

'We won't know for sure until the results of the autopsy later on today.'

'Well, whilst it's my earnest wish for it to emerge that the death was accidental, for the sake of you lot, let's hope you weren't barking up the wrong tree and causing a good deal of unnecessary distress.' It was the tone, rather than the words which gave offence.

Swift levelled his gaze with that of Parker's. 'In the meantime,' he said, ignoring the other man's challenge, 'it would be very helpful to have your observations of anything you saw or heard during the wedding reception which could throw light on Josephine's death.'

'Absolutely nothing,' Parker responded. 'I

can say that with confidence because, as I said before, I was expecting your visit and anticipating your questions. I had already given the particular one you have just asked a good deal of thought. I only wish I had something to report. Something which might go some way to illuminating the cause of this wretched tragedy — and the pain our son and Josephine's family must be feeling.'

'Yes, indeed,' Swift agreed. 'So, from your point of view, the wedding ceremony and the reception were proceeding smoothly?'

'Very satisfactorily.'

'There were no arguments? No tears? No little hitches?'

Parker's features tightened. 'I hope I am not hearing sarcasm in your tone, Inspector,' he said.

'If you did hear sarcasm, it was not meant and I apologize,' Swift said evenly. 'Would you be kind enough to answer my question?'

Parker sighed. 'Very well. There were no arguments, not that I heard, anyway. There were a few tears from the bride's mother at the marriage ceremony — which I believe are entirely normal, if not obligatory. And, as for hitches, no, I really don't recall any.' His fingers drummed on the desk, restless and impatient. He glanced at his watch. 'I don't have much time, Inspector.'

'How did you get to know about Josie's death, sir?' Swift asked.

Parker's frown made a deep diagonal cleft over his eyebrows. 'I was first alerted by the manager that there was a concern about her and that the doctor had been called.'

'When was that?'

'I can't be precise. In the region of nine o'clock, as I recall. Her death was communicated some time later to Josie's parents by the doctor. Melanie then advised Cassandra and myself.'

'Had the manager alerted anyone else in the wedding party before he first spoke to you at nine o'clock?'

'I truly don't know. Is it important?' Parker was now suspicious and increasingly displeased.

'All the details are important,' Swift said evenly.

'Right. Well now,' Parker said, giving one sharp tap on the edge of the desk with his fingers, 'I really must direct my attention to the day ahead. Cassandra and I are hosting a lunch party for those of our friends whom we were not able to invite to the wedding. As a number have flown in specially from Europe and the States we felt it was too late, and also uncivil, to cancel the event, and that the best thing was to go ahead, making the occasion an opportunity to pay tribute to Josephine.' Just for a moment his self-possession seemed on the point of crumbling. 'Dear God, this is all perfectly dreadful,' he murmured, staring blankly in front of him.

As Swift stood up in preparation for leaving, Cassandra Parker appeared in the doorway. She was dressed in an anklelength silk coat and dress in deep lilac and there were some nodding lilac plumes in her hair. 'Clive, have you finished with the inspector? We really need to get on,' she announced in staccato tones, directing a cursory nod in Swift's direction. There was a gloss about her appearance and a fierce determination in her manner which suggested that any feelings she might have about the disaster which had overtaken her son, and the family as a whole, were firmly corralled to some distant, inaccessible place.

'Good morning, Mrs Parker,' Swift said, his voice conveying sympathy and respect.

'This is really too bad,' she said, rounding on him now, her glinting grey eyes hard and challenging. 'To come here at a time like this when we are in such a state of shock. And with all the preparations we have to supervise.'

'I'm very sorry to disturb you,' Swift said. 'I've been asking your husband for his observations of anything unusual which occurred at the ceremony and reception yesterday.'

The grey eyes flared within the carefully mascaraed lashes. 'Let me think,' she said. 'Ah, yes. The bride died during the reception. And the police are putting it about that it was a murder. Yes, I think we can safely say something very unusual happened yesterday.'

Parker turned to his wife. 'The chief inspector was asking if there had been any arguments, tears or little hitches at the wedding yesterday,' he said.

Swift noted that his tone was perfectly steady and even. He guessed that Parker would be long practised and skilled in dealing with his wife's acerbity. 'Do you recall any of those, Mrs Parker?' he prompted.

'No,' she said. 'It was a lovely occasion, and it all went swimmingly. Until . . . ' She raised her hands in a gesture of utter weariness at having to answer such asinine questions. 'Really, that's all I can say.'

Swift paused for a moment. 'Thank you for your help,' he said, moving towards the door.

Cassandra Parker blocked his exit at the doorway. 'I hope you haven't been badgering our son. He's really not up to any extra stress at the moment.'

'Sergeant Sallis was planning to speak to

him again this morning. How is he coping?' Swift asked kindly.

Cassandra's face creased with a ripple of anxiety in which there was a faint trace of irritation. 'Obviously he's totally devastated. But we've tried to point out to him how vital it is to try to be strong now, both for his own sake and out of respect for Josie's memory and the way she would have wanted him to behave. When times are difficult, one has to simply think of getting through one day at a time with as much dignity as can be managed.'

'Are you expecting Jamie to be here for your lunch party today?' Swift asked.

For a moment she hesitated. 'Well, of course, in the normal run of things he and Josie would have been flying to Italy for their honeymoon today. Jamie was never intended to be a guest.' She glanced at her husband who was still sitting at his desk, his face grim and impassive. 'However, we did think it might be good for him at least to put in an appearance today. It would be an opportunity for him to begin trying to come to terms with what has happened. Putting on a brave public face isn't as fashionable with the young as it was with our generation, but it can be a very good way of preserving one's inner strength and facing up to realities.'

Clive Parker made a small sound in his throat. He moved from the desk and came to stand beside his wife, placing an affectionate, or maybe proprietorial arm on her shoulder. He said to Swift, 'You'll no doubt think we're hard-hearted, unfeeling parents. I can assure you that is not the case. We love our son — and value his talents. In fact, I recently recommended that he be voted on to the board of directors in my company. We simply want to help Jamie as much as we can at this terrible time, and allowing him to hide away and wrap himself in cotton wool doesn't seem to us the way forward for him.'

Swift gave a neutral nod. 'Will your daughter be here later?' he asked.

'Oh yes, Diana is always a huge support,' Clive Parker said, and Swift had a strong impression the daughter was held in much higher favour than the son.

'Actually she's rung to say she might be a little late,' Cassandra told her husband. 'Piers isn't feeling too well. He thinks he might be coming down with flu.'

Parker's face twitched with contempt. 'Typical Piers!' he muttered, then turned to address Swift. 'If you're thinking of talking to Diana, Chief Inspector, I suggest you see her at work rather than her home. The situation at our daughter's place is somewhat chaotic.'

Cassandra frowned. 'That's not fair, Clive. Diana just has a different set-up from the one we've always found works for us. She and Piers are a different generation, and of course they do things differently.'

'That's one way of putting it,' Clive Parker said.

Cassandra tightened her lips and stared meaningfully at her watch. 'We really must — '

'Of course. Thank you for your help,' Swift said as Cassandra stepped aside and enabled him to make his departure.

Walking out into the sun which was now beating down, parching the flowers and sucking the remaining greenness from the lawns, Swift began a mental review of the interview. He was doubtful that much of significance had emerged regarding the possible reasons for Josephine's death which he had not known already. But he had gathered in quite a good harvest of information on the Parkers' family dynamics. The parents' view of their daughter as clever and capable, whilst the son was regarded as vulnerable and possibly weak, was clearly of interest. Inadequates were well known for their capacity to display astounding levels of viciousness and violence if pushed too far. He had not yet had time to form an opinion on

Jamie Parker for himself, and he never tried to outdo professional psychologists at their job. He guessed, however, that those judged inadequate wrongly could be in even greater danger of turning nasty. They were thoughts he would keep to himself for the present.

In the meantime, there was an issue which needed to be cleared up without any further delay. He could telephone Sue Sallis to see if she had got any further information from Jamie. But then it might be counterproductive to disturb her if she were at a critical stage in an interview. He dialled John Ford instead, asking if he could confirm that he personally had made the call to summon the doctor to advise on Josie Parker's death.

'That is correct,' Ford told him.

'And who was the first person you told of your request for medical advice?'

'That was Mr Clive Parker,' Ford said. 'He happened to be in the foyer after I'd made the call.'

Swift was making rapid jottings. 'I see. And who alerted you to the need for medical input, Mr Ford?'

'It was one of my waitress staff.'

'And how had she discovered the need for a doctor?'

'One of the guests had told her. A young man. I'm afraid I don't know his name, and he left the hotel soon after. Obviously it was all terribly upsetting and the main issue was to get the doctor as soon as possible,' he added, becoming defensive now.

'Of course,' Swift reassured him. 'However, if you do have a chance to speak to your member of staff and gain any further information, it would be helpful.'

'She's not in this morning. I'll speak to her as soon as she comes on her next shift. It's not urgent is it?'

Swift considered the issue of urgency as he snapped his phone shut. With this investigation, at this stage, everything and nothing was urgent.

*   *   *

Pete was not having a good morning. The Parkers' daughter, Diana, had already slipped away with her husband and kids before he could talk to her. The bridesmaids were transfixed with shock and could hardly speak for staring tragically into the distance and bursting into tears. And Adrian Gowland, the best man, was in the grip of a massive hangover. Having found some clothes for Jamie to wear he sank into a chair, occasionally pressing his hand to his forehead, perhaps hoping to still the hammers that were beating in his skull.

'God, I feel as if we're all taking part in some horror movie,' he groaned.

Pete watched the other man with a disdainful pity he tried to conceal. Previously a heavy drinker and now reformed, Pete had no sympathy for those who were unable to control their need and greed for alcohol. He guessed Gowland to be in his early to mid-twenties. He had a chubby, amiable face and sparse dark hair which was already receding from his forehead. He was only too ready to answer questions, but as he hadn't seen or heard anything whatsoever amiss during the wedding celebrations, and had most likely been half-cut before the ceremony, and totally slaughtered before the wedding breakfast, Pete found it hard to glean anything of interest from him.

'How long have you known Jamie?' he asked, when the main agenda of the interview was over.

'Four years. We were at uni together in Bristol on a business management course. And Josie was doing law.'

'Is that where they met?'

'Yes. Although they only lived a few miles from each other, funnily enough. But she went to the local grammar school and he went away to school, so their paths didn't cross.'

'Did she have other boyfriends?'

'Nope. She was one of those beautiful, clever girls who've got so much going for them, they don't need to put themselves around — if you get my drift.'

Pete was not entirely sure, but he filed the thought away to ponder later.

A rap on the door heralded room service in the shape of a cafetière of hot coffee and several rounds of thick white toast. A cheery, beefy girl dressed in chef's blue and cream check trousers placed the tray carefully on the glass-topped table beside Adrian Gowland's chair. She glanced up at Pete. 'Shall I bring an extra cup, sir?'

'Er, no thanks.' Pete's taste-buds were quivering at the smell of the coffee but he felt a need not to be too pally with his interviewee, to keep his distance and be a true professional. Gowland might yet turn out to be a key witness — although Pete somehow sensed that was unlikely.

'She was a pretty amazing girl all round,' Adrian Gowland reflected, buttering a slice of toast and taking a huge bite. 'God, this tastes good! Nothing like a few slabs of grease and carbohydrate to clear the head.' He took a long swig of coffee. 'Yeah, Josie was great.

Fantastic looking. Very together and confident. But not a ball-breaker. Sympathetic type. Jamie couldn't believe his luck. He loved her to bits, worshipped the ground and so on. Quite honestly, I don't how the hell he's going to get through this.'

'What do you mean, Jamie couldn't believe his luck?' Pete asked.

Gowland speeded up his chewing and swallowed a huge wedge of toast. 'Hard to say really. He's a good-looking guy, he's no slouch on the brain front, and he's loaded, his father's worth millions apparently. It's just that he doesn't seem to know his own worth. Jamie, I mean, not his dad. And I'm talking person value, not bank balance size. Mind you, with a mother like that, what guy could ever crawl out from under without being a bit squashed? She's a real termagant. Scares me shitless.'

'Did Josie have any other boyfriends besides Jamie?' Pete asked, hoping to get something on the jealously angle.

'No. She had friends who happened to be guys, but, as I said, she didn't do casual sex.' He threw Pete a roguish glance. 'I should know, I tried quite hard. Not after they got to be an item,' he added hastily.

'Did she and Jamie ever row? Have a disagreement?'

'Do you know,' Gowland said, as though he'd just thought of it, 'I don't think I ever saw them fight. They really got on together. A perfect match if ever there was one.' He grimaced. 'Wish I hadn't said that, it makes them sound too good to be true. But they were.'

'Right.' Pete folded his notebook and looked thoughtful.

Gowland swallowed more coffee. 'You're not really thinking this is a murder?'

'Too early to say for sure. Thanks for all the information, anyway.'

'Sorry I can't tell you anything more sensational.'

'It's OK,' Pete said drily. 'We don't look for drama in this business, it just keeps rushing towards us.'

★　★　★

At three o'clock Swift held a further briefing meeting with Sue Sallis and Pete Fox, this time in his cramped cupboard-like office at the station. On his desk were word-processed accounts of the various interviews carried out that morning, copies of which had been left on Sue and Pete's desks earlier. Hopefully each member of the team would have had time to digest the findings of the others. As his team joined him, Swift was standing beside his printer which was still busy.

'The pathologist, Dr Blake, has just e-mailed a report through on Josie Parker's autopsy,' he told them.

'That was quick,' Sue commented.

'She told me she was swamped with demands,' Swift remarked. 'I would think she's no option but to work fast.'

'If she doesn't shift the bodies and the reports smartly she'll be sinking under the weight,' Pete suggested.

Sue grimaced at his poor taste. 'If you want something done quickly and efficiently then ask a busy woman,' she told him sweetly.

'If either of you have any interest in hearing the conclusions,' Swift interposed quietly, 'then I'll pick out the main points. Firstly Josie was a healthy young female with no history of medical conditions associated with sudden loss of consciousness. She did not have a significantly high amount of alcohol in her blood. She was not pregnant and she had been currently using oral contraception.' He paused to give those basic facts the attention they deserved. 'The cause of death was drowning. I quote: 'A significant volume of water had been inhaled in a short time, giving rise to metabolic catastrophe — probably in seconds — and death, most likely quite soon afterwards'. There are some physiological descriptions of the damage done to the red blood cells, which I can barely pronounce, so we'll take those as read. The second important point is that the clinical signs strongly suggest that death was quick, consistent with the woman having been pulled swiftly under the water thus causing a rush of liquid to invade her respiratory system.'

'The killer grabs the ankles and gives a yank,' Pete stated. 'If the bath is big enough and full enough the victim doesn't stand a chance. Apparently the technique was demonstrated in court when the brides-in-the-bath murderer was tried. They used a portable bath and a woman PC as the subject. The KC gave her such a heave she was on the point of drowning in seconds. When they set about reviving her it was touch and go for a few moments,'

Sue shuddered. 'Ugh!'

'Thanks for that, Pete,' Swift said, with a wry smile. 'You'll be glad to know your research findings are perfectly consistent with the extensive footnote in this report.'

'You'd have to grasp someone's ankles pretty tightly to pull their body under water,' Sue said thoughtfully. 'If that method of killing applied to Josie, then we'd expect there to be some bruise marks found on her legs.'

'According to Dr Blake there were faint signs of bluish, disc-shaped contusions around both ankles,' Swift told his listeners. 'Consistent with the pressure from fingertips.'

There was a silence.

'So, we're looking at a murder,' Pete said.

'The information we've got from the report does make accident or suicide seem remote,' Swift said. 'However, I've still got to convince Superintendent Lister that you two can be assigned to full-time assistance on a murder investigation. And he's not going to be pleased. Not with a significant number of his force down with flu. Nor with Sunday working and the overtime costs.'

'We'll need a plan of action,' Sue said, confident of Swift's ability to get his own way with the superintendent. 'We know the method of killing — '

'We have substantive information,' Swift corrected her. 'The method is not entirely clear cut. Only the killer can tell us for sure.'

Sue smiled. When she first worked with Swift she had found his liking for precision rather daunting. But once she had realized that his carefully stated corrections were not meant as personal criticisms or put downs she had become less anxious. 'Anything from forensics yet?' she asked him.

'No. Hopefully there could be something tomorrow.'

'But we can start formal interviews now, sir?' Pete asked.

'Oh, yes. We also need to get the people on the list of guests seen for preliminary enquiries as soon as possible. I'm thinking of asking Superintendent Lister if Geoff Fowler could be coaxed out of retirement to help us out on that.'

'Ooh, I don't know about that,' Sue said, grinning. 'Rumour is he's got a new girlfriend. And from what I can gather she's taking up quite a bit of his time.'

'Gossip girl!' Pete goaded her. 'Who's Geoff Fowler?'

'A retired sergeant with a lot of experience and a keen eye for villainy,' Swift said, recalling Fowler's sullen and reluctant co-operation when Swift had first joined the team; how he had gradually shed his hostility when he realized he and Swift had more in common than he thought regarding their determination to bring criminals to justice.

Pete's mobile chirped. Quickly flipping it open, he glanced at the read out. 'It's Jack Haygarth,' he said.

'Take it,' Swift mouthed. 'Go into the other office if you prefer.'

Pete shook his head, speaking out his name

crisply and frowning in concentration as he listened. Sue and Swift sat waiting, wearing the neutral expressions of those excluded from one half of a telephone dialogue. Pete's contribution was mainly attending to what was told him. There were occasional murmurs and brief comments conveying an appreciation of what was being said. Rapid jottings in his notebook. 'Thank you for this, Mr Haygarth,' Pete said, drawing the conversation to a close. 'I'll be over right away to talk to you in more detail. Thank you, sir.'

He snapped the phone shut and threw himself back in his chair. 'Well!'

Sue leaned forward. 'Well, what?'

'Josie Haygarth had a stalker. He'd been following her for months.'

5

Jack Haygarth was waiting at the door as Swift and Pete Fox arrived at his Victorian villa. It stood at the highest point of a hilly crescent, one of six carefully tended residences, each secluded from the others by overhanging beech and horse-chestnut trees, yet linked together by a communal green around which the houses were spaced. This Sunday afternoon the crescent was bare of people, and there was a sense of torpor in the sticky heat that had built up during the day.

Jack mumbled an acknowledgement of their presence, then struggled to move his big bulky body down the hallway and into a tall-windowed sitting room which Swift guessed Naomi would describe as shabby chic — and one which Mrs Cassandra Parker would have had redecorated and refurbished years ago. Jack sagged into the nearest squashy leather armchair, his frame crumpling as though all the bones in his body had softened into gristle. 'Melanie's gone out for a walk,' he said. 'We don't seem to be able to settle to anything. The time is just hanging. Endless.'

Swift and Pete Fox looked around for seating, eventually settling themselves on a large scuffed leather sofa adjacent to their distraught-looking interviewee.

'Mr Haygarth,' Swift said gently, 'thank you for inviting us to see you. Before we hear the information you have to offer, I need to tell you that we've received the report from the postmortem carried out on Josie. The findings indicate that we can rule out accidental death. This is now a murder investigation.'

Jack Haygarth sat quite still, his breathing slow and painfully audible. The muscles of his face barely moved, yet it was clear that he was hitting the rock bottom of despair. The infinity of his misery seemed to fill the room, to dim the gleam of the dust particles which drifted in the broad panel of light coming in through the window, to dull the impact of the sun itself. 'This is surely as low as it gets,' he murmured. 'We'd been expecting it, of course. But to hear that terrible word, in connection with my lovely daughter. How can that be?'

'We're very sorry to bring this news,' Swift told him. He glanced at Pete, and gave a brief nod.

'We shall be driving all our efforts into bringing the relevant aspects of this crime into the open, Mr Haygarth,' Pete said, the low gravity of his voice giving due respect to the father's inconsolable grief. 'And, of course, to bring the perpetrator to justice.'

'Yes, I'm sure you will,' Haygarth replied. He folded his hands in his lap and waited, as though he had completely forgotten that the interview had been at his own request.

Pete cleared his throat. 'You mentioned that Josie had been followed by someone in recent months. A young man called Saul Williams. Is that correct, sir?'

Haygarth nodded. 'Melanie didn't want me to say anything about it. But I couldn't get it out of my mind. I knew I had to tell you.'

Quite right, Swift thought. He wondered about Melanie Haygarth's motive in withholding information. He glanced at Pete, once again giving him the nod to proceed.

'You said that this young man had fallen in love with Josie and had in fact developed some sort of obsession for her.'

'Yes, that's right. At least that's how it seems to me.' Haygarth's voice was barely more than a whisper and his head dipped lower. His breathing was harsh and jagged.

'You said he followed her when she went out to the shops, or walking in the woods with the family dog. How often did this happen?'

'Three or four times a week, I think. Josie didn't say anything about it for quite a time. She wasn't afraid of him, you see. She used to let him walk along with her and they'd talk.' He pulled his shoulders back a little and became taller in his chair. 'She was that kind of person. She was so sociable and adept with people. People from all walks of life. She was interested in them and they would tell her things, confide in her.'

'Did Saul Williams try to contact her at other times, besides these walks you describe?' Pete asked.

'Not directly as far as I know. But in the past week, he'd begun to watch the house. I saw him on several occasions, standing behind the copper beech tree at the end of the crescent.'

'How long was he there?'

'I usually get up around seven-thirty, and when I looked out he was already there. That would be Wednesday, then again on Thursday and Friday.' He spoke slowly as though each short phrase was a heavy stone to be lifted. 'I'm not sure what time he left. It was a very busy week for Josie and the rest of us, as you'll appreciate. We seemed to be in and out all the time, always something to do. But he wasn't there in the evenings when I looked out after dinner.' He stopped, his chest heaving with the effort of communicating.

'Do you want to take a rest, sir?' Pete asked.

'No. Best to keep going.'

'Did you or anyone else go out and challenge this man?'

'I wanted to, but Josie said to leave him be. She said he meant no harm.'

'You didn't think to call the police?' Pete asked, a faint note of disbelief in his tone.

'Yes, of course. But it would have upset Josie.'

'What was your wife's view of the situation?' Swift interposed quietly.

'She didn't want the police involved either.'

'Why was that?'

Jack Haygarth slowly transferred his glance from Pete to his senior. 'She knows Saul from the past, you see. He used to visit the centre where Melanie works as a volunteer.'

'What centre is this?' Pete came in sharply.

'The Cardale Centre for Young People. It's a drop-in place. Youngsters can go there if they're in any sort of trouble. It's just down the road from here, on the way into town.'

Pete noted the details, then made a quick review of his scribbled notes. 'So, you're saying, Mr Haygarth, that Josie didn't seem worried about this young man following her around?'

'That's right. I suppose she'd made a friend of him.'

'And what did Jamie think about that, sir?' There was a buzz in Pete's manner, and Swift understood that he was experiencing the excitement of the hunter finding the scent of the prey.

Jack Haygarth shook his large shaggy head. Bewilderment flickered over his features. He was tiring now, the toil and stress of telling this simple but troubling story beginning to suck at his dwindling reserves of emotional strength. 'I really don't know,' he said. 'Maybe she didn't discuss it with him.'

Pete opened his mouth in a reflex jerk of astonishment. Noting Swift's sharp glance he quickly shut it again.

'Mr Haygarth, do you know if Saul Williams suffers from any learning or personality difficulties?' Swift asked.

'That's not my field at all,' Haygarth said. 'You'll need to ask Melanie. But I suppose all the youngsters who go to that kind of centre suffer from psychological disabilities of one sort or another.'

'Did Saul Williams ever threaten Josie?' Pete asked, leaning forward, eager and intent.

Haygarth stared at him. 'Threaten? I don't know. She never said so. You see he didn't seem to be a menacing young man at all. But then, you never know, do you? What people can do. The extremities of human nature.'

'No, indeed, sir,' Pete said, with heartfelt agreement.

'Was Saul Williams invited to the wedding, Mr Haygarth?' Swift asked.

Pete gave a little jerk of his head, wishing he'd thought to pop that one.

'Good heavens, no!' Haygarth exclaimed.

'Could Josie have invited him, by word of mouth?' Pete asked.

Haygarth's ravaged face registered intense dismay. 'No, of course not. We spent hours drawing up the guest list. Of course she wouldn't have invited anyone without telling us.' The brief flare in his eyes died away. His body drooped once more, his spine sliding down the smooth leather of the chair back. 'You'll have to go now,' he told them. 'I can't talk any more.'

Swift nodded and stood up, his example followed by a reluctant-looking Pete.

'See yourselves out, will you,' Haygarth said, in a low, flat voice. As he turned away the two officers saw his eyes close, returning him to the private black hell of his thoughts.

'I'm sorry, sir,' Pete said, as they closed the front door behind them. 'I'm afraid I put him off with that last question.'

'It was a good question,' Swift replied. 'And

I think he was already past the point of wanting to give us anything else. Of course the really interesting last question would have been whether Saul Williams was in fact present at the wedding — invited or not.'

'But surely Haygarth would have told us if he had been.'

'We didn't directly ask him.'

'No, but it was a relevant piece of information. And presumably he's given us what we've got so far on Williams because he thinks he's a suspect. He's no reason to protect him.'

'Agreed. But maybe he didn't see him, even though he was present. It was a large gathering with a number of assembly points. And also maybe he didn't recognize him. From what we know he's only seen Williams at a distance, half hiding in the bushes so to speak.'

'The CCTV footage might tell us.'

'Yes. Or Melanie Haygarth when we get to see her again. She presumably knew Saul Williams quite well.'

They climbed into Pete's ancient but trendily cool Ford Escort XR3. It had padded black leather seats and a steering wheel the size of a saucer. Swift suspected that Pete might be something of a speed merchant when on his own and out of the range of speed cameras. But with Swift as a passenger, the constable drove with impeccable regard to the speed limits, hardly ever getting beyond third gear.

'That was amazing stuff he told us!' Pete said, slotting his key into the ignition. 'Josie having a stalker who she then makes a friend of. Haygarth makes it out she's oh-so-sociable, but I bet that's not what he thinks deep down.'

'What *do* you think he thinks deep down?' Swift asked, bracing himself as Pete fired the engine and revved it into growling fury.

'That she was taking damned stupid risks.'

'Possibly. What's your take on it, Pete?'

'The same, obviously. And for sociable, read gullible. Plus, it's seriously odd she didn't tell Jamie.'

'We don't actually know that.'

'No, but Haygarth seemed to think it was quite likely she'd kept it secret.' He screwed his face up in thought. 'It's a very funny caper all round. Maybe she was simply a rotten judge of character. And secretive, to boot.'

'Mmm, but we haven't met Saul Williams yet. For all we know he could be an upright citizen of exemplary character.'

Pete grinned, feeling it might just be possible to feel relaxed in Swift's company in the not too distant future. 'I was assuming that was where we were going next, sir.' He had Saul William's address at the ready, underlined in red in his notebook.

'Yes,' said Swift with a sigh. His head was beginning to throb. He felt weak from not having eaten since breakfast, and he was worried about leaving Naomi on her own all day on a Sunday. Which was quite unreasonable as she had a good group of friends and had never shown any sign of moping around the house pining for her father. After all she was seventeen now. She'd recently passed her driving test and was fully mobile in the little Peugeot he had bought for her birthday. But still . . .

'We turn left at the main road and continue on for half a mile or so,' he told Pete, thinking it was high time they made a move before the Ford's twin exhausts filled the crescent with white smoke.

'There must have been something going on between Josie and Williams,' Pete mused. 'Most girls freak out if they think they're being stalked. Was she leading him on, do you think? We could be looking at a jealousy killing here.'

'It's possible,' Swift said. 'That's what's so frustrating and interesting at the beginning of an investigation: the possibilities are infinite.'

Pete's anticipation heightened as they

climbed the steps to Saul Williams's flat, even though he was surprised and a little disappointed that the block was newly built of golden Yorkshire sandstone, and had an air of peace and respectability about it which didn't quite match his image of the dwelling of an obsessed and possibly murderous stalker. He'd had an image of a concrete monstrosity with litter-strewn balconied walkways which, of course, was ridiculous. He should have learnt by now that there were not too many of those in this part of Yorkshire. In the countryside there were drystone walls and neat little stone houses and gurgling brooks skipping beneath hump-backed stone bridges. In the hearts of the villages there were bow-windowed post offices, tea shops with tinkling bells over the door and the occasional Michelin-starred restaurant. Maybe just the odd row of council properties bordering the edges. The small towns thrived: their once clattering mills converted into luxury apartments, the former millhands' cottages second homes for wealthy city dwellers, the outdoor markets stocked with asparagus and monkfish. There would be an underbelly somewhere, of course, just as he had found in Devon in the midst of moorland beauty and tourist havens.

Saul Williams's flat was number 14. Its door was freshly painted in lovat-green. There was no entry-phone, no spyhole, just a simple buzzer. Pete pressed it, his nerves twitching in expectation. Seconds passed.

'He's not in,' Swift said. 'It's funny, isn't it, how you get a feeling almost right away when a place is empty?'

'He could be lying low,' Pete said darkly. 'Pity it's up here on the second floor, so we can't look in the windows.' His face crinkled with frustration.

'He'll be in tomorrow, no doubt,' Swift said calmly, sensing there was no rush with this interview, having an instinct that Saul Williams would not turn out to be Josie's killer. He recognized that such an opinion at this stage was arrogant and to be treated with caution. And kept to himself.

'He could be halfway around the world!' Pete protested.

Swift smiled. He said, 'It's hard for murderers to hide anywhere on the planet in present times. And we're not at the stage when we can put out a widespread alert. What have we got on him? All we know is that Williams had followed Josie around, talked with her, and possibly fallen in love with her.'

Pete thought about it. 'I take your point, sir.'

'Look, I doubt if I'm going to get much further on this case until I've had some food and some sleep,' Swift said, suddenly crushed with weariness. 'So when we get back to the station I'm going to check on anything new that's come in and if there's nothing urgent, I'm going home.' He refrained from suggesting that Pete should do the same, but the implication in his voice was clear.

★   ★   ★

As Swift approached his apartment, Naomi was just ahead of him signalling to turn into the drive. She'd taken to driving with such ease, rarely panicking, showing a natural ability both for manoevring the car and for gauging the responses of other drivers on the roads. When she had passed her test and gone out for her first solo drive, he had sternly instructed himself not to worry. She would be fine.

'Hi.' He laid his arm briefly around her shoulders. 'Good day?'

She began to recite a résumé. 'Finished Maths assignment, read trashiest bits of the Sunday papers, took phone call from Marcus, had Lizzie round at lunchtime. We sunbathed in the garden, then when we were fully baked we went out for a drive into the Dales, windows full open to try to manufacture a breeze. And now — here I am!' Her vibrance and gaiety cheered and revived him. And then she threw him a highvoltage, witchy smile which made him worry afresh.

'So how is Marcus?' he enquired, guessing that an international call from Naomi's faraway boyfriend had probably been the main trigger for her buoyant mood.

'He's fine. Still doing his bit to save the world.'

Marcus was in Uganda doing something noble and very badly paid. Swift couldn't quite remember what. 'When's he back?'

'In four weeks.'

'Nice.' He smiled down at her as they went through the front door.

'There's cold chicken in the fridge and a pasta salad,' she said. 'I've already eaten and I'm out again soon. Lizzie and I thought we'd catch the latest Brad Pitt film. I won't be late, so you're not to worry.'

'Right.'

'How are you feeling, Dad?' She gave him a maternal, Kate-like appraisal. 'You still look a bit peaky.'

'I'm definitely on the mend. And looking forward to supper.'

'What about the investigation?'

'Oh, you know, the usual slow but steady progress.' He sank down on the sofa, leaned back and stretched out his legs.

* * *

Pete stayed on after Swift had left. He keyed the notes on the recent interview with Jack Haygarth into his computer. Whilst waiting for the printer to produce three copies he considered the attraction, or otherwise, of returning to his rented flat three miles from the station. He had only been in it for a few weeks and it still did not feel like a home. It was odd living on one's own again, he thought. There was freedom, sure — and that was great. But sometimes, when he was alone in the flat with nothing specific to occupy him, there was a sense of waiting for life to happen, rather than being out there living it. He was definitely going to have to do something about that. In the meantime, the thing he most wanted to do at this moment was beard Saul Williams in his den. He headed out to the XR3, fired the engine and roared out of the station car-park. He stopped at a nearby mini-market and picked up beef and pickle sandwiches and a can of Fanta which he consumed in the car. Minutes later he was bounding up the steps to Williams's flat.

Williams was still not in. Or alternatively still not answering the door. Pete walked slowly back down the steps. It was approaching seven o'clock now. The sun lay in thick golden slabs on the grass borders surrounding the block of flats. Pete laid a hand on the stones beside the main entrance. They radiated heat as though breathing out dragon breath. He walked around the side of the block, found a patch of shade and sat down on the grass, leaning up against a part of the wall which was warm rather than hot. From here he had a perfect view of the car park and the main entrance, but was not at all conspicuous himself.

He would just wait. Wait until Williams came home. The freedom to make this decision pleased him and he waited with perfect content whilst one hour passed and then another.

It began to grow dark. The temperature relented hardly at all. Pete had the idea that if it were to rain the drops would spit and steam on the scorched grass. The occasional car came into the car-park, and single flat dwellers disappeared through the entrance. As none of them seemed to be under the age of forty, Pete left them to their own devices.

A couple walked down the road from the direction of the town, arm in arm like old-fashioned couples in dated films. Pete watched them idly and then came on the alert

119

as they turned into the garden of the flats. There was a woman he guessed to be in her fifties from her ample girth and mumsy style of dressing, and a tall, bulky young man in his early twenties. The woman was doing the talking, her voice low and reassuring. Pete waited until they had passed through the entrance then followed them, treading softly in his rubbersoled shoes.

Sure enough they went up the staircase to the first floor. Pete followed and saw them stop outside flat 14. He got out his warrant card. The woman was slotting a key into the lock. Pete addressed the man, keeping his voice low and nonconfrontational. 'Saul Williams?'

The young man turned. His face was big, chubby and childlike, despite the adornment of a long, bushy beard. The hair on his head was dark brown and cut short in a stylish, jagged fringe. He was dressed in clean black jeans and a startlingly white T shirt. His trainers were the Puma brand in white and silver. Gear which was groovy and expensive. Pete had a pair himself.

Saul Williams's glance hovered between Pete's face and his warrant card, his plump face crumpling with anxiety.

'My name is Constable Fox. I'd just like a few words,' Pete said, aiming to combine authority with a degree of reassurance.

'What's this about?' the woman asked. She seemed innocuous to Pete in her long cotton skirt and flat beige sandals. Her query was polite but firm.

'We're making enquiries regarding a death at the Moorlands Hotel yesterday.'

Saul's eyes flared with panic. He looked desperately around him as though assessing a means of escape.

The woman grabbed hold of his arm. 'It's all right, love,' she said, her voice low and assured. 'There's no need to be alarmed.'

Pete could tell that beneath her quiet composure she was more than a little anxious. Adrenalin began to pump through his system. There was something going on here. Absolute dead cert. 'I'd like to come in,' he said, moving forwards. 'Ask a few routine questions.'

'Yes, of course.' The woman pushed the door open and guided her reluctant son inside the flat. She gently pushed him ahead of her down a narrow corridor tiled in black and white like a draughts board. They passed a tiny kitchen, which Pete noted was tidy and spotless. The living-room was simply furnished with a large sofa and two straight-backed chairs. There was a table with a smart new radio cassette on it and a wide screen TV in one corner. Also a small bookcase, the books stacked in neat rows. The floor was tiled like the hallway, the curtains cream cotton. It was a comfortable, pleasant, clean space in which to live. But it had an impersonal air about it, something odd in the atmosphere which Pete couldn't quite put his finger on.

The woman gestured to the sofa. 'Please sit down,' she said. 'I'm Caroline Williams, by the way. Saul's mother.' She threw her son a comforting smile. 'You sit there, love,' she told him, indicating one of the straight-backed chairs.

Pete would much have preferred to interview Williams on his own. He considered the ways and means of getting rid of the mother, but came up with no satisfactory strategy. He leaned forward towards Williams and noticed that he was rocking to and fro with a steady rhythm. What did that mean? It certainly didn't look good. He's a big lad, Pete thought, noting the young man's big shoulders, his fleshy belly and the huge splayed thighs straining against the fabric of his jeans. 'How well did you know Josie Parker?' he asked him, keeping his voice mellow and neutral.

The rocking accelerated. 'Josie Haygarth,' Williams murmured.

'Yes, that's right. How well did you know her, Saul?'

There was a long silence. Saul rocked backwards and forwards.

'You were friends, weren't you?' Caroline Williams prompted. She got up and put her hand on her son's shoulder. 'You used to go for walks with Josie. Didn't you, love?'

'And you followed her when she went shopping. And watched her house. Isn't that right?' Pete said, with brutal simplicity.

'Oh, love!' Caroline exclaimed, lightly touching Saul's face. 'You haven't started all that again, have you?' She turned to Pete. 'He used to follow a girl called Sally. He was very fond of her for a time. But that was three years ago.'

'Right. And was there any police involvement?'

'No. Neither Sally nor her parents wanted to make a formal complaint. They liked Saul, you see. They knew that he wasn't going to do Sally any harm.'

Jesus! Pete wondered where these naïvely trusting people had been all their lives. Wrapped in cotton wool in some snug little box with no windows to see out onto the big wide world? 'Stalking's not to be taken lightly,' he commented.

'Saul's lonely. He's never found it easy to make friends,' Caroline said, as though that explained everything. 'And he's not a stalker.'

'I see.' Pete turned once again to his interviewee who was rocking even more fiercely than before. 'Saul, I'm going to ask you an important question and I want you to listen carefully. Did you go to Josie's wedding yesterday?'

Caroline eyes widened in surprise. 'No! Saul went walking yesterday. He walks for six or seven hours every day except Sunday.'

'Mrs Williams,' Pete said sternly, 'I'm trying to question your son. I'd be grateful if you didn't persist in answering for him.'

'He's terrified,' she burst out. 'Can't you see that?'

'I can tell he's frightened, but that's no reason for not answering a simple question,' Pete came back sharply. 'If Saul has done nothing wrong, then he has nothing to fear.' It had seemed like a good thing to say until he said it. Hell, thought Pete, I've more or less suggested he'd do best to act dumb if he's got something to hide. Good one, Pete lad!

Saul began to speak. He was violently rocking now, but his speech was steady and clear. 'I did go walking yesterday. But not my usual route. I put on my navy suit and a tie. I bought a red rose and the woman in the flower shop pinned it to my lapel. I went to the Moorlands Hotel and I saw Josie get married to Jamie. It was a lovely ceremony. Josie looked beautiful. She always looks beautiful. I wished it was me marrying her. But she'd never marry me. No girl would marry me.'

Caroline stared at him in horror. 'You were there at the wedding. Oh God!'

'Why would she never marry you?' Pete asked.

'Because I get stressed out. And then I get depressed. It's called anxiety-depression.'

Pete wrote the words down. He'd come back to that later. The guy was clearly a madman, despite his ability to tell a coherent story. 'How long did you stay at the wedding, Saul?'

A long, uneasy silence. More rocking. 'Until about . . . half past eight.'

He's lying thought Pete, swallowing down his excitement. 'What made you decide to leave then?'

Another endless silence.

'Just tell the truth, love,' his mother said quietly. 'I know you've done nothing wrong, so you've no need to be afraid.'

'The manager said I should leave.'

'And why was that?' Pete asked. 'Were you causing trouble?'

'No.'

'I think you were, Saul. Why would the

manager ask you to leave if not?'

'No. I wasn't causing trouble.' He rocked furiously, his face contorted with feeling.

Pete had the sense that he was on the brink of some momentous information. 'I think you'd been trying to get close to Josie. Was that it, Saul? I think you were upset and jealous because Josie had married someone else. I think you started to make a nuisance of yourself.' He considered going further. No, it was too soon to get to the main agenda. 'That's the truth isn't it?'

Saul raised his head. Tears were standing in his eyes. 'I wasn't causing trouble. I just wanted to find Josie and make sure she was all right.'

Pete stared hard at him. 'And did you find her?'

Saul's cheeks flushed with panic. 'She was in her room. Jamie was there too.' He screwed his eyes tight shut and ground his knuckles into the sockets. 'I just wanted to help. Ask the waitress, she'll tell you.' His mouth went on working but no sound came. The chair was rocking with him now, its legs thumping the tiles with each impulsion.

Caroline snapped upright, swung round and squared up to Pete with a vengeance. 'I'm not happy with this line of questioning,' she told him, her face flashing a warning.

'And you won't get anything else out of him,' she added. 'Not now. He could be like this for hours. You'd better go now.'

Pete felt a stab of fury. He had been on the point of getting something interesting from the boy and this old cow had muscled in and spoiled the moment. 'This is a murder investigation, madam,' he told her. 'Josie Parker was found dead yesterday evening and we have reason to believe that your son might be a key witness.'

Caroline stared at him in deep dismay.

Suddenly the room filled with low groaning sobs. Tears came rolling from Saul's eyes, wetting his cheeks and running into his beard. He bent his head down to his knees, his body a heaving, moaning lump of grief.

His mother bent and wrapped her arms around him. As she comforted her son she turned her face to Pete, livid with fury. 'You crass, insensitive fool. What in heaven's name do you mean by springing that on him without any warning? Get out of here!' she hissed at him. 'Now — before you do any more damage. Just bloody leave us alone.'

Pete swallowed. 'We shall need to speak to Mr Williams further,' he managed, before exiting with slow and studied dignity. He ran down the steps and out to his car. Sitting behind the wheel he took deep breaths, acutely conscious of the wild boundings of his heart. There was something about frumpish, maternal women losing their cool that really stirred him up. After a minute or so he felt calmer. Glancing down at his notes he reckoned he had gained some pretty useful information during the brief mother and son interview. But just at this moment he was unsure whether to award himself a rosette or a booby prize as to the way he had handled it.

Back at the station he made himself strong sweet coffee then re-read Swift and Sue Sallis's notes on the information gained that morning. Swift's comment on the need to ascertain who had alerted the manager to call the doctor the previous evening suddenly sprang out at him. He wondered if the CCTV tapes from the hotel entrance had been looked at yet. They couldn't have been, there hadn't been time.

His customary self-esteem now fully restored, he slid behind the wheel of his car, arriving at the Moorlands Hotel some ten minutes later. Rather more speedy than the journey last evening with Swift at the wheel, he reflected. But then Swift had complied with the speed restrictions.

John Ford's shift had ended and there was a thirty-something woman in charge, attractively kitted out in a sleeveless cream shift dress which was both formal and sexy. Pete introduced himself. In another two minutes he was ensconced in the manager's room, reviewing the tapes which showed those entering and leaving the front door of the hotel from two o'clock onwards. He spent ten minutes conscientiously observing each frame, then started occasional fast-forwarding. After another few minutes he put in the second tape and wound on until the digits showed 20.30. There were not many people passing in or out by this time, presumably the dancing in the ballroom would now be in full swing. A party of four guests in their early twenties went out carrying wine glasses. A few minutes later they returned inside. 'Refills, guys?' Pete murmured, with a knowing grin. 'Why not? Any excuse, eh?' At 20.41 a silver-haired man went out. The tape wound on to 20.45 and there was no sign of Saul Williams's exit. Pete pulled his shoulders back and stretched out his arms, aware of the tension in his muscles. Returning his attention to the tape he watched through a blank period which seemed to stretch on endlessly. At 21.01 a group of five or six older guests came in from the garden. He found his concentration wandering, his eyelids droop-ing. He clenched his fingers and toes fiercely to restore full alertness. As the tape registered 21.12 a stooped, bulky figure made its way out of the hotel. Before reaching the steps, the figure turned, looking back into the foyer, his face filled with marked and unmistakable trepidation. Pete brought the tape to a stop, then zoomed in on a close-up of the face: the rounded features, the ridiculous beard, the haunted, frightened expression. He leaned back in his chair, a smile stealing up from his lips to his eyes. 'That's my boy! Rock on baby!'

★   ★   ★

Around the time Pete was making his way jubilantly back to the station, savouring the anticipation of relating the good news to DCI Swift, Jamie Parker was sitting in the flat he and Josie had decorated and furnished together in preparation for starting out on their new life together when they returned from their honeymoon. He had got so freaked out at the prospect of putting in an appearance at his parents' grotesque lunch party, he had come here instead. But the memories awakened in the place were not good, and now that the pills Diana had given him had worn off, he found himself raw and smarting, groping for the means to work out how he was going to exist in a world where Josie was no longer present. The pills had numbed the hurting and made him drowsy and disoriented. But as they worked their way out of his system the grief all came roaring back, even worse than before. How was he going to get through the years and years left of his life? His heart would starve.

In addition he found himself constantly groping for those crucial minutes which had been erased from his memory. The moment from when he had opened the door of the suite, calling out for Josie, to the time when he found himself on the bed, cradling her soft, dead body.

He went to lie down on the bed they would have shared together. He closed his eyes and tried to relax but he couldn't sleep. He wished he had some more pills. He poured a tumbler of neat whisky, but he was retching after a mouthful. Over and over he asked himself who could have wanted to kill Josie? No one. Not one single person alive. Surely.

He felt a sudden rush of agitation. He wanted to do something, not just lie here passively accepting fate. He wanted to jump up, to punch the air and roar and howl. He considered taking a run across the moors, but he guessed that the surge of energy would probably evaporate by the time he reached the outer door.

He took a stinging cold shower, then lay down again and tried to focus his thoughts. With persistent concentration surely he could get his mind to work for him and send him answers to the questions buzzing in his brain. He asked for nothing more than some shred of memory or understanding which would enable him to make sense of what had happened. No thoughts would come. He felt a rush of fear that he might lose touch with reality altogether, as if his brain were in some kind of meltdown. This is a medical thing, he told himself. And thus curable. His father had always paid hefty insurance to ensure that any ailment which befell a member of the family was instantly diagnosed and remedied. But he doubted if even his father's doctor in Harley Street would be available today. It was Sunday. And Harley Street was 200 odd miles away. Moreover he wanted nothing whatever to do with his parents' doctors or their money or their advice, ever again. Yesterday had changed all that.

He went out to his car, drove to the local hospital and presented himself at the reception desk in Accident and Emergency. It was quiet, only a handful of people waiting. He gave his name and details.

'What's the problem?' The receptionist looked up at him. 'Well?' she prompted, sharply.

'I've lost my memory. Not all of it,' he added quickly. 'Just some important bits.' His voice trailed off. He could see she thought he was either drunk, stoned or a simple time-waster. He was too stressed and exhausted to conjure up any sophistries which might persuade her to take him seriously. 'I've been talking to the police. I think I might have been involved in . . . an accident,' he said. 'But I can't remember. Please, please will you get someone to help me.'

Her eyes became wary. 'I see.' She was crisp, but she wasn't going to send him away. 'Right. Yes. Just go sit down. The doctor won't be long.'

He sat next to an elderly woman with a bath towel wrapped around her foot. Opposite was a teenage boy with a blood-soaked hand, his face shocked and white with pain.

Jamie waited. He had lost sense of time. He didn't mind how long he waited as long as someone would listen to him and help free him from the torment of his confusion and doubts.

A nurse came to fetch him, led him to a curtained cubicle and told him to sit on the bed. A boyish-looking white-coated medic eventually appeared. 'I'm Doctor Shaw,' he said, looking at the information sheet the nurse had left on the table and frowning in concentration. He banged Jamie's knees with a small rubber hammer. He pulled his eyelids up and down and shone a light into his pupils. He measured his blood pressure. He asked him to say the date, day, month and year. Then he asked him some very easy general knowledge questions. 'You appear perfectly fit and healthy,' the doctor told him, and Jamie had the sense the man simply wanted to get rid of him.

Jamie began to describe the incidents of the previous evening. The doctor sat down on the bed beside him, his attention now fully engaged. When Jamie finished there was a short silence.

'You're suffering from a short-term memory disorder,' the doctor told him. 'Most likely induced by the trauma you've described.'

Jamie struggled to make some sense of the significance of the diagnosis. 'Will the memories come back?' he asked.

'Most probably.'

'When?'

'It's hard to say. It could be days, or weeks. Maybe a year.'

'Isn't there any treatment I can have?'

'Not really. You need to take care of yourself and try not to expose yourself to more stress. I suggest you give yourself a day or so to rest and then go see your GP. He might recommend some medication for anxiety and depression, or perhaps some counselling.'

'Is that it?' Jamie asked, having a sense of being crushed and dismissed.

'I'm afraid so. You told them at reception you'd been involved with the police. Is that right?'

'I've been talking to Sergeant Sallis. She's with the CID. You can check with her if you want.'

'That's not my brief,' the doctor said. 'I'm sorry I can't be more helpful. Have you got someone to stay with. It might be better for you not to be alone. Family? Friends?'

'Yes. I've got family and friends,' Jamie said. He got up. 'Will you write it down for me? The diagnosis?'

'Sure.' The doctor scribbled on his pad. 'And I'll send a report to your GP.' He tore the sheet off his pad and handed it over.

Back at the flat Jamie laid the doctor's note on the table and secured it with the dolphin-shaped paperweight Josie had bought for him when she was in Spain for her hen weekend. He was overwhelmed with a sense of aloneness. There was no one to help him now that Josie had gone. She had been his friend and his helper and adviser, the one he turned to for everything. From time to time he had found himself looking around for her, fully expecting to see her restored to him. He knew that his behaviour was no more than a reflex, an instinctive habit, a trick of blind hope which might take months to be extinguished. She was not going to come back. And gradually he came to realize that if he was to survive and make some contribution to discovering the truth about losing her, then he had to find someone else who would be his helper.

6

Superintendent Tom Lister was well known for his florid complexion and the frequent presence of a cigarette clamped between his lips. Today, returning to work after an unprecedented absence of a week with flu, he was drained of colour, the small tin ashtray on his desk was empty and he looked a changed man.

'Fags and booze are totally out of bounds,' he told Swift with heavy regret. 'Doctor's orders, and I think he meant it.' He gave a hacking smoker's cough which seemed to confirm the wisdom of the medical advice. 'So, give me what you've got so far on this poor little bride in the bath. I haven't had time yet to go through the file notes to date. Oh, and by the way, have you seen the press this morning?'

Swift nodded.

'What can you do?' Lister said, shaking his head. 'No doubt one or two of the guests will soon be getting a nice little cheque for handing on what they'd gathered and what they'd made up. Plus the contents of their cameras. Jesus! Have people nowadays no decency — no respect?' He sighed. 'No need to answer that.'

Swift didn't. 'We've got a possible suspect, Saul Williams. He's twenty years old, unemployed and apparently not very bright. He turned up at the wedding uninvited. And he's been stalking Josie for some time.'

'Has he now? Any previous?'

'No involvement with us. He was known to Social Services for some years, but there's no regular contact now. Pete Fox thinks Williams had some kind of obsession for Josie.'

'Fox,' Lister mused. 'Ah, the new DC. How's he shaping up?'

'He's keen and a hard worker. And he seems able. It's early days yet.'

Lister smiled. He knew his colleague's disinclination to make judgements before he was fairly sure of his grounds. 'Good. So are you going to bring Williams in for questioning?'

'I'm going to see him myself as soon we've finished the morning team briefing. We need to clarify how it came about that he alerted a member of staff to the need for a doctor to be called soon after Josie's death. I thought I'd take Sue along with me. Williams sounds as if he needs careful handling if he's not to clam up.'

'Right. And how do you propose to fob off keen young Fox?'

'I'll think of something.'

Lister chuckled. 'Trust you to do it so he won't even know what you're about. You can be a devious devil, Ed.'

'If he doesn't put two and two together regarding what I'm about, then he's not going to make a good detective, is he?'

'And a hard taskmaster,' Lister said. 'Anything else I need to know on this case?

'It looks like the bridegroom could also be a suspect. He claims to be the person who discovered her body — '

'Which, of course, means he's quite likely to be the last person who saw her alive.'

'Indeed. He's in pretty poor shape — as you'd expect. He also claims a total loss of recall regarding the vital minutes around the time of the death.'

Lister sucked in a whistling breath through his teeth. 'That's bad news for him whether he's trying to pull the wool over our eyes or not. He's definitely one to keep your eye on. I mean, think about it — all those tensions around a wedding to wind a young couple up. Not to mention what could be going on between the two of them, and God knows who else. Motives galore! And you say the other lad was there at the scene as well?'

'I said that needs to be clarified.'

'There could have been some argy-bargy

between them,' Lister said. 'In fact, it would be damn strange if there hadn't been. Mmm, quite a bit to chew on there. Anything from forensics?'

'Nothing of particular significance, as yet. I phoned through this morning and they're still working through the victim clothes and luggage. The prints found at the murder scene were the victim's and groom's as you'd expect.'

'And on the door handle?'

'The same. There were also some blurred incomplete fragments, but then there had probably been quite a few people visiting the room during the day, quite legitimately. Staff, family, the bridesmaids and so on.'

'And what about her mobile phone? Those little sim cards sometimes tell some very interesting stories.'

'The phone hasn't been recovered so far. That's if she had one.'

Lister rolled his eyes. 'I thought the whole world had one. I'll get one of the IT boys to follow up with the mobile companies, see what we can dig up. Right, get on with it, Ed. Let's get this one tied up a.s.a.p.'

Swift gave the ghost of a smile.

'All right, all right. I know that's my staple parrot-cry. But this case is going to be frighteningly high profile in the press. It'll put the damn flu and the tropical weather well into the shade. And whatever else happens, we'll be in the spotlight.'

'I expect so.'

'Oh, by the way, I saw Geoff in the CID room earlier. He says he's been temporarily pulled out of retirement to do some legwork interviewing the list of guests.'

'I didn't want to bother you at home about it, Tom. I thought I could take it for granted you'd rubber stamp the extra expenditure, at least for a week or so.'

'Did you now? Have you got your sights on my job, Ed? I'm not clapped out yet, you know,' Lister said amiably.

★ ★ ★

Swift sensed the air of expectation in the atmosphere when he joined Sue, Pete and the recently retired Geoff Fowler in the CID room.

Fowler instantly got to his feet, his hand extended in greeting. 'Good to see you again, sir.'

'You too, Geoff. Thanks for agreeing to help us out.'

'It sounds a bit of a tricky one, from what Sue and Pete have been telling me. Around eighty suspects known to the victim present in the building at the time of her death. Plus any Tom, Dick or Harry around in the area. And no forensics to speak of. We should have it sorted by tea-time.'

'Hope is infinite,' Swift commented, perching on the edge of a desk. 'I was hoping you'd be able to find out where the various guests are likely to be now, and maybe get to see a number of them today.'

'Will do,' Geoff confirmed. 'I take it we'll need the relevant local forces to follow up with those guests in far flung parts of the country, or abroad.'

Swift nodded. 'I'll leave it to you to get their best co-operation.'

'Thanks, boss.' Geoff gave a crooked grin.

'Bet you're wishing you'd stayed at home doing the crossword,' Sue said.

'Ay! Watch it, young lass,' Geoff warned. 'Just because you've got your sergeant's stripes doesn't mean you can get lippy with me. I'm old enough to be your dad, besides which I've far more interesting things to do than spend me time puzzlin' over crossword clues.'

'Well, you certainly will, now you're on this case,' Sue retorted, amused that Geoff was putting on his broadest Yorkshire accent for the benefit of newcomer Pete. She looked across to Swift. 'What's the rest of the strategy for today, sir?'

Swift paused for a moment, marshalling his thoughts.

'You'll be wanting me to follow up with Williams, sir?' Pete was on the edge of his chair, psychologically poised for flight.

'I think I'd like you to get back to the Moorlands and follow up with the member of the waitress staff whom Williams allegedly spoke to, possibly only minutes after Josie's death. I'd like as many details as you can get as to what he told her, and also her view of his mood and general demeanour.'

The muscles of Pete's face drooped. 'Right, sir.' He was putting on a good front, but it was clear that his mind was racing in search of reasons for having been side-lined from a possible arrest scenario, a quick sewing-up of the case and a moment of treasurable glory.

'I'd be interested to interview Williams myself,' Swift told Pete evenly. 'Given that we've got nothing on our data base about Williams, and bearing in mind your full and detailed report, he's clearly a complex character.' He paused for a moment. 'I think it might be a good idea for Sue to come with me.'

'Oh! Fine.' Sue grinned with surprise and pleasure.

Pete looked down at his knees.

'Pete's report suggests that Williams is reliant on his mother,' Swift continued. 'A female presence could be helpful in getting him to talk.'

'Yeah! Good point, sir.' Pete was rallying bravely.

Geoff got to his feet. 'Right. Everything sorted. I'll be on my way then. See you all later.'

Pete maintained his brave face and followed the older man's lead.

Sue gathered up her notebook and slotted it into the one of the slim shoulder bags she always carried.

The phone on Swift's desk rang. He picked it up and listened for a brief moment. 'We'll be right there,' he said. He turned to Sue. 'That was the duty sergeant. Jamie Parker is in reception, asking for you. I think you need to see him. And now, before he changes his mind. I'll make a start with Williams and you can maybe join me later. Call me if there's anything vital.'

'Right, sir.' Sue headed off.

Swift grabbed his linen jacket and went out to the car park. Plates were spinning, he thought. But were they the right ones?

★ ★ ★

Jamie was sitting bolt upright in the reception area. On his knee was a pile of newspapers. He was resting the flat of his hands on them as though they might otherwise escape.

'Hello, Jamie.' Sue went to stand by him.

'Can I talk?' he said. He had that wild look of someone desperate with need and totally unconcerned about the niceties of social procedure. 'I need to talk to you.'

'Of course.' She led the way to one of the pleasanter interview rooms. There was a large oblong table with four neatly tucked-in chairs.

He pulled out a chair, sat down on it and threw the pile of newsprint on to the table where it landed with a fat thump.

Sue hadn't had chance to catch up with the morning Press. Sitting down opposite Jamie, she swivelled the top paper around — one of the national tabloids. There on the front page was a large picture of Josie and Jamie in their bridal gear. She was looking up at him, and he was looking down at her with heart-rending adoration. Their youth and beauty and joy sprang off the page, hitting Sue like a blow in the chest, reminding her of the awesome and catastrophic sadness of the case.

BRIDE IN THE BATH, the headline shouted. Beneath it the subtitle read, 'Tragic Josie drowns in the bath on her wedding night'.

The contents of the story were predictably dramatic and emotion-laden, and short on hard facts. But then we're pretty short on those too, Sue reflected.

She pulled some of the other papers out of the bundle. The tabloids were all pretty similar. The quality broadsheets made brief references to the drowning of a Yorkshire bride in her hotel suite some hours after her wedding, together with information that the police were treating the death as suspicious. They offered no pictures.

Sue looked across at Jamie's ravaged, defeated face. She said, 'Our Press Officer only gave out the briefest information.'

'I realized that. This other stuff must have come from someone who was there. God, people can be cruel.' He gathered the papers into a pile and dropped them on the floor. His breathing suddenly quickened. He pushed his chair back and stood up, his hand clutched to his chest. 'I need help.' His voice was raw and shaky.

'Do you need a doctor?' Sue eyed him with concern.

'I've seen a doctor. I went to the hospital last night.' He pulled out the note Dr Shaw had given him. 'Look.'

Sue attempted to decipher the puzzling scrawl.

146

'It says I'm suffering from a selective short-term memory disorder, induced by trauma,' he explained. He had kept re-reading the note and now had the jargon off pat. It kept repeating in his head. 'He said there was no treatment. Just rest. It might not come back for a year.'

'I see.' Sue paused to reflect.

'I just need someone to help me. Please, Sue, please?'

Hearing the panic in his voice, Sue got up and fetched him water from the dispenser in the corner of the room. She put the plastic beaker in front of him, and handed him a tissue. He slumped back on to the chair.

'I'm sorry to cry in front of you,' he said, as he began to grow calmer. 'I'm sorry. I'm so sorry.'

Sue's feelings were touched and she knew that was dangerous. 'What is it you want help with, Jamie?' She made her voice neutral with a touch of crispness.

'I don't know what to do. I can't sleep. I can't swallow any food. I keep breaking down.'

'You're in shock, Jamie. You've suffered a terrible loss.'

'You're trying to tell me this is all normal.' He rubbed the end of his nose and let out a few short gasping breaths.

'It's part of what you might expect in the circumstances.'

'Yes, all right, fair enough,' he agreed wearily. 'But these blanks in my memory are scaring me to death. I've got to get those moments back, Sue. I've just got to get them back or I think I'll go crazy, whatever that means.'

Sue's mind raced. What angle should she take now? 'I think I might be able to help you,' she said evenly. 'We have a witness who states that he saw you in the hotel suite, probably only minutes after Josie died.'

He stared at her. 'Who?'

'Someone who was . . . fond of Josie.'

'That could be anyone.'

'Someone young,' Sue said, concerned that her handling of this issue left a lot to be desired.

'What? You mean Barny?'

'Who's Barny?'

'He's Diana's son. My sister.'

'Right.' Sue shook her head. 'Not Barny. Someone older, around your age.'

He frowned in frustration and irritation 'It could be any number of people then.'

Sue sighed. 'Look, Jamie, I'm trying to help you get the memories back. It won't help for me to just hand you the information on a plate.'

'You want me to go through all the possibles, guessing which one it might be. That won't do any good, will it?'

Sue cursed her ineptness. 'Jamie, are you absolutely sure you don't remember speaking to anyone just after Josie died?'

'Yes.'

'Who's the first person you remember seeing and speaking to after Josie — '

'Don't say that word again,' Jamie interrupted. 'I've told you. It was the doctor. Don't you believe me? You don't, do you?'

'Yes, I do believe that you can't remember,' Sue told him firmly, despite her reservations. Pausing a fraction of a second, she decided to go for it. 'Did you know that Josie had a stalker?'

The instant, raw disbelief on Jamie's face was the only answer she needed. 'That's rubbish,' he said.

'According to this witness, he used to follow Josie around. Walking with her in the woods.'

'Josie had quite a few friends she met in the woods when she took the dog out. People who like dogs get chatting and walk along together.'

'He was watching the house last week. Waiting for Josie to go out.'

Jamie's eyes registered sudden understanding. 'Oh, you mean Saul! He's not a stalker.

Sure, he had a bit of a thing about Josie, and he used to hang around sometimes to say hello to her. But he's a nice guy, and harmless. He's one of Melanie's lame ducks. He used to go to the centre where she works.'

'If he was a friend of Josie's, then why wasn't he invited to the wedding?' Sue asked.

'You can't invite everyone. You see, Josie didn't want the kind of big grand affair my parents would have liked,' he added with a curl of disdain in his face. 'They did their best to persuade Jack and Melanie to accept financial help to have a big do in London. Dad has an OBE for services to British Industry and he could have swung it to have the wedding in the crypt of St Pauls.'

'I see.' Sue was impressed, but kept her expression impartial.

'All he needed to do was follow the procedure and write a formal request to the Queen. He has connections in high places, my dad. Anyway Jack and Melanie wanted a simple affair in Yorkshire. And Jack's an old-fashioned sort of man, he wanted to pay for everything himself.'

'You're very fond of the Haygarth family, aren't you?' Sue said.

'They're great people — and I was going to be one of them.' He became very still. Suddenly his body jerked as he was once again overtaken by wrenching sobs.

Sue waited through the painful moments until he was calm again.

He blew his nose. He said: 'The thing is, part of me wants my head to be clear and somehow force myself to remember what happened. And the other part wants to swallow a whole bucketful of pills and forget everything.'

Sue was torn between pity and suspicion. Whilst Jamie's plight and distress aroused her natural human sympathy, her police-officer's doubt and scepticism were also still at work reminding her that this could all be an act. Jamie could simply be trying to manipulate her. The hospital doctor's diagnosis seemed to be little more than a convenient label to describe Jamie's problem. And what actual physical evidence was there to prove it?

'You must see a lot of people in your job,' he said. 'Have you met anyone before who's got this loss of memory thing?' He was not merely asking, he was pleading and desperate.

Sue considered. 'No. At least not in the way you're describing it.' At the beginning of her work in the CID she had been involved with a suspect who'd claimed that whole chunks had been blocked out — days, weeks. But in the end compelling forensic evidence had shown that he was lying in order to save his skin and a possible life sentence. And then, of course, she had come across plenty of witnesses who would suddenly recall a small and significant detail which had not occurred to them earlier. But Jamie's loss of recall seemed more serious and more implausible than the simple over-looking of an isolated detail.

The attempt to understand Jamie's claims reminded her of the most recent training development conference she had attended. In addition to the plum-haired psychologist there had been a hypnotist talking of his techniques in unlocking blocked memories associated with trauma in childhood, mainly sexual abuse. He had not simply lectured, he had shown video recordings of his sessions. They had made the hairs on the back of her neck stand up.

'I've got to get those lost minutes back,' Jamie said. 'I've got to know . . . I've got to remember exactly what happened.'

Sue bent forward, resting her elbows on the table. 'Jamie, you think you might have killed Josie, don't you?' She braced herself for his shock, his outrage, maybe another storm of weeping.

He was very still for a time. When he spoke his face was filled with misery. 'I can't believe I could ever have hurt her. But no matter how often I try to remember what happened after

I went through the door and called to her, everything is dark. How can I go on living with that? Not knowing.'

For a moment, Sue was at a loss, personal sensations temporarily encroaching on the professional boundaries she was used to operating within.

'Can you help me, Sue? Please, Sue. Please help me.'

Sue leaned forward and began to speak.

★　★　★

Swift clicked the central locking on his car and looked up at the block of flats where Saul Williams lived. The sun, as usual, was shining at full strength as though some switch had been thrown in the heavens and locked it into permanently full-on mode. The sky was Mediterranean blue and the moors rising up in the background were veiled in a soft azure haze, their summits awesome and mysterious. Swift had worked in North Yorkshire for a year now. Just occasionally he found himself taking the dazzling scenery for granted and had to remind himself how beautiful it was, how fortunate people were to live and work here.

Saul Williams opened the door, still in his pyjamas, rumpled and sleepy-looking. But he was no down and out. The pyjamas were of pale-blue cotton braided with darker-blue satin, and were freshly laundered. Moreover his hair and beard were damp and glistening, giving off a gentle fragrance of soap. 'Good morning,' he said, like a well-tutored and polite schoolboy.

Swift smiled. 'Good morning. Am I speaking to Mr Saul Williams?'

'Yes.' Instantly fear flared in the young man's eyes.

Swift showed his ID. 'Might I come in to speak to you?'

'I don't know. I'll need to ring my mum.' His bulky frame blocked the doorway, rocking to and fro.

'That's fine,' Swift said calmly. 'If she wants to come and be with you whilst we talk, that's no problem.'

'Oh. Right.' He stood, wondering what he should do next.

'May I come in?' Swift repeated, mirroring Saul's old-style politeness.

'Er, yes.' He led the way into the living room. A radio was playing pop music Swift recognized, but couldn't place.

'Sit down, please.' Saul gestured to the sofa, then picked up a mobile phone from the low table. 'I'll go and ring my mum, then.'

Swift watched as he exited into the hallway,

poised for pursuit if there was any attempt to make a quick exit. But Saul turned into the kitchen, leaving the door slightly ajar. Swift located the volume button on the radio and turned it down. He placed his pocket tape machine on the table and switched it to record. He could hear the young man's voice agitated and rushed. 'Police are here again . . . Can you come? . . . No, not him, another one. No, he seems all right.'

Swift glanced at the books on the shelves. There were mainly battered-looking children's books presumably bought when Saul was much younger. There was a complete series of *Harry Potter* stories in hardback, two books on training and fitness programmes used in the SAS and a book on martial arts. Open on the table was a dauntingly fat tome on the philosophy and practice of Tai Chi, the page corners curled and well fingered.

Saul returned. 'Mum's coming. She's at work so she might be a few minutes. She has to get some photocopying finished.' He sat down. 'I'm sorry I'm not dressed,' he said. 'Would you like a cup of coffee?'

'Thank you,' Swift said. 'Milk but no sugar, please.'

He followed Saul's rocking progress to the kitchen and leaned up against the door whilst the young man pressed the switch on the kettle and got out mugs from the cupboard. 'I see you're interested in Tai Chi,' he remarked.

'Yes. I go to a class every Saturday. I've been going for three years now. My tutor's a master.'

'I see. I don't know very much about Tai Chi.'

'If you've seen the *Star Wars* films you'll have seen something about Tai Chi in there. It came from China in the sixties when people started worrying about throwaway cornflake packets and the emptiness of western life.' He began to elaborate, suddenly confident and apparently knowledgeable, although the agitated rocking still persisted. Swift slotted himself into partly listening mode, ready for any information that veered from Saul's chosen topic and at the same time assessing the young man and his surroundings. Much of what he was seeing and hearing was consistent with the contents of Pete Fox's report, yet it could also be argued that this young man before him was barely recognizable from the portrait Pete had painted.

By the time the coffee was prepared Swift had heard about monks and imperial guards, about yoga and the martial arts, pacifism and combat, positive and negative forces. Saul handed him a mug. 'You did say milk and no sugar?'

They went to sit in the living-room.

'You don't have a job at the moment, Saul, is that right?' Swift asked.

'My doctor says I can't work.'

'I see. How do you spend your time? Apart from your interest in Tai Chi?'

'I go out walking. Monday to Friday.'

'Where do you walk?'

'I go across the bridge over the river and then through the woods and then down to the cricket ground at Ramsden village.'

'That must take you around five hours there and back,' Swift commented.

'That's right. And I spend two hours doing Tai Chi movements. I've got permission to use the pavilion for that.'

'So, a seven hour day,' Swift commented. 'It sounds like a job.'

'That's exactly what my Tai Chi master says. It was his idea. I was getting depressed, you see, in the flat.'

'Are you going out walking today?'

'No, I haven't been for the last week. I'm on new tranquillizers and they're making me drowsy.'

'Why do you need the tranquillizers?' Swift asked, interested in the contrast between the childlike openness and unvarnished language with which Saul responded to questions and his eloquence and authority when he talked about Tai Chi. And how the rocking was perpetual.

'I get stressed out. Especially when I'm seeing ghosts and devils.'

'That must be frightening.'

'It is.'

Swift sat quietly for a few moments, sipping his coffee and reviewing the interview to date. He had the knack of being able to maintain short silences without creating embarrassment or tension. In fact he had found that highly anxious interviewees were sometimes reassured by an interlude of quietness and calm. Saul Williams interested him. He clearly had psychological problems, but his outward demeanour did not fit into any category of mental disability or illness which Swift had come across in his long career. He was co-operative, amiable and fluent. But there was a curious detachment about him, as though he were protecting some inner part of himself and keeping it guarded and secret. So far Swift had avoided challenging the young man and his responding manner had been pleasant, but there had been no real warmth, nor any shiny spark of the individual or personal. And if Saul Williams had been in love with the dead Josie Parker, he showed no signs of having been weeping for her.

He drained his coffee mug and set it down on the table. 'I'm sorry that you've lost Josie,' he told Saul. 'She was your friend, wasn't she? You used to walk along with her if you saw her and her dog walking in the woods.'

'He's a Westie,' Saul said. 'Mum used to have one like him when I was a kid. I think Melanie will have to take him for his walks now.' He fell silent.

So, Swift thought, no weeping for Josie, but an intense sadness at her loss.

'You went to Josie's wedding,' Swift said, sensing that he was treading on ice and approaching the brittle thin layer. 'What made you decide to do that?'

'To see Josie. To be there and have all that time to watch her on her wedding day. I just wanted to be there, looking at her. Just looking at her made me feel happy.'

'I think I understand. Did you have a good time?'

Saul frowned as though the notion of having a good time was alien to him. 'She came to speak to me,' he said. 'Just to say 'hello'.'

'That was good. What happened after that?'

'Melanie brought me some orange juice and some smoked salmon sandwiches. I don't really like raw stuff. I ate a few crisps and nuts from the bowls at the bar.'

'Did you have anything besides orange juice to drink?'

'I don't have alcohol because of my medication.'

'Did you join in the dancing later on?'

'No! I'm not a dancer. I just sat and watched everyone.'

A picture presented itself in Swift's mind. Saul at the Moorlands Hotel in his dark suit, a flower in the lapel of his jacket. A solitary young man, solemn and correct. Uninvited and out of place, an outsider and observer, yet playing the role of fitting in quite satisfactorily. And utterly, perhaps dangerously, alone.

'And you decided to go home about half past eight? I think that's what you told Constable Fox.'

A vicious twitch of anxiety. 'Yes.'

'There's a video camera in the entrance to the hotel. Did you notice that, Saul?'

'No, I didn't.'

'The tape has a picture of you leaving at twelve minutes past nine.'

Saul looked Swift in the eye, his rocking steady and rhythmic. He swallowed and his Adam's apple moved and swelled. 'Yes, that's right.'

'You made a mistake when you spoke to Constable Fox?' Swift asked evenly.

'I told a lie. I was scared out of my wits.'

'About?'

'Telling him what really happened.'

Swift nodded, indicating his understanding of this reluctance. 'I'd like you to tell me that now.'

Saul gave no immediate signs of anwering and Swift waited patiently.

'I'd been watching Josie all the time, thinking how lovely she was. It gave me a warm feeling to be there with her in the same place. She danced with lots of different people.'

'Do you know any of their names?'

'No. I only know the family, and Jamie.'

'So Josie was having a good time dancing?'

Saul nodded. 'At the end of one dance she went out of the ballroom. I followed her. Not close, not so she'd notice. I thought she'd go to the Ladies Cloakroom because she'd done that before. But she turned the other way and went down the corridor and then into another room.'

As Saul was speaking, Swift was calling up a mental map of the ground floor of the Moorlands Hotel. He had just reached the conclusion that Josie must have gone into the conference suite — which had not been in use at the reception — when he heard footsteps on the stairway outside the entry door to the flat. He guessed they would belong to Saul's mother and gave a silent curse. She could hardly have come at a more sensitive moment.

Saul was still engaged in his story, seemingly oblivious to the sounds beyond the interior of the flat. 'I hung about in the corridor waiting for her to come back. But she didn't.'

'And what time was that?' Swift asked, hearing a key turn in the lock and resigning himself to the likelihood of the interview quickly grinding to a halt.

'Just after eight-thirty. I remember looking at the grandfather clock near the stairs.'

It was all fitting. Swift remembered the clock: a chunky Victorian monster in dark mahogany with elaborate carving and a big greeny-gold face. He turned as a worried looking woman dressed in a long droopy skirt and a baggy, sleeveless white blouse came quietly into the room. She made instant eye-contact with him, concerned rather than suspicious.

His glance attempted to convey reassurance. *Your son is doing well and I'll give him a fair hearing. We're at a critical point.* Her eyebrows lifted a fraction and she stood very still just inside the doorway.

Saul looked across at his parent, his face neither smiling nor hostile. 'Hello, Mum.'

'Hello, love. Don't let me interrupt.'

'I've been answering some questions,' Saul told.

'Good.'

Saul got to his feet, a lumbering figure, pitching like a boat on a choppy sea. 'I'll make you a coffee, Mum.'

'Right, love. You do that.' She watched him leave the room. 'I'm sorry,' she said to Swift. 'I wouldn't have come in if I'd known he was this calm. If he gets really stressed, things can get difficult.'

'I see.'

She sat down on the sofa. 'Is he in trouble?'

'Not so far, Mrs Williams.'

'He's a suspect, isn't he?' She raised hands in the air. 'No, don't bother to give me the routine, politically correct answer. I can understand from what he's told me that he must be. Not that he's told me all that much. But I know that you know he's been following her and that he turned up at the wedding without an invite . . . ' She ran a shaking hand through her sensibly cropped greying hair. 'You'll probably have guessed there's a medical history here. He had a brain tumour when he was two. We nearly lost him during the surgery. And then there were all the problems about getting him to fit in at school. He doesn't have any learning problems, he just finds it impossible to get on with people

163

in groups. He gets extremely anxious and then he gets depressed. That's why he can't work. And if you need confirmation, you're welcome to look at the mountain of reports we've got on him from various specialists.'

Swift inferred from this calm, but damaging speech that the mother was making an early start on establishing grounds for the consideration of diminished responsibility should her son be charged and convicted of the murder of a young woman on her wedding night. He guessed he would do the same if he were ever in the appalling position of having to come to terms with the possibility that Naomi was a killer.

Saul appeared in the doorway. 'Do you want another coffee, Inspector?'

'No thank you.' Swift found the young man's politeness strangely troubling.

'Are you telling him my life story?' Saul asked his mother, with no hint of protest or irony.

'Yes, love. If you bring me my coffee you can hear what I've got to say.'

Saul completed four rocking movements back and forward and returned to the kitchen.

'The rocking?' Swift asked.

She shrugged. 'Some say it's anxiety based.

Others that it's a form of self-stimulation. And others simply put it down to the aftermath of brain damage. Whatever the cause, it's a terrible social handicap — to the extent that his father walked out because he couldn't bear to see him any more,' she added sadly. 'Still, he pays him a handsome allowance, so at least Saul doesn't go without the material comforts of life.'

Saul returned and gave his mother her coffee. For the first time he noted Swift's recording machine on the table. He made no comment.

'Can we go back to the time you were waiting for Josie to come out of the conference room?' Swift asked him. 'How long did you wait?'

'It seemed like ages. I looked at the clock again but it was coming up to nine. I went back to the ballroom but she wasn't there. Then I went back into the corridor and when there was no one about I opened the door into the conference-room. There were no lights on but you could see all right, even though it was getting dark. There was no one there, just rows and rows of empty chairs. I walked down the room and I noticed there was a door at the far end. I knew she must have gone out that way, because I'd have seen her otherwise, wouldn't I? So I went out there myself and I found myself in a little back corridor. There were some little stairs up to the first floor, so I went up there. There's a glass door at the top and when I pushed it open I was in a long corridor with doors on both sides. I walked along looking at the names on the doors. They're all called after the various dales. Except the one that's the bridal suite. I stopped there. I thought she must be in there. I wanted to go in and see, but I knew it was private.'

'What happened then?' Swift prompted. 'What did you do then, Saul?'

'I heard a noise. Someone crying and moaning. It was an awful sound. I felt panicky then. I was starting to get really stressed out.'

'Who was crying, Saul?'

'It wasn't Josie. It wasn't her voice. I wanted to get right away from that moaning. I must have knocked against the door.'

'You knocked on the door?' Swift asked, instantly realizing the blow would have been a consequence of Saul's rocking, probably increased and exacerbated by his fear and distress.

'No. I banged against it. It wasn't shut. I stumbled a bit and then I was in the room. Jamie was sat on the bed holding her. And she was all stretched out.'

'Did you see Josie's face?'

'No. Her head was hanging back and to one side as if she'd had an accident and passed out. I knew there was something wrong.'

'Did Jamie speak to you?'

'He told me to go away. He said Josie wasn't very well. He looked kind of shocked and frightened to see me.'

'So, what happened then?'

'I got out as fast as I could. I went back down the same stairs I'd come up into the back corridor. There was a waitress coming along with a tray. She asked if I was OK. And I said I was worried because Josie had had an accident and needed the doctor. And she said she'd ask the manager about it.' He placed his hands between his knees and bowed his head over them. His rocking was slow and dignified, a silent lament for the dead Josie.

'Thank you for that,' Swift said. Already he was experimentally putting flesh on the bones of information Saul had offered. 'I think that's all I want to know for now.' He guessed that the young man's exposition had exhausted him. Pressing him further at this stage would be unlikely to be productive.

He glanced at the mother. She looked wrung out with speculation and anxiety, as well she might. Her son had not made any clearly self-damning statements, but he had placed himself firmly at the crime scene around the time the crime was committed. He had admitted a preoccupation with the murder victim. He was in deep.

Swift stood up. He paused by the hunched figure. 'Goodbye, Saul,' he said gently, nodding courteously to the watchful mother as he walked past.

She pursued him to the door. 'I suppose there's no point in asking what you made of all that?'

'No,' he confirmed. 'Not at this stage.'

'I'll stay with him for the rest of the day,' she said. 'He'll probably sleep now, and when he wakes up he'll either be stressed or depressed, and those aren't good times for him to be alone.'

Swift walked down the stairs to the exit door, reflecting on the burden a parent carried when they had a son as vulnerable — and maybe as potentially dangerous — as Saul Williams. Opening his mobile he collected a message from the station. Clive Parker would like to see him. He had information. It was a matter of urgency.

7

Swift did not go directly to the Parkers, but returned to the station to collect Sue. On the way he stopped off at a green-grocers, bought a bunch of bananas and ate one whilst sitting in the car. He reflected that leads and the prospect of information seemed to have arrived in a steady stream since Josie Parker was killed, but as yet he saw no clear thread emerging. The absence of forensic evidence was a major concern. And his usual gut instincts regarding the identity of the guilty party had stayed disappointingly silent. He reminded himself that whilst his instincts had a good track record, they had never been one hundred per cent accurate. What counted was steady and insightful police work.

He found Sue Sallis at her desk, tapping her notes on the recent interview with Jamie into the computer.

'I hear I've been summoned to speak with Clive Parker,' he commented drily.

Sue looked up. 'According to the desk sergeant, Parker sounded pretty keyed up. How did you get on with Williams, sir?'

'I'll tell you in the car. I want you to come

with me to see Parker.'

Sue got up. She still felt a thrill of gratification when Ed Swift asked her to accompany him on a sensitive interview. When they had first worked together this hungry need for his approval had troubled her. She had asked herself if she liked him too much, if there was something which strayed beyond the professional in her admiration and respect for him. Having firmly told herself this was not the case, she had simply accepted the strength of her regard for him — both as a detective and as a person. Yet despite her regard, she never felt completely at ease with him. He was complex, and sometimes discreet to the point of secrecy. Unlike Geoff and Pete, Ed Swift was someone she would never claim to be able to read like a book.

In the car he gave her a brief summary of the interview with Saul Williams.

'He sounds to be a bit of a one off,' Sue commented.

'That's an apt description,' Swift agreed. 'He certainly doesn't fit into any neat category.'

'Which I suppose means he could behave in a random way.'

'Yes.'

'And he has a motive. Despair and perhaps

rage because Josie was marrying another man. You always hurt the one you love, and so on.'

'Indeed. So, what's the latest from Jamie Parker?'

As Sue related the interview in detail, she was wondering how she was going to tell her boss about the way it had closed. At the time she had believed she was acting with skill and imagination, setting up a scenario to further the investigation and also to offer the help for which Jamie had begged her. Very soon after he left the station she had realized that moving the investigation along and helping a key suspect were more or less mutually exclusive. She had been a complete bone-head. She felt a burn of heat mount up her neck, a physiological reaction which had nothing to do with the weather.

As they approached the Parkers' house the swarm of press and camera crews in front of the gates demanded instant attention. Swift braked and there was a surge forward. An army of beady eyes gazed into the car, flanked by fluffy microphones, TV cameras on stands and flashes on tripods.

'I'll go speak to them,' Swift told Sue as he switched off the ignition. 'You stay here.'

She watched the surge move back slightly as Swift got out of the car. She guessed he would be wearing his most solemn, sorrowful expression. It had a knack of disconcerting even the most hardened individuals. Far more effective than swaggering aggression.

He waited until the buzz of demands died down. 'Good morning, everyone. I'm Detective Chief Inspector Swift. I'll make a short statement and then I'll answer any questions you have. I can confirm that the young woman found dead in her suite at the Moorlands Hotel on Saturday night last, around nine p.m was Josie Parker, née Haygarth. She had been drowned in the bath. We're treating the case as murder. This was a particularly cruel attack, given that the victim was killed on her wedding day at a time when she was alone and defenceless. We would appeal to any member of the public in the vicinity who saw or heard anything unusual around the time stated to come forward. As soon as possible.' He left a fractional pause. 'Are there any questions?'

There was instant uproar.

He raised his hands. 'I can only hear one person at a time.'

A shaggy, dark-haired man at the front of the group spoke up, firing a volley of queries. 'Are you on to something? Have you come for Parker? Do you expect to make an arrest soon?'

'We're confident that we shall find whoever killed Josie. And hopefully soon,' Swift told them, well practised in the art of police speak. 'Our visit here is simply part of our routine work — talking with those who had a close connection with the victim.'

More clamour. Swift shook his head, indicating there would be no further dialogue until there was calm.

'Is it true you've been questioning Jamie Parker?'

'We're questioning everyone who had a close connection with the deceased. As I said before.'

'Where is Jamie Parker?' a voice shouted from the back. 'Gone into hiding, has he? We've been waiting a long time to get a glimpse of him.'

'You know I can't comment on that. When we get something relevant, you will all be put in the picture.'

There was a brief, reflective silence. Swift seized the moment. 'I'm sorry I can't tell you more at present. We will, of course, keep you informed of any further developments as they arise. And now I'd ask you to leave the families in peace. There's nothing more for you to see or do here. Please respect their grief. Thank you.'

He walked back to the car and asked Sue

to move into the driving seat. 'They won't leave straight away,' he told her. 'But I should think they'll be gone within the hour once they realize there's nothing going on here at the moment. I'll get the entry gates to open. Just keep driving, slowly and as if you mean it!'

He pressed the button on the panel beside the gates, and they began to swing open. One or two of the keener journalists moved forward, but were stopped by Swift's warning stance. As the car passed through the gates, he moved to follow it. The gates closed behind him.

'Well done!' he told Sue, slotting into the passenger seat.

'Likewise,' she said, then gave a low exclamation as the house came into view. 'Wow! That is a seriously wantable pile. It's beautiful! Must be worth an absolute fortune. I'd always thought the wool industry around here had died a death.'

'According to the local industries directory, Parker's mill specializes in luxury wool worsteds and mohair fabrics. Which apparently sell all over the world.'

'And there's the man himself,' Sue commented, spotting Clive Parker standing in the open doorway, framed between the magnificent white columns of the portico and wearing a darkly grim expression on his wolfish features. 'This promises to be interesting.'

Taciturn and unsmiling, Clive Parker led the two officers through to his study. Sue made the most of the few seconds it took to walk down the hallway to drink in the grand proportions of the entrance hall and marvel at the gold and white decor, illuminated from above by a high glass dome set into the roof. 'Parker's Palace', she murmured to herself.

Parker gestured Swift and Sallis to sit on the two chairs placed in front of the desk. He then settled himself in the tall chair behind the desk, viewing the visitors in the manner of a captain of industry about to upbraid two underlings for unsatisfactory performance.

Cutting into the dramatic pause Parker made the mistake of initiating, Swift said, 'I gather you have important information for us, Mr Parker.'

'I'd like to know first what you intend doing about the press and camera crews parked outside my house.' He spoke with menacing softness, spitting each word out with careful precision. 'I had intended to drive to my business premises for a meeting this morning, but was not prepared to run the gauntlet with those predators outside the gates.'

'I've already spoken to them,' Swift told him. 'I think you'll find that they will gradually lose interest and drift away. If you have any further trouble, let us know immediately.'

Parker was white and tight-lipped. 'I'd also like to know why you have been endlessly questioning my son. Clearly he had no part in Josie's death and my wife and I believe he should be given some time to recover from the blow he has suffered before he is subjected to any further interrogations.'

'This is a murder enquiry, sir,' Sue said. 'We need to question all those witnesses who can help us with information. And to do that as soon as possible whilst their memories are still fresh.'

'But surely not more than once?'

'As many times as are required in order for us to gain the information we need,' Sue persisted.

'I gather he was at the station this morning talking again with you, Sergeant,' Parker said.

'Jamie came to the station of his own accord this morning,' Sue said, being careful not to sound defensive, despite Parker's ability to arouse that sensation in spades. 'We had a frank and useful discussion.'

'Yes. That is something else I wish to speak about,' Parker said.

Swift thought it was time to intervene. 'Mr Parker, we came here with the expectation of learning something which will forward our investigation into Josie's death. If you wish to make complaints against me or any other officers on the case, then you are free to do so by contacting Superintendent Lister. So perhaps, now, you'd be good enough to give us the information you indicated was urgent and stop wasting police time.'

Anger and disbelief flared in Parker's face. Clearly it was a long time since anyone had dared to speak to him with such assertive frankness. He took some deep breaths, and Swift guessed it was important for him not to let himself down by losing his cool.

'I'm sorry, Chief Inspector,' Parker said, relenting a little. 'You must appreciate the strain I'm under — the strain we are all under. I don't actually have any useful new information, in the sense you seem to be expecting. Maybe your receptionist didn't quite understand my request to see you.'

'What did prompt your request to see me?' Swift asked.

'I had a call from my son earlier on. He said he was going up to Newcastle. He's made an appointment to see some kind of therapist. A hypnotherapist, I believe. He has some notion that this . . . therapist can help him retrieve his lost memories of the terrible moments after he found Josie dead.'

'I see. When did you take this phone call, Mr Parker?'

'At thirty-eight minutes past ten. He had just left the station after speaking with Sergeant Sallis.' He moved his gaze to rest on Sue, his manner clearly suggesting that he was wanting answers to a number of questions.

Swift also glanced at Sue, who moved uneasily on her chair.

'I gather that the suggestion to consult this hypnotherapist came from you, Sergeant Sallis. Is that right?'

Sue swallowed, living with that awful moment when clichéd phrases like 'this can't be happening' sprang into your head. 'I gave him details of a hypnotherapist whom I heard speak recently at a police training development course. It was purely information, not a recommendation.' She spoke with slow dignity, but her defensiveness was now running at the level of a fox about to be pounced on by hounds.

'Is this usual police practice?' Clive Parker asked Swift.

'We have procedures in place which I'm sure Sergeant Sallis is aware of,' Swift told him.

'That's no answer, Chief Inspector, as you well know. And I won't waste time trying to persuade you to break ranks and admit to the mistake of a member of your team in the presence of a mere layman. However, the situation we have now is that my son has gone racing off up the A1 to Tyneside. He is in a highly sensitive state. He is in no fit state to drive. I have no idea where he will be staying or when he will come back. Moreover, he is about to consult a therapist whose qualifications are not known to me, and who could possibly harm my son by practising some dubious 'memory retrieval' procedures which could result in God knows what. Who is to say that this therapist might not arouse or even plant false memories which could cloud your investigations? Worse still is my concern that such charlatan and spurious procedures might threaten my son's sanity.' He leaned back in his chair. *I rest my case.*

Swift was inclined to agree with much of Parker's concern. Besides which there was the worry that a key suspect was about to vanish into obscurity. 'How confident are you that Jamie will keep in touch with you?' he asked Parker.

'Reasonably. He's always done so before. But this is a rather special situation.'

'Yes, indeed. We'll alert the Tyneside

Division to this, sir.'

'Well, I suppose that's better than nothing. My wife doesn't know about this latest development yet, she went to her boutique as usual this morning in an attempt to keep her mind off all this terrible business,' Parker said reflectively. 'I dread to think what effect it will have.'

'I'm sorry for any extra stress she might undergo,' Swift said, keeping the apology as generalized as he could manage. It interested him to hear that Cassandra Parker, unlike her husband, had run the gauntlet with the press, which obviously Parker would have done if he hadn't wanted to stay at home for this meeting.

Parker considered for a few moments, then suddenly seemed satisfied. 'So perhaps, Chief Inspector, I haven't wasted your time after all. The information I've been able to offer on the misguided conduct of a member of your team — however well meant — is surely enlightening. A training point for future police personnel perhaps?'

Swift saw how easy Parker found it to get under the skin. 'Do you know if Josie usually carried a mobile?' he asked.

The change of tack had Parker on his mettle, and for a moment Swift thought he might refuse to answer the question. Would that be a resistance to answering any question at this point, he wondered, or specifically this one.

'She certainly possessed one,' Parker said. 'I can't say if she carried it regularly. Is this relevant?'

'Mobile phones can carry a good deal of information,' Swift pointed out.

'Of course.'

Swift got up. 'Thank you for your help, Mr Parker. I think that will be all, for now. We would, of course, be grateful to know if you hear from Jamie.'

'I'm sure you would,' Parker replied smoothly, rapidly retrieving lost ground.

He led the way through the hallway, looking around him as he moved forward, master of all he surveyed.

Sue, her pulses trembling with agitation, followed his gaze, seeing little more than a swirl of hazy colours in the huge gilded frames of the landscapes and portraits hanging above the staircase.

'Both the exterior and interior of this house were designed for me by Quentin Horley,' Parker told her. 'Have you heard of him, Sergeant Sallis?' He left a little pause. 'No? He's the finest architect working in Britain today.'

Swift and Sue didn't speak until they were

in the car and Swift had driven without hindrance through the electric gates. The crush of press had mainly dispersed and the road was free of any obstacles.

'I'm so sorry, sir!' Sue exclaimed. 'About giving Jamie information on this hypnotherapist in Newcastle. I can assure you he's a bona-fide guy. Well, he should be. It was the DCC who introduced him at the training conference. He's helped the police with one or two other cases of amnesia.'

'There are more orthodox procedures,' Swift observed, disinclined to give Sue a slating when she was already doing the job perfectly well herself. 'For example, referring the matter to our police doctor who could then liaise with the appropriate specialists.'

'Yes, I know, sir. I've been such a fool.'

'What was it, Sue? Letting your heart rule your head?'

'I suppose so.'

'That mustn't happen in our job. It's to be avoided at all costs. We're not priests, we're not psychiatrists, we're not social workers. Our only relationship with suspects and interviewees is as police officers.'

'Yes, sir.'

'We don't get emotionally involved — end of story.'

'I know that, sir.'

'And I haven't noticed it being a problem of yours before.'

'Well, that's reassuring,' she said regretfully.

'So is this something to do specifically with Jamie Parker?'

'I'm not attracted to him, if that's what you were thinking,' Sue said slowly. 'It's more that I feel so very sorry for him. I mean I feel sorry for plenty of our other punters, it's just that Jamie seems so vulnerable. And alone. Josie seems to have been his world. And, let's face it, his parents seem cold and distant for all Parker's protests about his fatherly concerns.'

'You're suggesting that he's in some way thinking of you as his ally, someone who will fight his corner?'

She sighed. 'Yes. That's a good way of putting it.'

'We could, of course, interpret his behaviour as a deliberate and cunning strategy to manipulate the police.'

Sue winced, more for herself than Jamie. 'Do you think Parker will make a formal complaint, sir?'

'Hard to say. He's a man who's worked long and hard on the way he wants to present himself to the outside world. He's got a powerful and well-defended façade. He's shrewd and he's cagey. He'll toy with the idea, then do whatever suits his purposes at the time.'

She sighed. 'Yes, I can see him jumping either way.'

'If he does make a complaint, I'll support you in any way I can,' Swift said. 'And in the meantime, Sue, remember to keep your personal feelings firmly under control when you're engaged in police work.'

'Yes, sir. Absolutely.' She sat in uneasy contemplation. 'I hope Jamie doesn't get himself into any difficult scenarios. Or disappear into thin air.'

'I'll second that,' Swift said with feeling.

'I spoke to the therapist this morning after Jamie had left. He said he'd let us know if . . . when Jamie turned up.'

'Well, that's something to hold on to,' Swift said drily.

'What now?' she asked, staring disconsolately out of the window. The view was a picture-postcard perfection of sunlit hill slopes beneath cloudless skies.

'A coffee and a hefty Yorkshire snack,' he said. 'And then we'll pay a visit to Diana Parker or Redmond as she is now. Jamie has a sister, and maybe she's someone who's able to tell us rather more than his parents can. Or are prepared to.'

★ ★ ★

Pete's interviewee sat with her legs daintily together, her lemon and caramel striped hair falling over one freckled cheek as she talked. Her name was Emma Goodall. She was sixteen, a skinny scrap of a girl who had been working part time at the Moorlands Hotel for one month. For the rest of the week she worked sessions at a nearby pub.

At first she had seemed overwhelmed by Pete's status as a policeman. Her eyes had widened with awe and alarm when she learned he was a detective. But his strategy of taking a soft and gentle approach had soon put her at her ease. He had broken the ice by asking her to show him the exact place where she had first seen Saul Williams. And then they had extended the tour to include the route Saul would have taken to return from the bridal suite down the back stairs and into the narrow corridor linking the kitchens with the main reception rooms on the ground floor of the hotel.

Now they were talking together in the cramped office the manager had earmarked for the use of the police when necessary. Emma recalled Saul Williams well and was able to give Pete a detailed and accurate description of his physical appearance. Her

185

recollection of the timing of their brief encounter was less precise.

'Ooh, I don't think I can tell you that. I'd forgotten to put me watch on that day,' she explained.

Damn! Pete muttered inwardly.

'I was in such a rush to get into work on time, you see. I'm always running late. The other lasses call me the late Emma.' She giggled, sending him a flirty glance to see if he got the joke.

Pete thought she might find the quip less amusing if she worked in his line of country where late often equated with dead. Nevertheless he gave an obliging smile.

'How about a guess as to what time it was? Just an approximation?'

'Ooh, mebbe half eight. Or p'raps nearer nine. Me feet were giving me hell, any road. It seemed like I'd been on 'em for years.'

'Right,' said Pete, entertained by her bluff Yorkshire accent. 'So, you were in the little back corridor when you first saw Saul Williams. I'd like you tell me just what happened, Emma. Take your time, there's no rush.'

'He came down them stairs I showed you.'

'Was he walking, or running?'

'A bit o' both, really. He's a big lad, I doubt he can do a right lot o' running.'

Recalling Williams's lumbering bulk, Pete was impressed with her observation. 'So, he was in a bit of a hurry?'

'Yeah. And he looked kind o' wild, and scared an' all. To tell you the truth I was dead worried he were going to knock into me and send all me glasses flying. Off me tray, I mean. I'd been goin' round gatherin' up all empties.'

'Right. Good. Go on, please, Emma.'

'Er, he kind o' stopped dead. He'd gone all white and funny looking, like he'd seen a ghost. And he were rocking, back and forrard, really hard. I said to 'im, 'Are yer all right, love?' And he looked at me, kind of puzzled. And then he said, 'It's Josie, she's had an accident. She needs a doctor.' And I said, 'Josie? Isn't that the bride?' And he said it was. He kept on about how she needed a doctor. I tried to calm 'im down and said I'd get the manager to see to it. I thought he were going to burst out cryin' then but he just turned and went off. Well! I went straight back ter kitchens and put me tray down. I didn't need to go searching for manager, 'cos he was there sorting something else out. So when he'd finished wi' that I told him what the lad had said. And he said, 'Leave this to me. I'll sort it'.'

'And where was Saul Williams then?'

'I don't know. I didn't see him again after that. I think he must 'ave gone 'ome.'

'Thank you for that, Emma. That was very helpful.'

'You're welcome,' she said. 'It's dreadful i'nt it? A bride being murdered on her wedding day? Me mum says it dunt bear thinkin' about.'

'No, indeed,' Pete agreed. 'It doesn't.'

'Do you want to know owt else?' she asked, with a winning smile, clearly encouraged by his praise and approval.

'*Is* there anything?' he asked, putting on a grave expression to remind her this was no girly, giggling matter.

'No.' Her smile had vanished.

He got up and thanked her once more.

'Can I go now?' she asked, regarding him with a respect which was disturbingly gratifying.

'Most certainly. Oh, there is something else, Emma. Is Mr Ford in today?'

'Er, no. He's on leave. Back Wednesday, I think.' She looked up at him, a hesitant smile quivering on her lips.

Pete restrained himself from telling her to run along.

★ ★ ★

The man who answered the door looked as though he had not slept for days. Dressed in battered jeans and a sweatshirt which bore marks of breakfast on its front, he was as far away from the suave, mohair-suited Clive Parker as could be imagined.

Swift showed his ID card. 'Mr Piers Redmond?'

The man gave a wan twitch of a smile. 'That's me. Come in.'

The house was large and airy. It had a mock Tudor façade, criss-crossed all over with heavily stained black beams. Swift recalled his house searchings when he moved up to Yorkshire the year previously. He had been sent brochures for one or two places like this. Estate agents liked to describe them as a gentleman's residence. They invariably had five bedrooms, at least two bathrooms and a generous number of reception rooms. Their price bracket had been way beyond his means and the price range he had specified. He guessed that estate agents lived constantly in hope, or employed staff who didn't take too much notice of the particulars of their clients' requests.

Piers Redmond guided them through a grandly proportioned dining-room furnished with a huge glass table and leather dining chairs upholstered in pale blond leather into a

189

conservatory where two children were playing with a doll's house. Sue hung back for a few seconds in the dining room, casting envious glances over the table and chairs which were very much to her taste, but wholly inconsistent with her income. She noted that the stylish effect of the room was spoiled by the clutter of young children's paraphernalia. Various items of clothing and a used disposable nappy were strewn over the table. There were shoes and toys on the floor, and a scattered trail of breakfast cereal and milk looked as though it would soon be well bonded into the cream Wilton carpet. She walked through into the conservatory.

Piers Redmond gave another wan smile. 'I'm sorry it's a bit of a mess. When you have three-year-old twins it's hard to keep things pristine.' He gestured to the children, two little girls, mirror images with identical blonde hair and big blue eyes. 'This is Laura and this is Claudine. You won't be able to tell them apart. Di and I have difficulty sometimes. Are you going to say 'Hi' girls?'

The children had been staring up at the visitors with mingled curiosity and instinctive infant suspicion. 'Hi!' they chorused.

Sue crouched down. 'I like your doll's house,' she said. The children assessed her for a few seconds in solemn silence. One of them reached into the house, took out a tiny model figure, regarded it thoughtfully then offered it to Sue.

'You'll have a job for life, now,' Piers remarked, sinking into a chair and stretching out his long legs. 'What can I do for you, Chief Inspector?' he said with a slight drawl. 'As the saying goes.'

'We were wondering if we could talk to your wife,' Swift said. He was wondering who provided the money for this luxurious house. There was a relaxed and reflective quality about Piers Redmond which made him seem a doubtful candidate for the role of go-getting money provider. So maybe Piers had private means. Or perhaps Clive Parker was the provider — and also pulling the strings. Or maybe Diana was a go-getter.

'She's at work,' Piers said. 'She's a partner with Sapphire-Chantry. It's a national accountancy group.'

Swift had heard of it. He was also aware that being a partner with a prestigious company of that stature would attract a very substantial income. So — Diana was the go-getter.

'I'm what's commonly referred to as a house-husband,' Piers said with an ironic smile. 'And a hands-on father. Three kids to date. Our eldest, Barny, is on holiday with

191

some friends so I've only got the girlies to mind for the next day or two. It's a tough old life being a parent.' A rueful grin. 'I've also some pretensions to be a writer. But, so far, I haven't got down to producing very much.' He began to yawn, tried to conceal it and then gave in. 'I'm sorry. The girls have been having me get up to them for the last few nights. They've got to the seeing monsters and nightmares stage. And, of course, we're all totally shattered by what's happened.' He leaned back in his chair looking drained and exhausted.

'Did you notice anything unusual on the night Josie was murdered?' Swift asked.

Piers raked his fingers through his thick, untidy-looking hair. 'I've been going over and over it. I knew you'd come round at some point — and I just wish I could give you some information. Dear God, if I could give any clues to help you find the lousy, cowardly bastard who killed Josie, I most certainly would.'

'But you don't think you can, sir?' Sue prompted him.

'No. I was heavily involved in dancing and getting wasted around the time she was killed. I wasn't noticing very much at all.'

'It was a good bash, then?' Sue suggested.

'Yeah. It was all going absolutely swimmingly. And, fair enough, I wasn't exactly at my most vigilant, but I truly didn't notice anything worth remarking on.' He sighed. 'I'm sorry not to be more helpful.'

'Did you know Josie well?' Swift asked quietly.

Again Piers raked through his hair. 'Diana and I really took to her when Jamie started going around with her. We thought she was just right for him. And we all became good friends, often went out in a foursome.'

'In what way was she right for him, sir?' Sue shifted her weight as one of the twins swarmed up on to her knee and patted her cheek.

'Jamie's a lovely guy, but he's nervy and unsure of himself. What my mother would have called highly strung. Josie was a steady sort of person, socially adept and very sure of her place in the world. I think Jamie must have found it tremendously reassuring to be with someone so calm and strong. And someone who really cared about him.'

Looking for a mother figure? Sue wondered.

'Jamie's always struck me as one of those people who can't help being driven by what others think and expect of him,' Piers reflected. 'Especially his parents. Don't get me wrong, I'm not knocking them. But they're both high achievers and they expected the same of their kids. Diana, of course, came up trumps. She always did well at school. She forged ahead with her own career. She's a great looking girl with a lovely personality who's earned lots of applause all round. Jamie's nine years younger than Di, and in my view he's simply never been able to catch up.'

'He's a director at Parker's,' Swift pointed out.

'Yeah. But only through being his father's son. Jamie's not cut out for business. He should have been an artist. Well, actually he *is* an artist. He's had one or two of his oils displayed at a well-regarded gallery in York. But there's no money or prestige in art, unless you get to the very top.' He held out his arms as the twin on Sue's knee squirmed off and climbed onto his.

'I suppose his parents were keen on the prestige aspect,' Sue said, her interest aroused by Pier's account of Jamie's strengths and weaknesses.

'Yeah. But don't run away with the idea they're ogres. They're people of their time and generation. They value status and social approval and they believe their kids won't be truly happy unless they too achieve that.

Clive's a bit of a power freak, but he's basically a decent guy. And Cassie!' He gave a snort. 'She started off as a burler and mender at Parkers who won beauty contests in her spare time and then married the boss's son and became grander than all the rich folk who used to look down on her. She's just a straightforward harpy and a snob. There are women up and down the country exactly like her.'

'What was your line of work before the children arrived?' Swift asked.

'Me? I was a dentist. Until I discovered I was in a career trap and I didn't want to spend the rest of my life peering into the malodorous mouths of moaning and terrified members of the general public.'

The second twin ran up to him and wrapped herself around his leg. He reached down, pulled her onto his lap and kissed the top of her head. 'Have you any idea who killed Josie?' Piers asked, in a low voice.

'We're following some leads,' Swift told him.

'Ah, yes. Following leads.' Piers gave a twisted smile. 'I've racked my brains to think who the fucking bollocks would do such wicked thing.'

Sue felt a jab of electric sensation. Not so much in reaction to the sudden swearing;

rather the contained, intense force in Piers's tone.

'Have you come up with any theories?' Swift asked.

'If only,' he said regretfully. 'Some twisted psychopath who has a fancy for killing brides maybe?'

'We thought of that too,' Swift said. 'But our data base doesn't throw up any similar homicides.'

'Yeah . . . well.' His stroked his hands over each of the twins' blonde heads, his expression distant and sad.

'Have you suffered from the flu that's going around?' Swift asked.

Piers jerked out of his reverie. 'What? Flu? No.' He glanced sharply at Swift. 'Why do you ask?'

'Cassandra Parker mentioned that you might be going down with it. That you'd had to miss the lunch party yesterday.'

'Jesus!' he said softly. 'Can you imagine the awfulness of such an occasion? Going through with it when Josie was lying in the morgue. Or more likely on the pathologist's slab. Dear God, Cassie Parker must have *life goes on* stamped through her like a stick of seaside rock.'

'So pending flu was a good excuse for absence?'

'Precisely.'

'Did Diana go to the lunch?'

'Just for a couple of hours. She thought the parents needed support, which I'm sure was true. I should have made an effort and gone with her. She's got a lot more backbone than me.'

Swift glanced at Sue. *Anything else?* She shook her head. He stood up and murmured thanks to Piers. 'We'll see ourselves out,' he said, gesturing to the now drowsing twins with a smile.

Piers got to his feet, a child balanced on each hip. 'No, no. I may not be a star at housekeeping, but I do try to preserve some standards,' he said with irony. As he went through the dining room he swept the discarded clothes and nappy on to the floor.

'You'll find Di in most days,' he told Swift and Sue as they passed through the doorway. 'If you come before eight a.m. and after seven-thirty in the evening.'

'Thanks,' Sue said. She glanced at the twins. 'I hope *you* manage to get some sleep before too long.'

Piers gave a ghost of a smile. 'Yeah, well. I'll just soldier on.'

'Oh boy, does he loathe the Parkers,' Sue commented once they were out of earshot. 'The parents, not Jamie.'

'Agreed. But he put on a good show of loyalty. And he seems to love his wife.'

Swift was making a start on pulling out the salient points of the interview, trying to assess their possible significance in relation to Josie's death. There was nothing which instantly claimed his interest. Piers Redmond was an agreeable, talented man who'd thrown up his career and settled for looking after his children. His liking for Jamie Parker appeared genuine, as did his sadness at Josie's death. Swift wondered how he felt about being financially dependent on his wife, and thus indirectly on the Parker parents.

'He's quite attractive, isn't he?' Sue remarked. 'A bit lizardy and laid back for my taste. And all that egg down his shirt. But still.'

'That's what I value,' Swift commented. 'That enviable female perspective no man can hope to match. And offered with such eloquence.'

Sue permitted herself a small smile in response to his veiled teasing, although she still felt bruised from Clive Parker's mauling.

'And what about Clive Parker?' Swift asked, as if tuning in to her thoughts. 'Do you think he is attractive?'

'Well . . . ' Sue made a rueful grimace. 'I have to admit that he is quite magnetic, in a wolfish, satanic kind of way. And I suppose his powerful position as a mill owner and his money are always a turn on. And not just that, the way he *believes* in his own personal power.' She glanced across to Swift. 'Have you got Parker in your sights as a suspect, sir?'

'We can't rule him out, can we?'

'No, that's true.' She waited for him to elaborate, but he stayed silent. 'Are you putting your money on any of the possible suspects we've seen so far?' she asked.

'If I were a gambling man I wouldn't be risking any bets at this stage. Would you?'

She shook her head.

'Nevertheless, I'm reasonably satisfied we're barking up the appropriate trees.'

'But do you think we're getting anywhere, sir?'

'I think we shall get much further once Jamie Parker resurfaces.'

Sue looked at his set face and fell silent. Bloody hell!

8

Jamie followed the directions the hypnotherapist had given him over the phone. They led him to a small basement flat in a Victorian terrace near the city centre. He paused before pressing the entry buzzer. Having been accustomed to grandeur from childhood he was instinctively doubtful about the professionalism and competence of someone who lived in such cramped conditions. He looked at the engraved brass plate beside the doorframe. Ian Homer. MA Cantab, Psychology. MSc Manchester. AFBPsS. That sounded reassuringly impressive. He placed his finger on the buzzer.

The man who opened the door was in his forties, dressed in dark-grey jeans and a black sweatshirt. His hair was cropped to around the same length as the dark stubble on his chin, and the glance from his eyes was stabbing and direct. He gave a fleeting smile of welcome. 'Are you Jamie Parker?'

'Yes.'

'Ian Homer.' He extended a welcoming hand. 'Plain mister, I'm not a doctor. Come in.'

He led Jamie through a narrow hallway into a low spacious room with pale blue walls and the minimum of furniture and ornaments. He gestured to a large yellow sofa placed against the back wall and Jamie sat down, tense and upright as though he had an iron rod strapped to his backbone. He braced himself for an introductory barrage of questions.

Homer settled himself into a chair facing his client, sat down deep into it and stretched out his legs. 'I'm going to tell you something about myself and the work I do,' he said. 'And if, after you've heard it, you feel you don't want to go ahead with the session, that's fine. In fact you can get up and leave anytime. OK?'

Jamie nodded. His eyes were stinging as though they had grit in them. He wanted this session to begin and then to be over, and for him to know the truth however terrible it was.

'I started my career as an educational psychologist,' Homer told his wary-looking client, 'but I got fed up with bashing out IQ results and fighting unsuccessful battles to keep unhappy kids out of residential special schools. I got a job driving a bus, and when I wasn't driving I studied the theory and practice of hypnosis.'

'Have you been practising long?' Jamie asked. He needed to know that this man had the ability to deliver him from the torment he was suffering.

'Five years. I think I know what I'm doing.' There was no smile, no eagerness to prove himself.

Jamie sat very still. His ears were humming and his heart was thumping insistently. He had only vaguely heard the information Ian Homer offered, but the man's direct, curt manner satisfied and reassured him. 'Don't you want to know all my family background and so on?' he asked.

'No,' Homer said. 'In order to do my work I simply need to talk to you when you're in a subconscious state. In fact I prefer not to be influenced by potted histories.'

This was not at all what Jamie had expected. But he liked Homer's response. 'You don't need to say any more,' Jamie told him. 'I just want you to go ahead. Do you want me to pay now? I've brought cash.'

'Later will do,' Homer said. He raised himself slightly, leaning forward. 'What exactly do you want to get out of this meeting, Jamie?'

'As I told you, there's something blanked out in my memory. I think it's there but it's as if it's locked away. I want you to unlock it. I want to find out what happened. Can you do that?'

'I think it's very likely,' Homer said. 'But before I help you into a trance-like state, I want you to take me through the few minutes before the 'blank' opens up. And then what's happening when you get to the other side.'

Jamie dully related the details he had given to Sue Sallis. 'So can you help me?'

'I hope and believe so. Ask me a more specific question, Jamie.'

'I'm sorry?'

'You've got one thing on your mind, one thing which you want to ask me about. Is that right?'

'Yes.'

'So tell me what it is. And I'll give you an answer.'

Jamie was aware of the base of his tongue, swollen and blocking the way for his words to emerge. 'I'm in hell,' he said softly. 'My wife was killed on the night of our wedding. I loved her so much, more than anyone or anything else I've ever known. But I can't remember what happened. I've tried and tried, and that's the honest truth.' Tears stood in his eyes.

'Take your time, Jamie. Stay calm. I'm here to help you.'

In a low monotone, Jame recited his account of how Josie had left the ballroom, how he'd begun to get worried and tried to find her.

'I pushed open the door of the suite and walked in. And then it's all blanked out. The next thing I remember is sitting on the bed. And she's lying in my arms, and she's dead. And I could have killed her.' He stopped, looking to Homer for a reaction.

'Yes, you could,' he said, his face impartial.

'Because if I can't remember what happened, then how do I know I didn't kill her?' Jamie insisted, his voice rising in panic.

'I can help you to recall what happened during those blank periods,' Homer said. 'If you truly want to work with me, then I can do that.' He sat waiting for Jamie's response. A dark, watchful figure, his face as grim as something hacked out of granite.

'If you find out I've killed my wife, what then?' Jamie asked.

'I talk you through the feelings the session has opened up. And I refer you to another professional if I think that will be beneficial for you.'

Jamie was puzzled. If he had done something as terrible as to kill Josie, then all he needed was punishment and eternal damnation. 'What about the police?' he asked.

'What about them?'

'You mean there's a possibility you might not tell them?' He was astounded.

'Jamie, I've already spoken with Sergeant Sallis.' Homer told him. 'She called me this morning after you and I made our appointment. I've agreed to give her and her team a full report on my findings.'

'Isn't that against confidentiality and so on?' Jamie asked.

'I'm not a doctor. I'm prepared to share my findings with other professionals when it's helpful and relevant.'

Jamie sat in silence.

'Do you still want to go ahead?' Homer asked eventually.

'Yes. Yes!'

'You're aware that I film all sessions. And that you will have full access to the whole of the recording?'

'Yes. Sue — Sergeant Sallis told me about it.'

'OK.' Homer paused. When he spoke again his voice was slow and deep. 'I want you to relax, Jamie. Let yourself go limp. Let your arms and legs feel heavy.'

Jamie's body jerked in alarm. 'Is this it? Are you going to do it? Right now.'

'Yes, it's nothing to be afraid of. All you have to do is think of yourself at the top of a long staircase. At the bottom there's a pool of golden light, welcoming you. You start to walk down, very slowly, no hurry at all. There are lights guiding you on your way . . . '

Homer's voice went on, low and rhythmic. Jamie became aware that the tension in his body was slackening, that a weight was lifting off him. There was a warm tingle in his fingertips, spreading into his limbs, up through his neck and into the hair at the base of his skull.

★　★　★

Geoff and Pete were the first to arrive back at the station in the late afternoon.

Geoff had found an empty desk at which to park himself and was now keying information into the computer, using the hunt and peck approach of those who have successfully resisted the pressure to become skilled typists. He looked up as Pete strode into the CID room. 'Now then, young sir!' he said in greeting, recalling the long gone days when he too had moved everywhere at top speed.

'Afternoon, Sergeant. Or is it evening? Seems like it's been a long, long day.' Pete threw himself into the chair behind his desk, leaning back and stretching his legs out. 'And it's hot enough in my car to fry an egg.'

'How's tricks, then?' Geoff asked. 'Got our

man, have you? Because I doubt very much if I have.'

'Yup. I do believe I have.'

'Oh, aye. Are we talking about the young guy you went to see yesterday?'

'The very same. I've been talking to the waitress he'd spilled the beans to.' He flipped open his notebook. 'Listen to what she said. 'He looked wild and scared. I thought he was going to knock into me. He was all white and funny looking, like he'd seen a ghost'.'

'Sounds promising,' Geoff said. 'Does the boss know?'

'Not yet.'

Geoff pressed his lips together. 'A word of advice, Constable. Don't hold your breath.'

'Sorry?'

'Don't get your hopes up about DCI Swift sending you straight out on a collar-feeling expedition.'

'We've got enough, surely, to make an arrest?'

'Oh, aye. I'm not disputing that. But you'll most likely find the boss isn't of the same mind.'

'Really!'

'Let's put it this way. He's not one for jumping in with both feet,' Geoff commented sardonically. 'I'm not criticizing, mind, just giving you the benefit of my experience.'

'Ah.' Pete looked thoughtful

'From what the boss said this morning, it didn't seem to me like your Saul Williams was at the top of his hit list.'

'Well, no, I agree. But with this latest witness statement . . .'

'Our DCI likes the psychological approach,' Geoff said, tapping his head to emphasize the point. 'He works on instinct rather than impulse. And I have to say, on occasions it works.'

Pete heard the mixed messages, the blend of respect and reservation Geoff was expressing for their team leader. 'Thanks for that, Sarge,' he said. Frowning and reflective, he made his way to the water dispenser and slipped a plastic beaker under the tap.

Sue Sallis came through the doorway and moved up softly behind him, dropping her shoulder bag on the floor and handing him a second beaker. 'One for me too,' she said. 'I'm parched and bushed.' She looked across the room. 'Hi, Geoff. Anything interesting come up?'

'Not for me, lass. 'Saw no evil, heard no evil, all was sweetness and light', seemed to be the general message from the folks I saw today. And it seems there are quite a few of the guests who are already in far flung corners of the globe. Looks like they put off their hols for the Josie/Jamie wedding and then drove straight to the airport. I reckon around a quarter of the folks on my list have jetted off. But then, it's the middle of August. What can you expect?'

'Yeah, but the ones who really matter are still around, aren't they?' Pete said, taking a long swig from his beaker, then placing a second one under the tap for Sue.

Geoff gave a wry grin. 'That's as mebbe. Are you suggesting I'm wasting me time, young lad?'

'Sorry, Sergeant,' Pete said. 'But if you want an honest answer, yes.'

'Aye, you're probably right. But I'm quite happy going around seeing folk again — and getting paid for it. Most of these wedding guests aren't villains. They don't live like pigs in muck. And they offer you tea and cakes.'

'Can't be bad,' said Sue. 'Won't your new girlfriend be missing you?'

'Ay! Cheeky! She's a very independent woman. She doesn't need me to hold her hand all the time. And it's her night out with the girls this evening.'

'Ooh, so you're fancy free again?' She flashed him a coy glance.

Geoff shook his head in mock despair. 'How was your day, then, Miss newly-appointed-Sergeant? Have you found out how to do joined-up thinking yet?'

Sue took the beaker Pete offered and stared down at it. 'I certainly wasn't using my brains properly this morning,' she said slowly. She sat down and sipped her water.

'Why? What's the problem?' Pete was eager and interested.

Sue's clipped and succinct account of her interview with Jamie Parker was followed by a short silence.

'I suppose that's basically colluding with a suspect,' Pete said.

'I suppose it is,' Sue agreed. 'It's also sending a suspect off into the unknown — maybe never to return. And saddling myself with a possible formal complaint from said witness's father.'

'Oh dear,' said Geoff.

'The boss is being very reasonable about it,' Sue said.

'But somehow, I suspect that only makes you feel worse,' Geoff shrewdly observed.

*   *   *

Swift needed some time to himself. He drove to the outskirts of Grassington, parked in a Forestry Commission car-park and walked down to the banks of the Wharfe. The air was heavy with heat and swarms of evening midges which gathered around him, taking

210

tiny bites at his forehead and scalp. The river's flowing majesty had been slowly diminished by the lack of rain, but its central force still surged and sparkled in the early evening sunshine. He watched the relentless movement of the water for a while, fanning his hand over his face to ward off the midges. Eventually he returned to the car, switched on the air conditioning, and took out a pad and pencil. After a few seconds he laid the pad down and closed his eyes.

There was something about the current murder case which prompted him to view it as though looking down on a half-lit stage. He saw Josie in the centre, and around her in the shadows were Jamie, Clive and Cassandra. A little way back were Jack and Melanie, their arms reached out in despair and grieving. Beyond were the dim figures of Piers and Diana, shoulder to shoulder. And in the wings, Saul Williams, alone and frightened.

This was a killing based on love or hate, he was sure. Love and jealousy, hate and revenge. So where did that lead him?

What if Jamie had discovered something about his bride which had shocked and revolted him? An affair with another man, past or present? Or another woman? Some other misdemeanour.

211

What if Josie had discovered something about her bride-groom which must never come to light? Something in his past no one knew about? What if she had challenged him and he had retaliated. There had been a struggle. Her death had been a terrible accident. Manslaughter not murder. Either way, it would be worth Jamie's while to attempt to hide behind a memory loss, either genuine or manufactured.

He turned the key and fired the engine. Theorizing about motives was not too helpful in the absence of strong witness or forensic evidence. What they badly needed now was a lucky break. But he knew only too well how slim the chances were on that particular front.

* * *

'He's coming now,' Sue announced, watching Swift's car park in the space reserved for him.

'You sound like a school kid spotting the teacher arriving at the classroom door,' Geoff commented, finding himself rewarded with an evil look from Sue who returned to her desk and stared fixedly at the notes she had made on the computer.

Geoff looked on with the impartial interest of one who is now out of the main arena of play, and happy to be so. He noted the attitudes of industry and unconcern adopted by the two young members of the team, aware that each was seething with their individual expectations and anxieties, which only their senior officer could satisfy.

Swift paused at the door of the CID room. 'Review meeting in ten minutes,' he said, before going through to his own office and standing for a few moments looking out of the window. He had seen the anxiety on Sue's face and he was concerned about her. The outlook was not good if Clive Parker decided to make a formal complaint about her dealings with Jamie. There would have to be an enquiry, and whatever the outcome of such an investigation there would be a permanent stain on Sue's record. Moreover, her confidence in her worth as a police officer could be badly eroded. Thinking back, he thought there had been a change in her during the last few weeks, a small alienation in her assurance, as if she was not quite as sure of the worth of the policing job as she used to be. And yet most of the time she was still the same eager, buoyant Sue who managed to combine enthusiasm with the wisdom and tolerance that came from a few years of hands-on police work.

Pete, of course, as a new recruit, was

running on a constant rush of adrenalin, hungry for the fifteen or sixteen-hour day which came with a new murder investigation. His confidence was boundless. He was like a toddler newly up on its feet and unaware of the bumpiness of the ground beneath him.

It went through Swift's mind that maybe Sue was finding Pete's keenness in some way undermining. Or maybe there were problems for her at home. He knew little of her situation, except that she was married — apparently happily — and had no children. He made a note to keep an eye on the situation, as much for the good of the team as for hers. But he cared about Sue, and he wanted her to be happy.

As he turned from the window, Sue and Pete came in together. Sue brought beakers of coffee on a tray. 'Geoff's slipped out to the mini market for some biscuits,' she said. 'And a quick fag, most likely.'

Swift smiled. 'I don't think he'll mind if we make a start. What have you got, Pete?'

Pete spoke with nerve and fervour, and his recital of Emma Goodall's description of Saul Williams brought a vivid picture of the damaged, fearful young man into Swift's mind.

Pete looked up from his notes. 'What do you think, sir?'

214

'It would seem from what Emma told you that Williams was in a highly emotional state,' Swift said. 'And one which could well be consistent with having just carried out a killing.' He paused, and Pete tensed, hearing the 'but' coming. 'Moreover we could argue that Williams had both motive and opportunity to kill Josie. He could well have construed Josie's marriage to Jamie as a betrayal of his own feelings for her. He gatecrashed her wedding, he stalked her movements; he went to her suite; then into her bathroom and remonstrated with her. And when her response disappointed him, he drowned her. But then where is the evidence? Our only way of placing him at the murder scene was by his own admission. We have no witnesses, no prints, no DNA, nothing of substance.'

'No, sir,' Pete said, unable to stay silent a moment longer. 'But if we brought him in for further questioning, we'd be able to break him down, no problem. He'd confess, I'm sure of it. He's the type.'

'The confessing type?' Swift echoed with a lift of his eyebrows. 'In my view Saul Williams is an ideal candidate for making a confession — whether he did the killing or not — simply to avoid the pressure we might put him under. In my book he's the typical false confessor.'

Pete looked down at his hands, rubbing clenched knuckles over his knees.

At this point, Geoff returned bearing slices of ginger cake on a plate. Observing the intensity on the faces of his colleagues, he sat down and kept shtum.

Swift continued. 'A further problem with Williams is how he came to see the dead Josie in Jamie's arms.' He looked directly at Pete. 'Have you had time to read the notes on my interview with Williams this morning?

'Yes, sir. I have seen your notes. But supposing after he'd killed Josie, Williams fled the scene, hung around for a bit and then went back to check.'

'Check that Josie was dead?' Swift enquired.

'Well, just check the scene.'

'Murderers aren't known for putting themselves back in the crime scene in public places,' Sue pointed out.

Pete maintained a short silence. 'Sure. I still think he could have gone back. I mean he's a few chips short of a sandwich, isn't he?'

'In fact, he's quite bright,' Swift said. 'I checked with a clinical psychologist who's assessed him on a number of occasions. Williams displays what is termed an uneven profile of intellectual abilities. He's high on vocabulary and general knowledge, not so good on spatial tasks. But overall he tests out above average.'

'Bloody hell!' Pete muttered.

'Never argue with trick cyclists,' Geoff commented. 'You'll only drop into the black hole of their jargon.'

Sue's phone began to play the opening bars from Mozart's Symphony number 40. She flipped it open and got to her feet. 'It's Ian Homer,' she said, sliding rapidly through the door and into the corridor.

'And who's he when he's at home?' Geoff asked.

'He's the hypnotherapist Sue put Jamie Parker on to,' Pete told him.

'Is he now? Yet another trick cyclist!'

Swift refused to be drawn in. He turned to his eager young constable. 'Pete, I recognize that we've got some good grounds for suspecting Saul Williams, but I don't believe we've yet got enough hard evidence to bring him in. And certainly not tonight.'

'Right, sir. Thank you.' Pete sat back. For a few seconds he nursed the wound of his deflation. And then told himself to move on.

In the ensuing silence, all three officers became aware of Sue's low murmurs of response to Ian Homer as she spoke in the corridor outside. An air of tense anticipation began to grow in the room. Swift reached out and took a slice of ginger cake. By the time he had eaten it Sue was back.

'Jamie's safe and sound at Homer's place,' she said, her relief palpable. 'Homer's going to let him stay there for the night. Apparently Jamie went into a very deep trance and Homer doesn't want to wake him abruptly.'

'Blood and sand! Rather him than me,' Geoff commented. 'What a carry on. The deep recesses of your brain in their hands.'

'Homer says Jamie's fine,' Sue countered. 'It's quite normal for some subjects to go into a deep trance state.'

'Three questions,' Swift said. 'Has any significant information emerged from the session? Do we have a confession? And do we ring the Parkers and tell them Jamie is safe and well now, or later?'

'Oh, God!' Sue groaned, the image of Clive Parker's wolfish features rising in her mind like a vampire with dripping fangs. 'I'll ring them,' she said, against all her instincts and desires. 'Now. Get it over with.'

'No,' Swift said quietly. 'We need to hear your information before we contact them. And I'll do it. I need to arrange interviews with Cassandra and Diana.'

'Besides which,' Geoff commented drily, 'from what I've heard, I reckon the Parkers are the sort who always prefer the top man.'

'You have a wonderful knack of giving with one hand and taking away with the other,' Sue told him, but the acidity of the remark was tempered with a smile. Being let off the hook of an imminent dialogue with Clive Parker had instantly lightened her mood.

'So what have we got from Jamie Parker's hypnotherapy session, Sue?' Swift asked.

'As far as I could gather, nothing conclusive. And certainly no confession. Homer's taped the whole session and he's sending it on to us by courier tomorrow.' She glanced down at the jottings she had made whilst on the telephone. 'The gist of it is Jamie was very receptive to the whole procedure. He went under very quickly and achieved a deep trance. Homer took him step by step through what happened. He answered most of Homer's questions, but the responses seemed to suggest that Josie was, in fact, lying dead in the bath when he first saw her.'

'Is it possible for a subject to fake responses?' Pete asked. 'Tell lies whilst they're under?'

Sue said, 'I remember that point coming up at the lecture Homer gave us at the conference. He said that lying is a deliberate act which requires the liar to be conscious and alert. In a trance a subject would simply recall happenings as their unconscious mind remembered them. Well, something like that.'

'That seems reasonable,' Swift said. 'Is it possible to fake the trance itself?'

'I suppose you could make a show of trying to. But Homer has a way of testing the level of consciousness.' She paused.

'Go on!' Pete urged.

'He sticks pins in the back of the subject's hand, without warning them first. If you stick a pin in someone when they're not expecting it they give an automatic reflex response. Homer demonstrated it with one of the officers in the audience. He put him under, linked him to a bio-feedback monitor, then stuck the pin in. The machine registered a significant shock, but the subject showed no response at all.'

'So I wonder what we've got here?' Swift mused. 'Given that we can assume the trance was authentic and Jamie was not deliberately lying or withholding information, it doesn't sound from what Homer told you as though we're much further forward.'

'Homer said he'd transcribe the audio part of the tape and e-mail it through to us first thing in the morning. He seemed a bit wary about giving detailed information on the phone.'

'From my admittedly sparse knowledge, I don't believe that e-mail carries any better assurances of privacy,' Swift remarked drily. 'However, if we're going to receive a full account within hours I'm not inclined to argue. So I suggest we call it a day, and you three go to our local and get a beer.'

'And you, sir?' Sue asked.

'I'm going to speak to the Parkers. I'll be along later. Order me a whisky.'

★ ★ ★

It was Cassandra Parker who answered the phone with a barked, 'Yes!'

Swift got straight to the point, reassuring her that Jamie was in Newcastle with a bona fide therapist. And that he was safe and well.

There was a pause and Swift braced himself for an onslaught.

Cassandra gave a low moan. 'Oh, thank God! Thank God he's all right. I'm really grateful to you for letting us know, Inspector. I've been calling his mobile phone all day but it's been switched off. I've been frantic with worry. I mean to lose Josie was terrible, but to think of losing Jamie . . . '

'Were you concerned he might not return home?' Swift asked.

'Quite honestly, I didn't know what he might do, he was in such a state the last time I saw him. He's always been a rather nervy person. And this has been such a blow. I just pray that when he gets over it, he can start to build his life again.'

Swift made an appropriate murmur of agreement.

'Has the therapist . . . found anything out from Jamie?' she asked.

'We've no details as yet, Mrs Parker.'

'I know nothing about hypnosis,' she said dismissively. 'It's always seemed to me a very dubious activity. Some of my friends have tried it to help them stop smoking. And to tell the truth, it seems to be a bit of a dead loss.'

'We won't have the therapist's report until tomorrow,' Swift said. 'But in the meantime Jamie is quite safe. He's staying at the therapist's house overnight.'

There was a pause. 'I'm just wondering if I should drive up to Newcastle now and fetch him back home myself,' Cassandra said, with uncharacteristic hesitancy. 'It's so difficult when your children are adults, isn't it? You want to do your best for them, but they don't always welcome your help. And sometimes it's impossible to know what to do for the best.'

'I think we should wait and see how he is in the morning,' Swift said, having plans of his own about getting Jamie back to Yorkshire.

'Will you be at your shop in the morning, Mrs Parker?'

'Yes. Unless there's something urgent, of course. We all have our lives to live, don't we?'

'And your husband?'

'He'll be at work too. We must all try to carry on as normal.' Her voice was stronger now. 'Please feel free to call us any time,' she said graciously. 'And, by the way, Inspector, Clive and I are of the view that, providing there are no unpleasant sequels to this wild goose chase suggested by Sergeant Sallis, we shall not be lodging a formal complaint.'

Swift guessed she would be expecting an intimation of gratitude for their clemency. 'Good night, Mrs Parker,' he said.

Clicking the connection off he then phoned through to the Tyneside division and requested surveillance on Ian Homer's flat and Jamie Parker's car. If Parker left and attempted to board a ferry, plane or train link overseas, he wanted him stopped. There mustn't be any risk of this suspect slipping through their fingers.

*　*　*

Jamie woke to find the lights in the room dimmed and Ian Homer opposite him, dozing in his chair.

He glanced at his watch and saw that it was 4.30 a.m. He'd been asleep for ages. He struggled to orient himself, gradually recalling where he was and why. The hypnosis session must be over. He had no idea how long it had lasted.

Homer stirred and spoke. 'How are you feeling, Jamie?' He got up, poured chilled water from a steel flask and handed Jamie a filled glass.

'I feel kind of warm and relaxed,' Jamie said. 'Is that normal?'

'It's how I tell my clients they will feel when they come out of their trance.'

'It must have worked, then,' Jamie said. 'What happened in the session? What did you find out?'

'You're tensing already,' Homer said. 'Breathe deeply, Jamie. Take some mouthfuls of water. There's nothing to be anxious about.'

★   ★   ★

Swift let himself quietly into his apartment. Naomi was curled on the sofa, asleep, her head resting against an open, dogeared copy of George Eliot's *The Mill on the Floss*. He touched her hair lightly and she opened her eyes.

'You have been working far too many hours,' she said. 'I might have to report it to your senior officer.'

He smiled.

'Any progress?'

'At least it's more forward than back,' he said.

Naomi stretched and looked at her watch. 'God! Is that the time?' She glanced up at him. 'If I didn't know you better, Dad, I'd think you'd been out on the town with a secret girlfriend.'

9

Homer's e-mail was timed at 6.46 a.m. Swift was in at 7.30 to pick it up and by 8.15 the team were assembled to read and then discuss the contents.

Re: James Parker's session
From: 'Ian Homer' <ih@ihhc.com>
Organization: Ian Homer Hypnosis Consultancy

For attention of DCI Swift and Sergeant Sallis

The following is a literal transcript of the audio sounding taken from the audio/video recording of the session yesterday evening (video to follow by courier).

The transcript begins at the time Jamie entered a full trance state and ends when his account reaches the point where he is retrieving memories he can readily access when conscious (Cf. Sergeant Sallis's information e-mailed yesterday)

IH — I want you to relax, Jamie. I want you to feel safe. There is nothing for you to worry about. I want you to nod to show that you are relaxed and not afraid. (pause — Jamie nods). I want you to take yourself back to the day of your wedding.

I want you to think about the party in the evening. You and Josie are dancing, you are happy, everything is going right for you. You dance with the guests and you're having a fine time. Then you notice Josie is no longer in the ballroom. You tell yourself she'll soon be back. But she doesn't come. You start to get worried. You go to find her. You can't find her downstairs or in the garden so you go up to your suite. I want you to concentrate on this moment. You're standing in the corridor. Now you're pushing open the door of the suite. The door opens easily for you, doesn't it?

Jamie — Yes.

H — You're walking in now. What can you see and hear?

Jamie — I can't see anyone in the room. The bathroom door's open. I can smell a strong scent. Bath essence. I'm calling out for Josie. She's not answering. I'm getting a terrible feeling that something's wrong. Something really really bad. My legs feel like they can't move. I'm looking around the bathroom door. It's steamy in there and so hot. My heart is exploding in my chest. I can see dark hair waving in the water. I know it's Josie's. I'm so scared I think I'm going to be sick. I don't think I can move. But if I go away someone else will find her. My Josie. My lovely Josie-Jo. I'm going to do it. I'm going in. Oh God, oh God, oh God! She's lying in the bath and I'm frozen, nothing will move. (Jamie starts to sob) **H** — I want you to stop crying, Jamie. I want you to tell me what happens next. **Jamie** (shuddering, trying not to cry) — I'm putting my hands in the water. She's warm, she's still alive. I'm trying to get hold of her, but she slips out of my grasp. I've got to let the water out! *Let the water out.* I can feel her now. She's not breathing. Her eyes are blank like a dead fish. (Jamie breathing very hard) I'm putting a towel on the floor. My hands are shaking so much I don't think I can get her out. But she's not heavy. Oh God! She's dead. She's dead! What do I do? I don't know about first aid. God! Help me, God. Bang her chest, bang her chest. Breathe air into her mouth. Breathe, breathe. Breathe life back into her. (long pause — Jamie still breathing hard) There's this sweet, sweet smell. It's making me sick. God, I'm going to throw up. (Jamie makes sounds of retching — then falls silent)

H — What are you going to do next, Jamie?

J — I'm wrapping her in the towel. I'm taking her through to the bedroom. She's not heavy. I can always lift her quite easily. I'm sitting there with her. I'm still thinking she might not be dead. Hoping. Oh please. (pause) My mind is empty, I can't feel anything.

H — Is there anyone else in the room Jamie?

J — Just me and Josie. (gulps and sobs) Oh dear God! I can't stop crying . . .

H — Who comes to find you?

J — That boy Saul. I don't want him there. I just want her to myself.

H — What's Saul doing?

J — Just looking. (pause) Now he's gone away.

H — Is there anyone else in the room?

J — No. (pause) Someone's coming, knocking on the door. It's the manager.

H — What does he want?

J — He wants to know if everything is all right. I can't speak. I can't talk. He's coming into the room. He's looking at Josie. (12 minute pause, Jamie appears exhausted — so no questions attempted)

H — What's happening now, Jamie?

J — The doctor's here. He says Josie's dead. I'm trying to tell him what happened but I keep feeling sick again. I just want to be left alone. (10 minute pause)

H — Jamie, I want you to come out of the dark place you've gone into. I want you to move on in your thoughts and tell me what's happening when you come out of that dark place.

J — There's a woman here talking to the doctor.

H — Can you tell me what she's like?

J — She's got dark hair like Josie's, only cut short. She's wearing a pale blue shirt and cream trousers. She's looking around and asking questions.

H — Let's move on a little, Jamie. This woman with dark hair. Did she talk to you? After the doctor had gone?

J — She spoke very quietly. She told me she was from the police. She said I must let go of Josie . . .

At this point Jamie's recalled information is very similar to that previously offered to Sergeant Sallis and is therefore not included. The completed video recording should be with you mid-morning. However, in my view the basic information you require is contained in this partial transcript although the video images might possibly offer further insights.

I hope that this report will be helpful in furthering your enquiries. Ian Homer (M.A. MSc)

The team read through their individually printed-out copies in total silence. As each one finished reading they laid their copy down on Swift's desk. Geoff was the last to finish. He shook his head in disbelief. 'Well, it beats reading Dandy and Beano.'

'It's unbelievable!' Pete exclaimed.

'You don't believe it?' Swift asked.

'I'm not sure what I believe, sir. It's certainly something I've never come across before. Impressive, but a bit voo-dooish to be honest. Would it be admissible evidence?'

'Homer's experienced at giving evidence as an expert witness in child abuse cases,' Sue responded. 'His comments and supporting videos have been used in court on a number of occasions.'

'Leaving that particular issue aside for a moment,' Swift said thoughtfully, 'where does this transcript leave us with regard to Jamie Parker?'

'In my book it strongly suggests he's innocent,' Sue said.

Swift turned to the constable. 'Pete?'

'I'm sceptical about the validity of hypnosis, sir, have to admit that. But if we ever got as far as getting an indictment on Jamie then this work Homer's done would certainly help to get him off in court. Especially if we can't come up with hard evidence against him.'

'I agree,' Swift said. 'And it's worth reminding ourselves we're in great difficulty generally with this case, because of a lack of provable facts. What's your view, Geoff?'

'Basically, I'm with Pete,' Geoff said. 'A confession with some good corroborative evidence would be nice. And pigs might fly. So, what now, sir?'

'I'd like you to continue with your PC Plodding, house to house.' Swift gave the retired sergeant a rueful smile.

'Champion by me. Nice steady job,' Geoff concluded.

'I'm going to see Cassandra Parker,' said Swift. 'It will be interesting to find out whether the concerns about Jamie have prompted something to emerge from her memory. I want Sue and Pete to interview Diana Parker, for the simple reason she's the

232

one member of the Parker family we haven't yet got around to seeing.'

'We'll get her angle on Josie,' Sue said. 'As the saying goes, to find out how someone died, first find out how they lived.' She glanced round the group. 'Does anyone know where that quote comes from?'

'The harrassed detective's manual,' Pete suggested.

'Her husband indicated that he and Diana were pretty chummy with Josie and Jamie,' Swift said. 'It could be useful to get her view on that. And we also need to see the Haygarths and bring them up to date. Hopefully that might work as another memory prompt.'

'What about Jamie?' Sue asked. 'When's he coming back?'

'Very soon, I hope,' Swift said. 'I've asked the local police to keep him under surveillance. We're waiting to see where he sets off to when he leaves Homer's place. And wherever it is, he'll have a tail on him. Until he gets home.'

'You're still regarding him as high priority?' Sue asked, a faint note of disquiet in her voice.

Swift turned to look at her. 'He's not out of the frame yet,' he said quietly. 'And I'm getting a hunch that whether Jamie Parker is our man or not, he's the key to whoever is.'

Cassandra Parker's fashion shop, *Arabella*, was situated at the north end of a prestigious row of shops serving the Dales town of Ilkley. It had a frontage double that of the shops surrounding it. Ebony-faced manikins dressed in flowing pastel-coloured gowns and exotic headgear decorated the brightly illuminated windows. The outer paintwork was white and pristine, the door handle gleaming.

Trying the door, he found it locked. Through the glass he could see Cassandra sitting at a delicate gilt desk, engaged in paperwork. On seeing him she got up and came forward instantly to let him in.

'Good morning, Inspector Swift,' she said. She turned and walked ahead of him, leaving a trail of sugary fragrance in her wake as she led him past racks of gowns and sweaters and suits to a small office at the back of the shop. 'Or should I say, *Chief* Inspector?' she enquired, gesturing him to a chair with courteous smile. He gave a brief confirming nod, noting that he was still in her good books since their talk the previous evening.

'Have you heard from Jamie, since we spoke yesterday evening, Mrs Parker?'

'No. Not as yet.' She sat down, crossed her legs, smoothed the skirt of her beige linen suit, then patted the back of her smooth, bobbed hair. Her fingers were large and capable, made feminine with long nails painted a deep pink. 'Would you care for coffee, Chief Inspector? I've asked my assistant to bring some along.'

'Thank you.' He sat quietly for a few moments.

'I don't open the shop until ten o'clock on a Tuesday,' she said. 'So we shall be able to talk in private for a few minutes. How can I help you, Chief Inspector?'

'You must be very worried on Jamie's behalf,' he remarked with sympathy.

She took a few moments to assess his words. 'I take it you're referring to this business of his being advised to rush off to see some dubious therapist?'

'That was clearly a concern for you.' He looked thoughtfully down at his hands.

'What other concerns would we have about him?' she demanded sharply. 'Apart from being anxious to help him through his grief?'

He fixed her with a grave look. She had vividly blue eyes, accentuated by grey eyeshadow, and a remarkably velvety ivory skin. Hostility slowly faded from her face to be replaced by a tremor of fear. 'You know something! Something about Jamie? Is it to do with this hypnotist's findings?' Suddenly anger broke through and she was firmly back on the offensive. 'If anything's been suggested which is incriminating for Jamie, then Clive and I will challenge and fight it all the way. I can be a tigress where my children are concerned.' She spat the words at him.

'I've seen the transcript of the session,' Swift told her. 'In my view the results are interesting, but inconclusive.'

'Oh my God! I'd thought that at least all this ridiculous hypnosis thing would clear things up for Jamie and get you lot off his back.'

'We haven't yet got all the information we need to make an arrest,' he said in neutral tones. 'Because we haven't yet asked all the questions we need to ask.'

'Just leave Jamie alone!' she said, furious now. 'You couldn't be more wrong in believing him to be the murderer. He adored Josie, and he's such a gentle boy. He would never hurt *anyone*.'

Swift dipped his head in acknowledgement of this gallant maternal defence.

There was the sound of teaspoons clinking on china. A well-dressed middle-aged woman came quietly forward and placed a tray with coffee and chocolate biscuits on the desk. 'Thank you, Janice,' Cassandra said with a gracious smile which indicated that Janice could now return to whatever she had been doing prior to preparing coffee.

Cassandra poured. She looked at Swift. 'Let me guess,' she said, 'milk and no sugar?'

He nodded. He said: 'Mrs Parker, whereabouts in the hotel were you at the time Josie was killed?'

She frowned at the change of tack, then gave a little smile. 'I was in the garden, talking with friends and getting a little air. Probably from around eight-fifteen to nine o'clock. I'm sure quite a few people could vouch for me.' A smile, the arching of a well-shaped eyebrow.

'And your husband? Was he with you in the garden?'

'No.'

'Do you know where he was?'

'You'll have to ask him. We were both constantly here and there, talking to our guests and making sure they were happy.'

'Of course.'

'Oh, and Diana will also have plenty of people to attest to her presence in the ballroom until the news broke about Josie. She and Piers are rather super dancers.' She shot him a look of warning and triumph.

'Thank you,' he said.

She rose. 'And now that I've been able to assure you that none of the Parker family are murderers, perhaps you would allow me to get on with my work.'

'You carry a large stock,' he commented, as she walked him to the door.

'People come from miles around to buy their clothes here,' she told him. 'I stock some beautiful Italian, German and Danish designer clothes, but I also stock the latest collections of two British designers which are not readily available in many other outlets.' She paused and pulled a wisp of a skirt in chocolate brown silk from the rack. 'This is a Janey Morrell. It came in last Friday, and I shall be very surprised if it's still in the shop by tomorrow evening.'

Swift noted the price tag — £379.

'Are you married, Chief Inspector?' she asked him. 'You should bring your wife to look at my stock.'

'I'm a widower,' he said, imagining Kate's smile of mockery at the prospect of buying her clothes in this stifling, perfumed emporium for the seriously rich.

'I'm sorry,' Cassandra responded stiffly, her face showing the discomfiture of being wrong-footed and made to retreat from the high ground. She released the latch on the door and pulled it open for him. 'Good morning, Chief Inspector.'

Walking to his car, Swift reflected on

Cassandra's obvious concern to have made a slight social gaffe. Social skills were important to her — tools with which to manipulate her world. And not only was she articulate, she was also a careful listener. She would have missed nothing he had said.

Heading back to the station, he took the road up the Ilkley Moor and pulled into a lay-by noted as a breathtaking view point, the aspect sweeping along the river valley from the north through to the south east. As he switched off the ignition and prepared to allow himself a few moments' contemplation, his mobile chirped.

'Joyce, duty sergeant, here, sir. We've got a Mrs Melanie Haygarth at the station. She's been asking to see you.'

'I'm on my way. Has she said anything of interest?'

'She's not said much at all, sir. She's been brought in by the foot brigade, accused of shop-lifting.'

10

Sitting in interview-room 4, supervised by an impartial, uniformed constable, Melanie Haygarth looked sad and defeated, smaller than Swift remembered. She glanced up when he came through the door. In the frame of her spiky dark hair her eyes were watery bright, drowning in helplessness and despair. She wore a crumpled navy linen jacket, the creases folding into deep consecutive waves over her hunched shoulder blades.

Swift sat down, facing her across the table. He saw that she had been given tea and biscuits which stood untouched in front of her. 'Melanie?' he said quietly.

'They're bringing a charge against me,' she said with a weary smile. 'Theft of twelve items of cosmetics from Colston's Chemist on Church Street. Eyeshadows, foundation bases and moisturizers, the brand Josie liked. The colours she used to prefer. They said it came to sixty-one pounds fifteen. I was pretty stroppy with the woman who stopped me. She'd been far too busy to serve me when I was in the mood for paying. Completing her stock list seemed more important than serving customers. I got fed up waiting, so I grabbed a few more items and chucked them in my bag. Suddenly she was all action. She followed me to the door and suggested I might like to pay up. And I said I wouldn't. There was a bit of a scuffle. She had to get help.' She shut her eyes and took some deep breaths. 'The bitch. I'm not sorry about any of it.'

Swift said, 'The shop will most likely drop charges when they know the full circumstances.'

Melanie shrugged. 'I couldn't give a bloody damn what they do. When I think of Josie lying there in the mortuary, dead, I feel like screaming at the top of my voice — NO, NO, NO! I feel as if my heart is going to burst. And sometimes the pain is so bad, I simply want to die.'

'Have you consulted your GP?' It was a routine question. It needed to be asked, but Swift winced at its banality, at the suggestion that advice and medication could go one millimetre towards compensating this mother for her loss.

'My GP's a devotee of librium and diazepam. I could be drugged to oblivion if I chose. But being fully conscious is a way of being with Josie again, even though she is lost, even though the pain of not having her here in the world any more is a living hell. She deserves to be remembered, to be mourned to the full. And, anyway, Ludo needs me to be at least half functioning. Poor boy, he doesn't know what's hit us all. His sister gone, his mother going slowly crazy, his father completely out of it. Fortunately he's the kind of boy who's always had a bunch of good mates, and they're rallying round. Plus the new girlfriend.'

'And how does your husband cope?'

'He's taken himself into another life. He's still at home, but he's not there with us in spirit. For the past three mornings he's gone out early and bought every single newspaper he can lay his hands on. He takes them up to his study and pores over them, searching for any mention of Josie. He's making a scrapbook of the cuttings.' She stopped talking as though she had run out of steam and just sat, miserably still.

Swift waited.

'I think the loss of Josie will kill our marriage,' Melanie said. 'People don't grieve in the same way, do they? And that can drive them apart, because their personal suffering is so fiercely private. And somehow the level of heartbreak you are experiencing can become some kind of competition. You find yourself guarding these intensely secret thoughts — I loved her more than you did. She and I were closer. I miss her more than you. Your pain is terrible, but mine reverberates through the universe and all of time.'

Swift left a silence, then said, 'Will you answer some questions for me?'

'Of course.'

'We've been interviewing Saul Williams. I believe you know him.'

'Yes, I was aware that you'd spoken to him. Caroline phoned to tell me. She's pretty unnerved about it. Well, who wouldn't be?' She gave a little shrug.

'You realize that Saul had the opportunity and possible motive to kill Josie?'

'Oh, yes. I think he was utterly fascinated by her. And she was probably the first attractive young woman he'd come across who hadn't given him the brush off once he started getting keen.'

'Are you saying that you believe it's possible that Saul killed Josie?' Swift asked. 'That he's capable of killing?'

'We're all capable, aren't we? A moment of pure rage, a moment when against all odds we can get even. Kill the one we love most because they've let us down in some way. Of course Saul was capable. But I don't believe he killed Josie.'

'Why?'

'OK, you could argue he was jealous and angry because Josie was marrying someone else. Well, maybe he was jealous, although I doubt that in Saul's case. He would simply be sad and resigned, because that is how he's learned to cope with the knock backs he's had in life. He would never have believed he would ever get a prize like Josie. And I don't believe that his feelings towards Josie would include aggression. You probably know he suffers from spasmodic clinical depression. And from what I've picked up from the psychiatrists involved with kids at the centre, depression is thought to hinge on turning all the anger and guilt you feel on yourself, rather than others. The love Saul offered Josie seems to me like the unconditional love of a young child or a pet. He'd go on loving whatever the love object did. I don't mean to patronize him by saying that. He's a very intelligent young man, but emotionally he's less well developed.'

'Infantile rage?' Swift suggested, following up her last point.

'No.' She looked across to him. 'Forget about Saul. You're wasting your time there.'

'Where do you think we would be spending our time more fruitfully?'

She sighed. 'I've no idea.'

He said, 'After we spoke for the first time at the hotel, where did you go?'

She fidgeted with the sleeve of her jacket for a moment. 'I went to see Jamie. I was worried about him. I stayed with him until he dropped off to sleep.'

Swift raised an eyebrow.

'I thought he might consider trying to kill himself. He was so besottedly in love, so deeply attached to Josie. I had this dreadful feeling he wouldn't be able to face the next day without her. He's very sensitive and vulnerable. Well, you'll know that from your conversations with him.'

'Was Josie besottedly in love with him?' Swift asked.

She frowned, looking down at her hands. 'She loved him, certainly. But there is always one in a relationship who loves more, who is more attached and needy. And that means the other partner has the power. I could see that with Josie and Jamie. She was the one with the power. Jack was like that for me, at the beginning of our relationship,' she said reflectively. 'And then later, things turned and it was the other way round.'

Swift waited for a few seconds and then said, 'Melanie, do you know where Josie's mobile phone is?'

'No,' she said, startled. 'Should I? Your

people took her luggage away. And I presume they'll return it to Jamie.'

'I wondered if she might have left it in her room at your house, before the wedding.'

'She normally carried it around with her. I'm pretty sure she had it at the Moorlands.' She frowned, thinking. 'Yes, she definitely did. She used it before the ceremony whilst she was having her hair done to phone a friend who couldn't make the wedding. I remember because I was with her at the time. Is it missing?' she asked sharply.

'It appears so. As is her wedding ring.'

'Oh, no!' she exclaimed in dismay. 'What can that mean? Does Jamie know?'

'Not yet.'

'Do you know how he is? I phoned him a couple of times yesterday, but he wasn't answering.'

'He's been to see a hypnotist in Newcastle.' Swift watched her reaction closely.

'Really!' She let out a long sigh. 'Then I just hope he's found someone who can help him.'

'Were you having an affair with Jamie?' Swift asked softly.

Melanie seemed to be expecting the question: she made no show of incredulity or indignation.

'No,' she said with tenderness in her voice.

'It's true that I was holding him in my arms on the night of his wedding. And it's true that I loved him. But we weren't having an affair. I had a certain compassion for him. He's had a rough deal. There's no one to blame, it was just an accident of fate. Cassie was thirty-six when he was born, and apparently suffered bad post natal depression afterwards. From what she once confided to me it seems she never really bonded with him. She hadn't wanted a baby at that point in her life and was perfectly happy just to have her daughter whom she idolized. Poor Jamie, I don't think he got much love from either parent, and I think he finally found what he was seeking with Josie. He's a good person, and I loved him for that, and because he was Josie's choice.' Her eyes levelled with Swift's. 'Do you believe me?'

'Yes.'

'I'd like to go now,' she said. 'I need to check on Jack. Can you get me bail, or whatever?' There was a frail touch of humour in her voice.

'You'll have to endure a short session of paperwork,' Swift told her. 'And then you're free to go home.'

Having left her in the care of the uniformed constable, he went to his office and stood in silent thought for a moment. He had the impression Melanie Haygarth had been honest with him in her answers and her opinions, and he had enough experience to be pretty accurate in his judgement of when people were lying. He also knew, however, that a wise witness or suspect answered those questions which involved the truth and kept their counsel on more complex issues.

He felt a sudden exasperation with the lack of progress they were making in the case. Turning to his desk he saw that a bundle had been brought through from reception. The first packet he opened was from the IT department. There were several sheets inside showing incoming and outgoing calls made through Josie Parker's mobile phone in the past three months. A quick glance revealed no tell-tale bombardment of calls to and from one particular number. He laid the papers on one side, delaying the decision as to whether to follow up with the Haygarths or Jamie Parker until later. The videotape of Jamie Parker's interview with Ian Homer had also arrived. He took it through to the VCR in the CID room, slotted it in and set it to play.

Instantly Jamie Parker's face appeared in close-up. His eyes were closed and there was an expression of still serenity on his face. As Homer began to question him his features became mobile and elastic. These were not images from a melodrama; Jamie's face was never creased or distorted with violent emotion, and yet the feelings were clearly shown through small flickers and twists on the skin.

At the point of realizing Josie was dead, his sobs were wet, gasping moans of despair. And then he became still, his face smoothing into blankness as though he had slipped into some deep level of unconsciousness. Swift wound the tape forward. It had reached the point where Jamie mentioned the presence of a sweet smell in the room and of how it was making him feel sick. Swift watched closely as Jamie's face became contorted with a mixture of emotions — fear, revulsion, disbelief. Swift rewound the tape and watched again. And once again. He paused the tape and sat back in his chair.

Something fell into place. It came through some mental process by which the coalescence of ideas, sound, vision and thought all came together. Jamie was hiding something. Even under hypnosis he was unconsciously still holding down some forbidden memory in a dark inaccessible place. Something he had sensed and understood. Something he shied away from. Something too terrible to give voice to. Suddenly Swift understood: Jamie

Parker was protecting someone. Or maybe simply himself.

A call through to the division in North Yorkshire confirmed that Jamie was still driving south on the A1. There had been no attempt to make for any airports or coastal areas. It looked very likely that he was heading home.

Swift wondered whether Jamie would make for his flat rather than the family home. An arrest at the former would be less complex and problematic. But apprehension at the latter venue might be far more revealing.

* * *

Diana Redmond welcomed Sue Sallis and Pete with smiling courtesy, even though she had had to be pulled out of a partners' meeting in order to speak to them. She took them through to her office. The room was large enough to accommodate a vast desk, and also an attractive sitting area furnished with three comfortable armchairs upholstered in pale-green tweed. She gestured Sue and Pete to the armchairs and sat down herself, placing her hands loosely in her lap. She was impressively tall like her mother, and elegantly dressed in a simple navy skirt and white tailored shirt. But the lines of her face, although strong, had none of the hawkish qualities of her parents. Her nut-brown hair was cut to fall in a diagonal sweep over one cheek. Her eyes were grey and her mouth wide and full.

She's a bloody attractive woman, Pete was thinking, as Diana directed her steady, intelligent gaze first at Sue and then at him.

'I've been expecting you,' she said. 'My husband mentioned that you would need to see me.'

Sue kicked off with the necessary expressions of sympathy then moved on to the standard introductory questions about the interviewee's memory of events at the time of the murder.

Diana confirmed that she had been in the ballroom from around 8.15 until the news of the need for a doctor's advice on Josie broke.

'Was your husband there in the ballroom with you?' Pete asked, leaning forward.

Diana gave the smile of an affectionate and tolerant wife. 'He was a bit woozy after the reception. I got him to drink a few glasses of iced water and tread a few steps around the floor.'

'But was he there with you all the time?' Pete insisted. 'During the time Josie was murdered?'

Her eyes darkened with concern. 'Well, I'm

not in the habit of keeping a constant watch on him. Maybe he slipped out to the cloakroom while I was dancing with other guests.' She looked from one officer to the other. 'Piers didn't kill Josie,' she said, her voice trembling with the shock of realizing what lay behind the constable's insistence. 'We were both very fond of her.' She threw up a hand and pressed it against her chest.

'Are you all right, Mrs Redmond?' Sue asked considerately.

Diana nodded. 'It's just that after the terrible shock of Josie's death, we're all dreadfully on edge. My parents are deeply shocked. Poor Mother really feels these things, she's quite highly strung, and Dad puts on a brave face, but underneath . . . ' She took up a pen from the desk top and twisted it in her fingers. 'You don't really mean it about Piers, do you — that he's in some way involved?'

'We need to eliminate as many people as we can from the investigation,' Sue reassured her.

'Of course. I understand.' She fell silent.

'You said you and your husband were fond of Josie,' Sue remarked. 'How well did you know her?'

'We went out for drinks a few times. And invited them to our place for supper once or twice. Josie was very easy to get on with. And the kids liked her. She had that knack of knowing how to talk to them. Getting on their wavelength without being patronizing.' She stared ahead of her, temporarily lost in a private reverie. 'Do you have any idea who might have killed Josie?' she asked. 'No, I'm sorry,' she said, correcting herself. 'That's not the sort of question you can answer, is it? I mean do you have any leads at all? The whole thing seems utterly incomprehensible. Piers and I still believe Josie must have been killed by some outsider. I know the statistics tell us most murders are done by spouses or lovers or the family. But truly, I simply can't believe it with Josie. I've been trying and trying to remember if I saw anyone behaving oddly at the wedding and afterwards, but I saw nothing. I had no bad vibes. It was all just perfect. But then maybe I'm the stereotypical accountant, only sensitive to number crunching.' Belying her last statement, her eyes filled with tears. 'Poor Josie. And poor Jamie,' she said softly. 'One with their life taken away, the other with their life ruined.'

Sue and Pete looked at one another, rose from their chairs, and having thanked Diana for her time made their way back to the car.

'How old do you think she is?' Pete asked, glancing up at the blue sky and noting that there were a few quite hefty clouds about. A phenomenon not seen for some weeks.

'Thirty-two, give or take a year or so.'

'But women aren't like trees, are they? There aren't any concentric rings to count?'

'Trust my female intuition about other women's ages,' Sue told him. 'What did you make of her? And I don't want to hear about your lustful fantasies for the older woman.'

'Nice person. Very bright, very female, secure, grounded.'

'Yes, I thought so too. But she'd no useful info to offer us.'

'No. But that's because she hasn't got any.'

'Odds on her turning out to be a likely suspect?'

'Extremely low.'

'I agree.'

'You know,' Pete mused, 'what we've unearthed from our digging around about Josie has all been infuriatingly normal, nice, and boring.'

'Too good to be true?'

'Not necessarily. Maybe it's the simple truth. She was a nice, pretty, clever, lovable girl. But she got killed. It does happen. And that's why my money's still on Williams as our killer. He had a motive, he was there at the scene, he had the opportunity.'

'True.'

'Well, if it's not him and it's not your golden boy Jamie, then the field's open to about eighty per cent of the world's male population.'

'Jamie Parker is not my golden boy,' Sue said with some severity.

'OK. Fine.' He held his hands up in surrender. 'Listen, don't get me wrong, I respect the boss, but I have to say I think he's pussy-footing around regarding Williams. Arrest the guy, for God's sake. Put him under a bit of pressure and he'll crack like a nut. Which is, of course, what he is.'

'End of story?' Sue suggested with a whiff of sarcasm.

'Watch this space, Sarge.' Pete said, unlocking his car and gallantly pulling open the passenger door for Sue.

'Easy on the loud pedal,' she told him as he fired the engine and revved it within an inch of its life.

* * *

Superintendent Tom Lister's ruddy physiognomy went through a variety of rubbery gyrations as he listened to Swift's proposal.

'A sprat to catch a mackerel eh?' His grin was wily and roguish. 'I've no objection to that strategy, Ed. The only thing is, if your little plan doesn't work we could be left with egg on our faces. The proverbial dog's breakfast. The press would make a real meal of it.' He chuckled at his play on words.

'But if it works, we shall have a dainty dish to set before the Deputy Chief Constable,' Swift pointed out.

'Quite.' Lister was suddenly reflective and deadly serious. 'And let's face it, we're going to be truly bogged down in the mire with this case if we don't move it on a bit.' In need of comfort, his hand automatically reached out for the ever present packet of cigarettes. But it wasn't there. He heaved a sigh and drew his paw back. 'What's the worst scenario of the possible fallout?'

'The Parkers throw their money and their might about and make things difficult for us.' Swift said. 'Worse, we don't get our murderer. And the publicity is enough to put tabloid sales up by a hefty percentage.'

Lister winced. 'I can see it all as clear as day.' He fished a stick of mint chewing gum from his pocket, unwrapped it and popped it in his mouth. 'Do it, Ed. And do it now!'

★ ★ ★

Jamie drove down the motorway keeping his speed at a steady seventy. He was concentrating hard on his driving, suspecting that if he allowed himself to shift into automatic pilot mode he might cause an accident. He knew that the police were following him. He knew also that he must be a prime suspect for Josie's murder. For a time he had been his own prime suspect. But since the session with Homer he had found himself in no man's land. Lost and rudderless, not knowing what to think, what to believe. The idea of continuing to exist in this wilderness made him wretched, and yet he was terrified of moving forward.

He turned off the motorway, killing his speed to a steady thirty as he drove through residential built up areas and then into the country suburbs. Cars and vans overtook him, some of them cutting in so sharply to avoid oncoming traffic that they almost carved him up. His hands gripped the wheel more tightly. The effort of concentration was making his head throb. He longed to be home, to drink a long glass of iced water, to lie down with the curtains tightly drawn. He turned into the driveway leading to his flat and saw a bevy of police cars. A haggard-looking man with auburn hair got out of a silver saloon and began to walk slowly towards him, his face solemn and still. Sensing what was coming Jamie felt an overwhelming sense of relief.

11

In reception at the station, Swift waited in the background whilst Jamie was booked in. Duty Sergeant Joyce Rugg, an experienced officer with neatly cropped hair and a stern, yet impartial expression, asked him to empty his pockets, intoning the words of the admission procedure as she gathered up keys, a wallet, a brushed steel pen and a gold watch. 'You have the right to have someone informed of your arrest. You have the right to legal representation. And if you want to see a solicitor — '

'Yes,' Jamie cut in. 'I'd like Louise Rushforth from Haygarth and Rushforth.'

'Right.' The sergeant pushed a sheet across the desk. 'You'll need to sign there.' She handed him a pen. Swift noted that his hand was steady as he made his signature.

'Is there anyone you would like informed of your arrest?' the sergeant enquired.

There was a pause. Jamie shook his head. 'No.'

The sergeant looked at him with fresh interest. 'You're new to this, aren't you?'

'Yes. What happens now?' he asked, his

voice composed and polite.

'You'll be put in a cell until an officer is ready to interview you.'

Jamie nodded, and allowed himself to be led away.

★ ★ ★

'It was one of the quietest, most civilized arrests I've ever made,' Swift told the team. They had gathered in the late afternoon for a further review and planning meeting. The details Swift had offered regarding Jamie Parker's arrest and the reasons underlying it had been brief and concise.

Pete, enlivened and excited by the arrest, even though the suspect was not the one he would have chosen himself, was eager to forward matters. 'So how do we play it, sir? Aggressive, proactive interviewing to move things forward and get a result?'

'That is certainly an option,' Swift said. 'Do you want to have a go with him, Pete?'

'Surely that's not the right approach with a suspect like Jamie,' Sue put in with some force. Her face was white with the shock of what had happened. She had not before known Swift to act unilaterally. Fair enough, she appreciated that once the decision to make an arrest had been made it had been right and proper to proceed without delay. Moreover, as she had been occupied talking to Diana Redmond with Pete, she recognized that it would not have been helpful for him to have called her away. She recognized also that there were no grounds for being critical of her boss in terms of procedure. And, of course, she knew that it was her emotional over-involvement with Jamie which lay at the heart of her discomfiture about his arrest. But the knowledge did little to lessen the unpleasant jolt of surprise at Swift's actions, and the sense of having been side-lined.

Swift turned to face her. 'What would you suggest, Sue?'

'A more subtle approach, sir. For a start, I'd like to question him on the hypnosis session.'

'With what purpose in mind?'

'Basically to discover if the work Homer did with him has clarified Jamie's current, conscious memory of just what happened when he found Josie. As you pointed out earlier, sir, you didn't consider the hypnosis tape to be convincing evidence either way.'

'Yes, I think your line of questioning would be useful.'

'We could, of course, simply ask him if he drowned Josie,' Pete pointed out. 'And keep asking him. Maybe sketch out a strong scenario of just how things would have happened if he did, in fact, drown her. That might be a very good jog to his dodgy memory.'

'OK, so we bully him into a confession?' Sue suggested with some sarcasm. 'Which he would later retract on the advice of his solicitor. Or even simply of his own accord.'

'Your two approaches don't rule each other out,' Swift said. 'In fact, it might be interesting to try them both. I'd suggest Sue starting things off, and then Pete following up. Not too much switching from one approach to the other. Jamie might simply shut down.'

'You want us to work together on this, sir?' Sue asked, keeping any suggestion of incredulity firmly under wraps.

'Yes, I think I would.' He paused. 'What's your take on this, Geoff?'

Geoff threw his boss a whimsical glance. 'Are you suggesting I have a go too, sir?'

'Why not?'

'Because, basically I don't want to set foot in a cell or an interview room ever again. I'm well past all that. Let the young 'uns show us what they can do. I'm happy to carry on with my bit of semi-retired foot-soldiering.'

'Oh, come off it, Geoff,' Sue said with a coaxing smile. 'Tell us what you make of all this, even if you don't want to do any questioning.'

'I think you and Pete will make a good team,' Geoff told her. 'If he can stop himself champing at the bit too hard, and you can make sure you save all your natural maternal instincts for babbies of your own, and not Jamie Parker.'

Sue closed her eyes for a moment. 'If anyone can make me blush . . . '

Geoff turned to Swift. 'Do we need to send a team to search Jamie's flat?'

'They're already on their way.'

'And when and where do you come in, sir?' Geoff asked, his voice laconic, a glint in his eye.

'I'll bide my time until we see what Sue and Pete can come up with,' Swift responded. 'And what the findings are of the team I've sent to search Jamie's flat.'

Geoff caught his senior officer's eye, a split-second shimmer of connection. He guessed that Swift was playing a slightly devious game and wondered how much had been revealed to the two youngsters. Well, he certainly wasn't going to give anything away. Better for them to believe the Jamie Parker arrest was in good faith if they were going to interrogate with full zeal. Geoff sat back, put his hands behind his head and reflected that the role of veteran onlooker and sage had a lot to recommend it.

★ ★ ★

Louise Rushworth hurried through the car-park to the entrance of the station, her cheeks flushed, her long honey-blonde hair flowing out behind her in the sharp breeze which had sprung from nowhere. On the voluptuous side of curvy, she was wearing a cream knitted silk top and conker-brown trousers. She had the looks to turn heads. And at this particular moment she looked both hot and bothered.

Louise had been at Haygarth and Rushworth Solicitors for no more than a year. She knew that she owed her effortless securement of a job in the firm to her father's position as a founding and senior partner. She also knew that she was talented: the first class honours in law had to mean something. But she was keenly aware of still being a novice as far as the practice of law was concerned.

The duty sergeant arranged for her to be taken to an interview-room and for Jamie to be brought to see her there. He came in looking wan but in surprisingly good command of himself.

Louise sprang up from her chair. 'Jamie!'

She reached out and shook the hand he offered with vigour and sympathy. 'Are you all right? Oh, God, what a fatuous thing to say!'

'Yes, I'm all right.'

'Has anyone questioned you yet?'

'No. Not since I came here.'

They sat down, side by side. Louise took out an A4 notepad and a pen with a chewed end.

'Jamie,' she said, 'I haven't read through the casework file yet, and I really don't know if I'm the best person to advise you. My current speciality is family stuff and the drawing up of wills and so on.'

'You were Josie's work colleague,' he said. 'You work in her father's firm. I've got every faith in you, Louise.'

'Well, thanks. I've been doing a bit of boning up before I came here, and, of course, I'll try to get more up to speed as we go on.'

He was only half listening, concentrating more on watching her. Her eyes connected briefly with his. They were hazel and bright with vigour and flair. 'You'll be fine,' he said.

She glanced over the details the duty sergeant had given her. Dear God! 'They've arrested you on suspicion of Josie's murder, Jamie.'

'Yes, I realize it's serious.'

'You seem pretty calm about it,' she remarked, anxiety taking hold.

'I don't think I did it,' he said.

Louise blinked. She had been anticipating a firm, maybe passionate, denial. Which she would probably have believed. Which would have made a difficult situation a little easier to handle. 'Don't you know?'

He rehearsed the story he had told to Sue and Ian Homer and explained to her about the blanks in his memory.

Louise's mouth fell open. God! An amnesia case. She'd read up on a few of those when she was an undergraduate. Fiendishly tricky. Knowing she must think on her feet, she made an instant decision to regard Jamie's 'don't know' as 'didn't do it', and to regard the amnesia as genuine.

'We're going to go into the interrogation on the basis that you're innocent, Jamie,' she told him firmly. 'Expressing half-baked doubts is akin to lying down and dying.' She fixed him with her nutmeg-flecked eyes. 'Is that agreed?'

There was a beating pause. 'Agreed.'

The door opened and a young man swung in, dropping his papers on the desk with a loud slap. He was followed a few moments later by a young woman with a serious and expressive face and an air of gentle authority.

266

Louise eyed the two up as they introduced themselves and sat opposite her and Jamie. She had a sudden thought of a mixed doubles in tennis, a game she was rather good at. He would be all big serves and flashy volleys at the net, whilst she would be steady and competent from the baseline.

The constable leaned forward and began to speak. Louise's theory seemed to have been spot-on. She put tennis out of her mind and straightened her backbone.

★   ★   ★

In the viewing-room, behind the one-way mirror, Swift followed the progress of the interrogation with close attention. Jamie Parker's quiet, peaceful demeanour interested him. The transcripts from Sue's previous interviews with him had painted a picture of a grieving, troubled and possibly psychologically disturbed young man. The sorrow, naturally, was still apparent. But there were no signs of agitation or serious unease, not even when he was under fire from Pete, who had the ability to work up a good head of steam. In some way Jamie had moved on in his emotional state, possibly as a result of the hypnosis session with Homer. Swift was not a psychologist or psychiatrist, but in police work one learned a good deal about human motivation — its contradictions and complexities. He had the impression that Jamie was in some kind of transitional state. The fears he had expressed before — and for the purposes of building a theory Swift was working with the assumption that the blanks in Jamie's memory had been genuine — no longer seemed to be tormenting him. And yet, so far in the interview, he had still not directly denied killing Josie. He had let his solicitor do that for him, however, and she was standing firm, giving him rock solid support. There was no question of Pete's being allowed to have all his own way.

Swift reflected that they would have a maximum of seventy-two hours to question Jamie, providing they were granted a magistrate's extension, which was by no means automatic given the paucity of evidence. Would it be possible in that time to get Jamie to the point of making a firm statement of his innocence, and then to name the real killer?

He turned as a uniformed officer came quietly into the room and handed him a note. Immediately he got up and went to the reception area.

Melanie Haygarth was standing at the desk, her face ashen. 'I need to talk,' she said, her voice no more than a faint croak.

Swift took her to his office. For a few minutes, she was barely able to speak. He poured her a glass of water and set it in front of her, but she seemed not to notice. She took two envelopes from her bag. Swift noted that they were business envelopes franked with red ink. Her hand shook as she pulled out the contents from one of them. She pushed them across the desk. 'Look!'

They were airline tickets, made out for the use of Miss Josephine Haygarth and Mr Piers Redmond. The destination was Barcelona, the date five weeks ahead.

The possible significance of the tickets slotted instantly into Swift's mental framework of information on the case. He was aware of a thrill of exhilaration: the investigator's joy of uncovering a gem, to be going forward at last. He kept his face still and solemn in respect of Melanie's silent agony.

'And this,' she whispered, handing him the contents of the second envelope.

There was one single sheet, a letter from an estate agent in London confirming the lease of an apartment in the Sant Just area of Barcelona for one year. The starting date coincided with the date on the airline tickets. The lease was in the joint names of Mr P

Redmond, and Ms J Haygarth.

'Is there anything else?' Swift asked gently.

She shook her head. 'Have I made a mistake?' she asked, gesturing in despair to the materials on the desk. 'Have I read something into this stuff which isn't in fact there?'

'My initial reaction to this is that Josie and Piers were going to go away together,' Swift said. 'They were planning to set up house in Barcelona.'

'Yes. It's as simple as that, isn't it?' A nerve beneath her lower eyelid began to flicker violently.

'And presumably to dissolve or annul the marriage to Jamie as soon as possible,' he added almost to himself.

'I thought things couldn't get any worse,' she said bitterly. 'How can things get worse after your daughter has been killed? But they have.'

'Does your husband know?'

'No. I've only just found out myself. I couldn't bring myself to open the post until now. And to be honest I don't think I can face telling Jack.'

Swift looked at the envelopes. They were addressed to Josie, in her maiden name, at her parents' address. 'Why would she allow these letters to be sent out in her name, to your house?'

'You're wondering why she didn't make more devious and secret arrangements?' Melanie said. 'You see, over the years, from being a student, she's always asked me to keep her mail for her when she went away. She knew I wouldn't open it, or interfere. It's not that I'm a saint; I'm just not the sort of mother who needs to know every detail of my children's life. I've always had a good enough life of my own not to need to interfere in theirs. Josie was aware of that and she trusted me. Well, at least I hope she did. I hope that's something I got right.'

'She couldn't have these items sent to the flat, nor to Piers, nor to the Parkers,' Swift mused. 'She must have trusted you very much, to give you the chance of uncovering a secret like this.'

'Yes. But, of course, if she had still been alive, the secret would still be intact. I wouldn't have given those envelopes a second thought.' She stared at Swift with deepening disquiet. 'How could she think of doing this to Jamie? Why didn't she call the wedding off before it was too late? She was never a coward. What was going on?'

'I'm assuming you had no idea of her plans?'

'None. Absolutely none. She was so excited before the wedding. So hyped up. Radiant.

Just as a bride should be.' Her shoulders slumped. 'And it must all have been to do with the prospect of being with Piers.'

'From the dates on the envelopes it would seem that she and Piers must have made up their minds only a week or so before the wedding.'

'She couldn't face Jack,' Melanie said flatly. 'She couldn't tell him the wedding was off. It would have been like telling a kid Santa Claus wasn't coming. He was so looking forward to the day. He'd been far more involved in the planning than I was. And they were so close. She was his darling girl, the person he loved most of anyone who had been a part of his life.'

'Maybe she couldn't face Jamie, either,' Swift pointed out.

'That's certainly true. He was another needy one. And totally enchanted with her.' She raised her glance, avoiding his gaze and staring unseeing out of the window. 'Maybe the idea was to simply steal away and leave a note or whatever. What a trail of destruction. Jamie, Diana, the children. Oh, God! *The children!* Clive and Cassandra. Jack and me.'

A silence fell. The little room seemed charged with Melanie's wretchedness, as though it were too restricted to contain it.

'What now?' she asked him. 'What are you going to do?'

'Clearly we need to talk to Piers. And to Jamie.'

'Where is Jamie? We've heard nothing from him or from the Parkers. You said he'd been to see a hypnotist. Is he back?'

'He's here at the station,' Swift told her. 'Helping us with our enquiries.'

The well known euphemism took a moment to sink in. 'Oh God! No! Oh, no! Not Jamie. He wouldn't kill her, not even if he'd found out about all this. He wouldn't. He'd simply have fallen to pieces.'

* * *

Swift walked with Melanie to her car. 'I'll be all right,' she told him. 'I've got one or two very good friends whose shoulders I can cry on if I need to. And I have to think of Ludo. It's so easy to block out your other children when one of them has been taken from you.' She slipped behind the wheel and inserted her keys.

'When will you tell your husband?' he asked.

'After a few large glasses of wine,' she said, firing the engine.

Walking back into the CID room, Swift

noticed that Geoff was still at his desk. He went to sit with him and shared the news which Melanie had broken.

'Bloody hell!' Geoff commented at the end. 'That's a rum carry-on! With bells on. So what next?'

'I'd like to get Redmond's story first. Sue and Pete can keep up the pressure on Jamie until we're ready to confront him with the elopement plan.'

Geoff sucked in a breath through his teeth. 'Rather you than me!'

'I was thinking it would be helpful if you'd come along with me to meet Piers Redmond,' Swift said.

Geoff raised his eyebrows. 'Were you now, sir? Was that inspiration or desperation?' He twisted his lips into a grin. 'Give me a minute to phone the girlfriend. And another two to brush the rust off my brains.'

⋆   ⋆   ⋆

Pete was determined to get something out of Jamie Parker. If not a confession, then at the very least a new piece of information. But Jamie had been quietly resistant about spilling any beans. And not just because his solicitor was infuriatingly good at picking him up before he fell, but because he somehow

274

seemed to have grown a non-porous skin of self-possession. Which, when Pete thought about it, was rather remarkable. To be arrested on suspicion of murdering your bride, banged up in a cell and made to face a tough interrogation was hardly a bed of roses. He had to admit he'd be pretty bothered about it himself in Jamie's shoes.

Eventually Louise Rushworth had insisted that Jamie had a break. 'My client has been very co-operative and helpful,' she had told the two interviewers, addressing her remarks mainly to Pete. 'And I have to point out that you have offered no forensic evidence against Mr Parker, nor any clear witness statements to back up your allegations. Moreover, if you ask for an extension of custody beyond the forty-eight hour period, we shall challenge it very forcefully.'

'We're not getting very far very fast, are we?' Pete said to Sue as they left the interview room and gave themselves chance to take stock.

'On balance I don't think we are.'

A uniformed constable was coming down the corridor. He handed Sue a note which she scanned rapidly. 'The search team have drawn a blank at Jamie's flat,' she told Pete. 'No phone or ring found. Nothing of any significance.'

Pete gave a shrug. 'Failure to find anything tells us very little. He's probably smashed the phone to bits with a hammer, dropped the sim card down the sink waste-disposal and put the ring and any other leftovers down a very deep drain.'

'Would that be your preferred method of disposal?' Sue asked.

'Well — you have to admit it's a pretty foolproof method.'

They decided to make their way down to the canteen. Pete fancied a bite to eat.

Sue threw herself into a chair. She was hot, sticky and weary.

'From what I'd heard, I'd got the feeling Jamie was a bit of wimp before we brought him in,' Pete said. 'But he's no pushover. What do you reckon about the amnesia, do you think he was just faking it?'

'I don't know what to think,' Sue said irritably. 'I'm absolutely whacked. You be mother and get the coffees and grub, Pete.'

'What? Oh, OK, then. Put your feet up, Sarge. What are you having?'

'Just coffee. I'm past being hungry.'

Sue closed her eyes. It was gone 7.30 and she longed to go home and soak in a cool, scented bath. She wanted flickering candles around the side of the bath, and for her husband to prepare a beautiful supper. Oh, for goodness sake! She'd never been a girly girl who craved pampering. And when had he ever cooked supper?

Pete came back with coffees, chips and an Aero Bar. He settled himself down, his face alight with speculation. Sue thought he looked as if he could keep going for another twelve hours at least.

'So,' Pete said, 'to sum up — I don't think he did it, you don't think he did it, and the boss doesn't think he did it either. Does he?'

'I don't think he does.'

Pete said. 'So why arrest him?'

Sue sliced him a knowing glance.

He held up his hands. 'No. Don't tell me. Let me work it out. I've been to training school and passed my assessments.'

Sue smiled. She couldn't help liking Pete, even though she sometimes wanted to slap his wrists.

'He wants to flush someone else out! Yeah! That's it. And clever stuff — if it works.' He unwrapped the chocolate, broke it in two and gave half to Sue. 'So who has he got in mind?'

'I really don't know.'

'He hasn't confided in you?'

'No. To be fair, there hasn't been much opportunity. And I'm only guessing about the arrest being some kind of ploy. It's certainly not a card he's played since he's been here.'

'He's a dark horse,' said Pete. 'I like that.' His face became rapt and thoughtful as he ate his chips.

Sue fancied she could see into his brain, track his thoughts as they carried him along to the heights of DCI and beyond, his dark-horse antics becoming increasingly daring and successful. 'I've just an inkling the boss may have his sights on Clive Parker as a suspect,' she said pensively.

'No kidding!' Pete's eyes lit up. 'What makes you think that?'

'He made a point of asking me if I thought Parker was attractive.'

'As in sexy, fascinating, beddable and so forth?'

'Yes.'

'And you said?'

'I said I thought he had a certain magnetism about him. OK, I'm very wary of him, and I still don't trust him not to make a formal complaint about me. And I don't like him. But I'll bet a quite a few women would find him compelling.'

'Well now!' Pete drummed his fingers on the table. 'So, what's the boss thinking? And where does Daddy Parker fit in?' His features twitched with conjecture. Then he clicked his fingers. 'How about this? It's a blackmail scenario gone wrong. Parker and Josie are screwing each other, maybe they've been at it for ages, but Parker won't leave his wife. So Josie throws him over for Jamie. And before the wedding she gets greedy and threatens to out the affair with Daddy-in-law if he doesn't pay up lots of dosh! He's loaded isn't he? And a pillar of society and such forth. So, what choice has he but to shut her up for good? Right?'

'It's a possible storyline,' Sue agreed.

'Parker's all fired up after the reception and all the booze. He wants to have things out with Josie. He goes to find her. He goes up to the suite. She's there. They have a row. Maybe they have sex. Yeah, that's it! They have sex so Josie needs to take a bath to wash off all the traces, because later on she'll have to be doing it with Jamie.'

Sue winced. 'Pete!'

'And Parker hangs about, goes into the bathroom and takes the opportunity to grab her ankles and pull her under the water. A few seconds of madness, and it's all over. No problem.'

'But there's no evidence either,' Sue pointed out. 'Nothing to place him at the scene at the time Josie died. And even if they were having an affair, which, I grant, would give Parker a possible motive, how do we prove it? I don't see him rolling over and telling us.'

'Hmm.' Pete frowned into his coffee.

'Of course, if Parker *had* been having an affair with Josie, and Jamie had found out — '

'Then he'd have a motive to kill Josie from rage and jealousy.'

'Exactly.' Sue broke off a corner of her chocolate and regarded it thoughtfully. 'And, of course, we know Jamie was at the scene, by his own admission and from Saul Williams's account.'

'And there's all the business of the so called amnesia, which could be one big cunning scam to avoid conviction.'

'Yes.'

Light came back into Pete's eyes. 'Do you think we should pitch the scenario to Jamie? Get his reaction?'

'Maybe. But I think we should discuss it with the boss first.' She paused. 'I wonder where he is. He said he was going to observe from the viewing-room. I'm surprised he hasn't come to join us. I'll go and see if I can track him down before we start the next round.'

Pete bounded up the stairs ahead of her and dashed off to the CID room. He was already reading the memo Swift had left on her desk when she caught up with him. He handed it to her in silence.

No cool bath, no leisurely supper, thought

Sue, absorbing the powerful new information and Swift's subsequent instructions. But ah, the exhilaration of fresh evidence and a new window opened up in a murder investigation. And then she thought of Jamie.

'Well!' Pete said, rubbing his hands. 'We've certainly got something to get our teeth into now.'

'You mean confronting Jamie with all this elopement and betrayal stuff? Don't look so bloody excited, Pete.'

'Sorry. Poor bloke. Even my stony heart's leaking the odd drop. Although I can hardly believe he didn't know anything. But maybe the amnesia was conveniently at work again. Do you want to break the news, or shall I? It's almost worse than delivering the death-o-gram.'

Sue gave a shudder. 'I'll do it. I wouldn't trust you to deliver a newspaper.'

12

'Nice little place,' Geoff commented as he drew his car to a halt outside Diana and Piers Redmond's house. 'Must have cost a bob or two.'

Swift nodded agreement. 'Whatever the difficulties in the Parker family, a lack of money doesn't seem to be one of them.'

'You'll have heard the Yorkshire saying, 'where there's muck there's brass',' Geoff said. 'And there's some truth in that. It works the other way around too, if you take my meaning.'

'Very true,' Swift responded. 'But I'd be surprised if money turns out to be the main motive in this case.' He swung his legs from the car, glancing up at the house and the arch of sky above it. Thin streaks of cloud had been building up all afternoon and the sun was veiled, its burning heat tamed for the first time in weeks.

Swift put up his hand to the gleaming brass bell push. There was a pause and then Diana appeared in the doorway. She was wearing a long green sarong and a white crêpe-de-chine shirt through which the outline of her bra could be faintly made out.

Swift showed his warrant card. 'Mrs Redmond? I'm Detective Inspector Swift and this is Sergeant Fowler. I believe you met two of my other colleagues earlier on.'

Diana's face showed concern, but her natural composure and politeness worked against any display of alarm or resentment. 'Please come in,' she said.

Swift noted the low, melodious quality of her voice, her quiet, calm demeanour, her air of being comfortable with herself and her life. He reflected on the curious phenomenon of genetic inheritance, that unique blending of the genes of two people which could create individuals so different from themselves — and from the other children they produced.

'Is your husband in?' he asked, before moving forward.

'Yes.' Her eyes clouded with unease. 'Is anything wrong?

'We'd like to speak to him,' Swift told her, reflecting on the bomb he was about to detonate which could blow the Redmonds' marriage into pieces.

She stood aside to let him and Geoff pass through the doorway. The scent of roasting chicken and garlic drifted from the kitchen. 'We're having friends in for supper,' Diana murmured as if talking to herself. She was clearly anxious now. 'Piers!' she called up the stairs. 'There are people here to speak to you.'

There was a short delay and then a shouted: 'OK, just coming.' Diana and the two officers stood in the hallway looking upwards and hearing the soft murmur of Piers Redmond's voice behind a door somewhere on the first floor.

'He's putting the children to bed,' Diana explained. 'It sometimes takes a while to get them settled.'

Swift nodded courteously, indicating that he and his sergeant were quite prepared to wait.

'I'll go and take over,' Diana said. She walked up the stairs, her gait measured and graceful.

'Good-looking woman,' Geoff commented, as she opened a door on the landing and disappeared. 'Seems to have the personality to match.'

Swift had no time to respond as Piers Redmond appeared at the top of the stairs and ran quickly down. 'Hello there! What can I do for you?' He was barefoot and dressed in battered but very clean jeans and a white open-necked shirt. His automatic smile of welcome faded. 'You're the police,' he said softly, instantly sizing the visitors up.

Swift had the impression that Piers Redmond had been half expecting a visit. He showed his ID. 'We'd like to ask you some questions, Mr Redmond,' he said. 'You might prefer to talk to us in private.'

Piers Redmond slanted the two officers a quick, sharp glance. 'Fine,' he said, walking ahead and gesturing them to follow. He took them into a corridor-like room which adjoined the sitting-room on one side and the kitchen on the other. An old oak refectory table took up almost one side of the room. On it were a laptop computer, a printer, a lamp, CDs of Mozart and Tchaikovsky and around a hundred books, stacked together in random tottering heaps. There was only one chair. 'My den,' Piers said. 'This is where I was going to write my first book, when I finally got around to finding a subject worth writing about.' His voice trailed away and he stood looking around him with an air of puzzled appraisal as though he hadn't been in the room for some time. 'I'll get some more chairs,' he said.

In his absence Geoff and Swift made a quick inspection of the contents of the room, but apart from the books — dictionaries, a Thesaurus and a host of novels, there was little to see. The desk diary, open at the current week, was blank apart from a brief note of the supper arrangement that evening.

Piers Redmond returned with two wrought iron kitchen chairs. 'Hideously uncomfortable,' he remarked, as he lined them up against the desk, which was the only option as the room was so narrow. 'Please sit down.'

They sat in a line: Piers at the far end of the group in his desk chair, Swift on his right, and Geoff to the right of his senior.

'You'll know that I spoke to Sergeant Sallis and Constable Fox earlier on,' Piers said. He seemed composed, unnaturally calm.

'We have the details of that interview,' Swift confirmed. He opened his notebook and slid out the the airline tickets which Melanie had given him. He laid them on the desk in front of Piers. 'It appears that you and Josie Haygarth had an arrangement to fly to Barcelona in a few weeks' time.' He waited for the inevitable resistance of the truth which was a common response in the initial stages of a sensitive interview.

Piers's long frame slumped slightly. There was no attempt to battle. 'Yes,' he said quietly.

Swift placed the tenancy confirmation beside the tickets. 'And that you were planning to set up house together?'

'Yes.' He gave a sigh. He had gone a ghostly white.

'Who knew about this, sir?' Geoff asked,

his voice filled with a disapprobation he made no attempt to conceal.

'No one. Except Josie and me. At least, as far as I know. I certainly hadn't told anyone.'

'Your wife has no idea of this?' Geoff followed up.

'No.' Piers's face seemed to crumple in on itself. 'And, if at all possible, I hope she never needs to know.'

'That will depend on how the issue affects our investigation. This is a murder investigation, Mr Redmond,' Swift said, with cold impartiality.

'Yes, of course.' Piers stared at the wall above the desk, as though frozen into immobility.

'So, what was the plan, sir?' Geoff asked, his voice heavily laced with contempt. 'How were you and Josie going to do it? How were you going to get around the thorny problem of breaking up two marriages, abandoning your kids and running off to Spain together? It's a bit of a tricky one, you have to admit.'

'We were planning to tell Jamie and Diana that we had fallen in love and that we needed to be together,' Piers said. 'I recognize it sounds totally banal, but that was the plan.'

A silence fell. 'Look,' Piers said, his voice heavy with the burden of remorse and grief, 'let me tell you how all this came about.'

As he prepared to launch into his account, Swift could sense Geoff's anxiety to tear into Piers Redmond and try to break him down into some kind of confession, whether the sin were moral or mortal. He knew the sergeant would have little patience with the notion of two police officers listening to some pathetic tale of illicit, doomed love and playing father confessor. He made a small gesture indicating restraint.

Piers began to speak. 'I first met Josie a year ago when she and Jamie got engaged. But I didn't get to talk to her individually until Diana invited the two of them for an informal supper here. I wasn't downstairs to greet them when they arrived. Jamie and Diana had gone into the kitchen to fetch drinks. She was standing on her own in the sitting-room when I went in. She was very simply dressed and her hair was loose around her shoulders. She was beautiful in a simple, natural way and she had this air of being filled with a sheer, unadulterated joy and eagerness for life. I remember that she simply said, 'Hello. I'm Josie.' She had a rather metallic, nasal voice. There was something about that voice and about her whole being that enchanted me. There was a rush of excitement, and yet the main feeling I had was of suddenly being at peace with myself.

My body felt warm and relaxed and it was as if I'd been waiting all my life for Josie to join me. It was as simple as that, and by some miracle it turned out she felt the same.'

Swift heard Geoff let out a long, weary sigh. Piers Redmond's eloquence was not to his taste. But Swift judged that Piers had a desperate need to talk about his feelings for the dead Josie. Only when those feelings about the living Josie had been released would he be able to talk about the circumstances leading up to her death.

Piers was continuing. 'She didn't allow me to come anywhere near her at first, and I'm not just talking about sex. She wouldn't meet me on my own. She wouldn't talk on the phone — '

'So how did the two of you manage to get together?' Geoff interrupted with some acidity.

'I started to engineer meetings between the four of us. Me and Diana, Jamie and Josie. It wasn't difficult. Diana is fond of her brother and she was pleased that I wanted to make a friend of him. And Josie.' His face twisted in pain. 'I know this sounds utterly crass,' he said quietly. 'Those meetings were magical. I'd snatch moments to be alone with her, to tell her how I felt. She wouldn't let me sleep with her for over six months. She wouldn't even let me kiss her. I just had to keep working at it, wearing away her resistance. She was a very moral person. She didn't believe in sleeping around. And she wanted to be loyal to Jamie. She loved Jamie, but basically he was still a boy and he needed mothering. Gradually she began to realize the attraction of being with a man who'd gone beyond all that needy stuff for a mother figure. The first time we made love it felt like the most natural thing I'd ever done in my life. She was my woman, my soul-mate. I didn't really feel I was being unfaithful to Diana, it seemed so right to be with Josie. In fact when I was with Di I felt unfaithful to Josie.'

'Where did the two of you meet?' Geoff asked, ever practical.

'At a hotel in Leeds. On the day the twins go to nursery. How tawdry,' Piers said sadly. 'She didn't deserve to be cheapened in that way.'

'When did you and Josie first discuss the idea of going away together?' Swift asked.

As he was speaking there were sounds of footsteps coming down the stairs. Piers lifted his head like a dog hearing an intruder. The footsteps came close to the door of the den, then passed on. Seconds later the tinkle of crockery and the hiss of running water came from the kitchen. Piers let out a long shuddering breath. 'After the first time we made love,' he said, his voice so low and faint it could hardly be heard. 'But Josie wouldn't throw Jamie over. She went along with the plans for the wedding and I began to get frantic. I begged and pleaded, and in the end I wore her down. She said she would go away with me, but that it was too late to cancel the wedding — '

'You had a row about it,' Geoff cut in. 'You didn't believe she was going to go away with you; you thought she was chickening out.'

Piers lifted a hand in denial of Geoff's suppositions. His response was clear and direct. 'No. I simply couldn't believe she would put herself through the farce of marrying Jamie. But in the end, if those were her conditions for agreeing to be with me afterwards, I was prepared to accept it.'

'You thought she was dumping you,' Geoff insisted. 'You thought she'd finally come down to earth and realized what it was she truly wanted to do. And that was to marry Jamie.'

'No,' Piers said, his voice calm and intense. 'No, you don't understand it at all. We had complete confidence in each other. We knew that what we each had with our other partners was flimsy and shallow-rooted. We knew we had to be together. In the end I told Josie that I'd accept a lifetime of her being my mistress if she couldn't bring herself to hurt Jamie. And I meant it. It was after that she finally made her decision. It was Josie who made the arrangements for the flights. It was Josie who organized the tenancy of the flat in Barcelona. And she meant it.'

There was a short silence. 'How were you going to manage for money?' Swift asked.

Piers's face took on a strange look of causticity. 'My mother died last January. She left me what my father had left her two years back. He was a tight-fisted old bugger, my father. He worked as a clerk in the finance office of the local council. He used to take us on rainy, penny-pinching holidays to Wales when I was a kid. My mother used his old vests for dusters and constantly worried about money. And when he died it turned out he had around three-quarters of a million sitting in different building society accounts, and the same again in a low-risk portfolio. The money came from way back in his family but he'd always kept it quiet. Poor old Mum, I think it was the shock killed her.'

'Double lives seem to be something of a theme in your family,' Swift remarked.

Geoff registered a grimace of approval, but Piers kept silent.

'You told us that despite insisting on going ahead with the wedding, Josie was still all set to go away with you just a few weeks after marrying Jamie,' Swift said. 'And yet your plans all went wrong. They ended up provoking a terrible tragedy. So what happened to make Josie's wedding day end with her death?'

'I don't know,' Piers said. 'I truly don't know.'

'Come on, Mr Redmond, you must know something,' Geoff pressed.

Piers sat back in his chair. 'The only thing I can tell you is that we confirmed our plans at the reception. It was all still on.'

Swift and Geoff exchanged a brief glance. The mists surrounding the few minutes before Josie's death had begun to shift.

'Where did you meet?' Swift asked.

'In the conference suite. It's just off the main reception area. It was empty and we'd identified it as somewhere to meet earlier on in the day.'

'What time was this?'

'Around eight-thirty. I'd been dancing with Diana and one or two of the other guests in the ballroom. I'd kept my eye on Josie and when I saw her leave to go to the conference-room I told whoever I was dancing with that I was slipping out to the gents. Which I did. And after that I had a quick few moments with Josie.'

Swift leaned forward. 'How many moments?'

'Maybe five minutes or so. We knew we had to be very careful, but we felt reasonably safe. The room has only one window looking into the reception area and that and all the other windows were covered with venetian blinds which were shut.'

'Did you and Josie embrace?' Swift asked.

'Yes. A kiss. As we parted.'

'So, someone opening the door and seeing you with Josie might have drawn some interesting inferences.'

'It's possible.'

'Do you know where Josie's mobile is?' Swift asked evenly.

'No!' Piers shook his head, frowning slightly. 'Why do you ask?'

'It's missing. As is her wedding ring. Do you know anything about that?' Swift's tone was pressing now.

'No.' Piers's face darkened and crinkled like cellophane collapsing in a fire. 'Oh, sweet Jesus! Her ring! I've no idea where it is. I swear!' Suddenly he was overcome with grief. He bowed his head. His shoulders shook and he began to sob.

There was a sharp rap on the door, and then suddenly Diana was in the room, running up to her husband and putting her arms around him. She swivelled her head as she comforted him, looking reproachfully at Swift and Geoff. 'Oh, God! Surely you don't think he killed Josie? That's just not true.' She stroked Piers's thick hair and kissed the back of his neck. 'Darling, it's all right. It's all right.'

'We are simply making enquiries, Mrs Redmond,' Swift told her, rising from his chair in the knowledge that the interview had run its useful course.

★　★　★

Geoff slotted his keys into the ignition. 'He's not our murderer: he hasn't the guts.' The words burst out of him in a low vicious hiss. 'Although I wish to God he were, and that he'd soon be seeing the grim side of life from the inside of a prison cell.'

'I don't think he murdered Josie, either,' Swift said.

'But he was the bloody catalyst. If it wasn't for him that poor, silly girl would still be alive.'

'I get the impression you don't rate Piers Redmond very highly,' Swift observed.

'Too right, I don't. Every time he jumps he falls on his bloody feet. Lovely wife, lovely kids, lovely bit on the side. Lives the life of Reilly and then he gets left a small fortune to top it all off.' Geoff stopped to draw breath. 'And after all this is done and dusted he'll be wanting to stay with his wife because he knows which side his bread's buttered with a lovely woman like her. And d'you know what? I bet she lets him.'

'It wouldn't surprise me.'

Geoff fired the engine, eased the car into first gear and set off with commendable restraint, given his ferocious mood. 'And how he fancies himself. Not only a successful ladies' man but an armchair psychologist and a would-be writer to boot. And such a gift of the gab. The way he told that love story it could go straight into a Hollywood film. And as for that guff about just giving her a kiss at the end of their little tryst in the conference-room. I'll bet he gave her a quick seeing-to up against the wall. Which is probably why she went upstairs to have a bath. After all there'd be the hubby wanting his oats a bit later on.'

Swift gave an absent nod, only half attending now.

'They always say wickedness will out,' Geoff said morosely. 'But I don't go along with that. Wickedness can easily stay in, minding its own business for eternity, if the right situation doesn't arise. And it's the lucky ones like Piers Redmond who get away with it!' He thumped his hand on the steering wheel. 'Right then, now I've got all that of my chest, I'll talk some sense.'

'Do you believe Piers's story?' Swift asked reflectively. 'The love story of Piers and Josie. A mutual obsession, doomed from its inception?'

'Funnily enough, I do. Despite the fact it makes me cringe to think of that idle, pampered creep getting off with a young lass like Josie — even if she was a bit gullible to let herself be taken in. He must be almost old enough to be her dad.'

Swift was momentarily preoccupied in recalling his early days wooing Kate. The sensations Piers Redmond described had awoken a number of analogous memories. 'There was something about the story that rang true for me too,' he said. 'So, if we assume that Piers's story was true, and if we further assume that someone did, in fact, see him and Josie together in the conference room, then it's hardly rocket science to form a theory of what might have happened next.'

Geoff drew the car to a halt at traffic lights The engine purred softly. 'The observer, onlooker, stalker whatever, is furious to see Piers and Josie hugging and kissing, and maybe a bit more besides. He waits for a few moments and then follows Josie to her suite, by which time she's in the bath. He has it out with her. Josie spills the beans. Our villain loses control. And drowns her.'

'Yes, that works for me,' Swift agreed slowly. 'In the main.'

'And it does put young Jamie well and truly back in the frame again,' Geoff said. 'Finding out that your bride of a few hours was planning to leave you for an idle bastard like Piers Redmond would be enough to inspire a saint with murderous thoughts.'

'But why would Josie spill the beans to Jamie?' Swift said. 'Why wouldn't she simply calm him down, making light of the kiss in the conference-room? After all everybody kisses everybody at a wedding. Surely it was in Josie's interests to keep things quiet, as she and Piers had agreed.'

'What? And face a honeymoon with a guy she didn't fancy any more? Why not grasp the nettle and face the music there and then?'

'True, that does seem hard to understand, but then the whole story is pretty incredible. But on the other hand blind infatuation doesn't bow to all the usual social pressures.'

As he was speaking a few enormous raindrops suddenly hit the windscreen like exploding eggs. Geoff switched on the wipers which instantly smeared the dust of weeks of drought across the screen.

'You see,' Swift said slowly, 'I have the impression that whoever went to Josie's suite to confront her was someone who was able to provoke Josie to rise to the challenge. And whilst that by no means rules Jamie out, it somehow doesn't fit with what we know about their relationship. It seems to me that Josie cossetted and mothered him. She would have met his anger and distress with feminine diplomacy.'

'OK. So who are we left with?' Geoff said, pressing a stalk on the steering column and releasing a torrent of detergent from the windscreen washers. 'Who would be hopping mad at what they'd seen and at the same time be someone Josie felt a need to stand up to?'

'Certainly not Saul Williams,' Swift said.

'Agreed. Diana then? The betrayed wife about to be abandoned?'

'She'd have every reason,' Swift said.

'Clive or Cassandra Parker?'

'Very possibly. They would both be angry and affronted.'

'What about the Haygarths?'

'Yes,' Swift said quietly. 'What indeed?'

'But we're still up a gum tree with no witnesses and no forensics.'

'Exactly. And so far no one has been

flushed out by Jamie's arrest. So — any gut feelings, Geoff?'

Geoff shrugged. 'God alone knows who did this one. Or how we're going to prove it when we find out.'

Swift clipped on his seat belt and looked out of the window. The rain was now streaming down the windscreen in a broad sheet. The scent of dampened, parched earth filtered in through the air vents. He closed his eyes and mused on the four most likely suspects. One of them was beginning to step forward from the rest, fleshing out a suspicion which had been steadily growing since watching the tape of Jamie's hypnosis session. Unfortunately there had been nothing in the interview with Piers Redmond which could be used to pin down that particular suspect, and the question of hard evidence still remained stubbornly elusive.

★   ★   ★

Jamie stared down at the tickets and letter Melanie had given to Swift. Brief documents which told a whole story. He took up each slim, plastic-encased piece of evidence in his hand, one by one, turning them around, examining them from every angle as though the search might change the terrible nature of

300

the message they held. In frozen silence he passed them to Louise Rushworth. She turned to him, her face stunned and compassionate. Very briefly she laid her hand on his.

Sue steeled herself. 'What did you know about this, Jamie?'

He gave her a look of deep reproach and shook his head slowly.

Pete leaned forward. 'You do appreciate that this gives you a strong motive to have killed Josie,' he said. 'In addition to your having had the opportunity and being there at the scene.'

Jamie nodded, passive and dumb.

'I suggest you found out about this at the wedding,' Pete said. 'I suggest you were so angry you lost control.'

Jamie's head drooped. He was the portrait of a man defeated.

'Come on, Jamie!' Pete protested. 'What bridegroom wouldn't feel crazed with jealousy and humiliation to be jilted on his wedding night? And that's how you felt, wasn't it? Shamed and used. And you couldn't bear it — the idea of Josie going off with another man. She was betraying you, Jamie. She was acting like a selfish, evil bitch. You had to get rid of her, didn't you? *Didn't you?*'

Jamie remained still and hunched.

'Did you kill Josie?' Pete demanded, emphasizing each word, his tone loud and insistent.

Jamie shook his head.

Louise Rushforth touched his arm. 'I think you should answer the question, Jamie. So we can all hear.'

Jamie raised his head and thrust his chin forward. 'No,' he said. 'I did not kill Josie. I know that now.'

* * *

Swift and Geoff found Sue and Pete slumped at their desks. Pete sprang back into life first.

'We've been getting nowhere fast with Parker, sir,' he told Swift. 'Any luck with Redmond?'

'He was certainly talkative.' Swift loosened his tie. The air in the office was sultry and oppressive. 'And you were right, Pete. About Josie having chosen the wrong man. That was one of the first things you mentioned in our team discussions.'

'Oh, yeah. One of my throwaway gems of intuition!' Pete acknowledged. 'But where has it got us?'

There was a dull silence.

Whilst Swift gave the two young members

of the team a brief summary of the interview with Piers Redmond, Geoff used his powers of persuasion on the coffee machine. As they talked and sipped the hot tasteless liquid, Swift was making a number of decisions, the first of which being that they should all go home and get some rest as there seemed to be a sense of quiet frustration in the team which further discussion would only exacerbate.

Sue had been sitting in silence, still reflecting on the enormity of the plan Josie and Piers had hatched together. 'Are we making any progress at all?' she said eventually, her expression harrassed and weary.

'Yes,' Swift said firmly. 'Every interview, every comment from an interviewee or a suspect must inevitably move us forward — even if it doesn't seem so at the time. But for now — well, I think we'll call it a day.'

Pete grinned, stretched and glanced out of the window. 'Bloody hell. It's raining. An answer to all the farmers' prayers!'

'A change in the weather. Maybe it's an omen.' Sue got to her feet and slipped the strap of her bag over her shoulder. 'Well — good night all.'

She and Pete walked off together. The room seemed very still and quiet. Swift drummed his fingers on the desk, already projecting ahead to the morning and formulating plans.

Geoff gathered up his keys. He looked across to Swift. 'Ed,' he said quietly.

Swift glanced up. Geoff Fowler had never before used his Christian name. The breath caught in his throat. 'What is it?'

'There's something I need to say. And it doesn't give me any pleasure, and that's the honest truth.'

'Go on.'

'It's about your daughter, sir.'

Swift had guessed as much. He braced himself.

'I've seen her at my local pub a couple of times in the last week or two. She was with a bloke I know at the snooker club. He's not a bosom chum, or anything, but I know a bit about him.'

Swift absorbed the information. Foreboding lay in his stomach like a bad meal. 'Is he married?'

'Yeah. He used to have a bit of a reputation with women.' Geoff was avoiding Swift's eyes. His unease was palpable.

Swift pulled in a long breath and let it out.

'I mean, it could be quite innocent,' Geoff said, trying to reassure but sounding unconvinced. 'They weren't up to anything untoward, but they seemed pretty friendly.'

'I see.'

'I don't want to interfere,' Geoff said. 'I just thought you should know, in case you didn't already. I think I would in the same position. If I'd got a daughter.'

'Oh, yes. You were right to tell me. And I didn't know.' Swift was suddenly painfully aware of his position as a lone parent, with a daughter who was part girl, part woman. And, of course, perfectly free to form relationships as she pleased.

'His wife has cancer,' Geoff said. 'Prognosis not good.'

★ ★ ★

Swift drove home through a thundery atmosphere lit with a livid yellow sky. He let himself into the apartment. The rooms were empty yet filled with a silent sense of expectation, waiting for someone to arrive. There was a note on the kitchen table.

Supermarket pizza and bag of salad in the fridge. Gone to Lizzie's brother's birthday bash. She's aked me to stay over. See you tomorrow. Hope the case is going well. Love you lots, N XXX.

Swift poured himself a glass of chilled mineral water and paced about the kichen taking desultory bites of pizza. He resisted the need to telephone and confirm the arrangements with Lizzie and her family. He resisted the urge to ferret around in Naomi's room. He left a message on Lister's voicemail advising him of the new developments, then poured himself a stiff whisky and resisted the impulse to do any further detective work of any sort for the rest of the evening.

13

'The Super wants to see you,' Duty Sergeant Joyce Rugg informed Swift as he arrived at the station the next morning. 'Immediately, if not sooner.'

Swift raised an eyebrow. He had expected that the superintendent would want to discuss the progress of the Haygarth/Parker case with him. But not as matter of urgency.

'He's running at full throttle,' the sergeant elaborated.

'I'll be right there,' Swift said.

Joyce returned to her paperwork. 'Oh, by the way,' she called after him. 'That young man you've got in the cells.'

Swift turned. 'What about him?'

'He's the politest custody customer we've had in years. A real gent.'

Swift smiled.

'And such a sad, sweet face,' the sergeant continued. 'If you don't release him soon, I think I'll take him home with me.' She grinned. 'Strictly maternal intentions, of course. He looks as though he needs a good dinner and a lot of TLC.'

'And they say the police are cruel,

unfeeling bastards,' Swift commented, putting on a touch of speed as he made his way down the corridor.

'Thank God you're always an early bird, Ed,' Lister said by way of greeting as Swift opened his door. He was holding a sheet of paper in his hand and frowning at it ferociously. 'Clive Parker's lawyer has filed a complaint against us. Concerning Sue.'

'Ah.' Swift took the sheet Lister passed across the desk.

'Harrassment and lack of professional competence,' Lister barked, in the event of Swift's failure to read for himself. 'What the devil's all that about?'

Swift offered a brief explanation.

'Oh, bloody hell! What got into her? She's usually such a level-headed lass.'

Swift said, 'I wonder if Clive Parker is serious about pursuing this, or whether it's simply a piece of manipulative sabre-rattling.'

'You're the amateur psychologist on the team, Ed, you tell me.' Lister subsided on to his chair with a thud.

'Maybe Parker thinks this is a way of putting pressure on us to release Jamie from custody,' Swift commented.

'Well, if he thinks that, he's another think coming,' Lister snarled. 'We're not puppets to be manipulated by Parker and his delusions of power. Or his cash.'

'We had hoped that Jamie's arrest might flush someone out to give information, or maybe even to confess to Josie's murder,' Swift reminded his superior. 'I can't help thinking the filing of this complaint is somehow connected with Parker's anger — and fear — regarding Jamie's arrest.'

Lister considered. 'Fair enough. So what we do now? I'll have to carpet Sue, of course, which I'm not looking forward to.'

'No. Indeed.' Swift was still concerned about Sue, sensing that she was nursing a personal anxiety. And he understood only too well how that could affect one's work and personal attitudes.

'I think it would be helpful if you had a word with Parker,' Lister said. 'Use your cunning diplomatic skills.'

'I had, in fact, planned to visit the Parker household today,' Swift responded. 'With a search warrant — given your approval, Tom.'

Lister's eyes sharpened. 'You're thinking Josie's missing mobile phone and wedding ring could be at the Parkers' place?'

'I'm fairly confident that whoever is in possession of those items, even if not the murderer, is privy to the identity of who is.'

'Fair enough.'

'And as we found nothing at Jamie's flat,'

Swift concluded, 'I think we shall have to release him.'

'Mmm. It always bothers me having to release a strong possible suspect,' Lister said with a certain gloom. 'But, it's your call, Ed. I'm not going to block you. Not that it would do any good, you always do what — ' He broke off at the sound of the telephone. Irritated by the interruption, he grabbed the receiver and snapped out a challenging, 'Yes!' He drew his bushy eyebrows together as he listened. 'I see.' He gave a wince. 'You mean now? Very well, then. Tell her to come right away.' He put the phone down and grimaced at Swift. 'Apparently Sergeant Sallis is asking to see me. A.s.a.p.'

Swift raised his brows. 'Do you want me to leave?'

'No! For goodness' sake, stay.' Lister reached for the pen which lay at the side of his desk, then pulled his A4 pad towards him. Picking up the pen by its point he tapped it rhythmically on the pad. 'I'm not looking forward to this,' he muttered. He glanced down at the tapping pen and forced himself to lay it flat on the desk.

Swift kept calm and silent, knowing Lister's distaste for contentious or emotional interchanges with female officers. It would be pointless to make any kind of suggestion at this point.

Sue came quietly into the room and sat in the chair Lister gestured her towards. She was looking drawn, but her hair, as usual, was shaped and glossy and there was no sign of a wrinkle in her cream trousers and jacket. 'There's something I have to tell you, sir,' she said to Lister. 'And Chief Inspector Swift as well.'

Lister was taken aback. He had expected to take the lead. 'Right then, Sue. Fire away.'

'I'm pregnant, sir,' she said. 'Sixteen weeks.'

So that was the problem, Swift thought, with an accompanying sense of relief. He supposed if he had been a female officer he would have guessed long ago. Or been confided in. He noticed Lister flinch, unsure how to proceed and invariably at a loss when faced with matters relating to the female reproduction system. 'That's good news, Sue,' Swift told her.

'Yes, indeed,' Lister followed on, booming out the words. 'Congratulations! Well, well! Happy days, eh?'

'I didn't say anything earlier,' Sue explained, 'because there was some risk of a miscarriage. But that seems to be past.' She gave a faint, wistful smile. 'I'm not sure what I want to do regarding the job. Whether I want to be a full time mum for a while, or . . . ' She was on the point of crying, but struggled to keep control. 'I love this job,' she burst out.

Lister was looking at her as though she were a bomb about to go off. 'Listen, Sue, no need to rush things. You just take your time to make up your mind. Talk to Joyce, she's an expert on juggling kids and the job. She'll give you some tips.'

'Yes.' Sue sounded shaky and uncertain.

Swift glanced at Tom Lister and decided that there was now no chance of his broaching the complaints issue. 'Sue,' he said quietly, 'I'm sorry to bring this up now, but Clive Parker has filed a formal complaint against you through his lawyers.'

'Oh,' Sue said in a flat voice. 'Well, I suppose he has grounds.' She folded her hands in her lap with the air of one miserably resigned to her fate.

Lister rushed in. 'Don't you trouble yourself, right now,' he told her. 'You and I will have a little talk about the matter later on. I'm confident we can get it sorted out without things going any further. In the meantime, what you have to do is take good care of yourself and make sure you give Ed one hundred per cent on helping to crack this Josie Haygarth case.'

Sue looked steadily back at the superintendent. 'Yes, sir, I will. And thank you for saying that.'

Lister leaned back, his face resounding with deliverance and satisfaction. He addressed himself to his SIO with fully restored command and vigour. 'Right, Ed. Let's get on with it. And get a result.'

★ ★ ★

Following a short briefing meeting, Sue prepared to embark on a final interview session with Jamie, Pete set off to see John Ford at the Moorlands Hotel and Swift and Geoff started out for Clive and Cassandra Parker's house with a duet of uniformed officers and a search warrant.

The door of the house was opened by a nervous-looking elderly woman with a thin face and a cupid-bow mouth exaggeratedly defined with dark red lipstick. 'Oh, the police!' she exclaimed, looking at Swift's warrant card. 'I expect you'll be wanting to see Mr or Mrs Parker. But they aren't here. They're both out at business.'

Swift nodded. 'And you are?'

'I'm Mrs Dryden. The housekeeper.'

'We have a warrant to search the house, Mrs Dryden,' he told her.

Mrs Dryden's anxious face went pale. 'Oh dear. I don't know whether I can let you do that. I think I should telephone Mr or Mrs Parker. They wouldn't be at all pleased if I did anything against their wishes.'

'They don't have a choice, Mrs Dryden,' Swift said gently. 'We have a legal right to conduct a search in connection with a murder investigation.'

'Oh heavens!' Mrs Dryden stood to one side. Her hand shook as she pointed soundlessly down the hallway. 'Just go where you have to,' she said, her eyes widening in horror as the implication of what was happening began to sink in. 'I'll be in the kitchen if you need me,' she whispered, scuttling away as though she could not bear to witness the house being ransacked.

Geoff looked around him: at the columns and pedestals and vases, at the high dome of the ceiling; at the rows of doors leading off the hallway and the broad corridor at the head of the stairs. 'Needle in a haystack job, this,' he commented. 'I was hoping to get a bit of a break at the weekend. Do you think we'll be halfway by then?'

Swift went out into the garden with the purpose of identifying possible sites where small objects might be hidden. Thoughts of Naomi and Sue were intruding into his concentration, distracting him from his focus on the murder investigation. A call from Pete soon brought him back on track.

'Ford says it wasn't him who sent Saul Williams packing just after he'd told Emma Goodall something was wrong: it was Clive Parker. Apparently Parker was hanging around in the reception area just before Williams came through after speaking to Emma. Ford was coming out of his office to go to the kitchens to sort out some problem. He saw and heard what was going on. He says the lad was pretty upset, wasn't making much sense. Parker didn't intimidate the lad, just guided him in the direction of the entrance and said it would be best for him to go home.'

'We don't have this interaction on camera, do we?' Swift asked, mentally reviewing the video Pete had shown the team.

'No, we don't, sir. Pity about that. I've had another look at the tape and it definitely shows Parker leaving the hotel to go into the garden at 8.41. Then there's a group come in just after nine and Parker's probably amongst them, though it's hard to be sure as they were all bunched together.'

'So Parker was possibly in the garden — or missing — for twenty minutes?'

'Looks like it. Interesting, don't you think, sir?'

'Yes, it is.' As he was speaking, one of the uniformed officers came out into the garden to find him. 'The drawers in the desk in the study are locked, sir,' he told Swift. 'Do we break it open?'

Swift shook his head. He finished the call with Pete and went back into the house with the officer in search of Mrs Dryden. She was, as promised, in the kitchen and engaged in polishing a silver candelabra, rubbing furiously, her face pink with the effort. 'Oh!' she said when she saw them come in.

'Do you know where the keys are for Mr Parker's desk?' Swift asked her with a gentle smile.

She bit on her lip. 'Oh, dear. Well, yes.' She gazed at him, consumed with misgiving.

Swift waited.

'He keeps them about his person,' she explained. 'But there's a spare set.' She gazed at him with a mixture of fear and appeal which Swift had seen many times before in the eyes of those caught up in a murder enquiry.

'Could we have them, please?'

'Oh! Yes, of course.' She pulled open a drawer in one of the cupboards beneath the polished granite work tops. After some rummaging she extracted two tiny bronze keys on slender split ring. 'These are the ones.'

Swift took them with a nod of thanks. He felt Mrs Dryden's eyes on his back as he and the uniformed officer made for the study. In the third drawer down on the left-hand side of the desk they found a small bundle wrapped in a man's white handkerchief. Swift drew on a pair of protective gloves and gently pulled open the handkerchief.

'Gotcha!' the officer exclaimed.

Swift looked down at the slim phone and the gleaming ring, its surface virgin and unscratched. 'Well, well,' he murmured. Moving out into the hallway, he called out for Geoff to come.

Mrs Dryden hurried from the kitchen door where she had been waiting. 'Oh! What is it? Have you found something?'

'We have. There'll be no need to search further,' Swift told her. 'For the present.'

★   ★   ★

Geoff stayed on at the house in the event of Clive Parker's returning there unexpectedly. Whilst Josie's phone and ring went off to the forensic lab for examination, Swift, Sue and

317

Pete set out to apprehend Parker at his place of work.

'So old man Parker did it after all,' Pete said with musing satisfaction.

'We don't know that for sure yet,' Swift said, sounding a warning note. 'But it's certainly not looking good for him to have been keeping and hiding Josie's belongings.'

'And he's got a clear motive,' Sue pointed out. 'Taking revenge on the woman who was going to betray his son with his daughter's husband.' She slanted a glance at Pete. 'Not quite the motive you dreamed up!'

'You can't get it right all the time,' Pete said with a grin.

'Is this something I should have heard about?' Swift asked.

'Not in the light of what we now know, sir.' Sue told him. 'Just a flight of fancy.'

'You know,' Pete said, 'everyone thought Josie was such a nice girl. A conniving little bitch, more like. I mean it's going it a bit to go through a wedding and a honeymoon when you're planning to run off with another chap.'

'Be warned, Pete, there are quite a few other conniving little bitches around, just waiting to deprive honourable chaps like you of your happiness and well-being,' Sue told him, relishing the sting of her sarcasm.

'Yeah, yeah. Very amusing. But what baffles me is how she had the nerve to do it. What was driving her?'

'Besottedness,' Sue said. 'And raging hormones. They can drive a girl mad.'

* * *

Parker Mill stood on its own on a quiet stretch of upland bordering on a moorland road which had once carried carriages from the north of Bradford to the Dales town of Skipton. It had been built in the early part of the nineteenth century, and had been extended on several occasions in order to accommodate the new machinery and expanded workforce necessary to keep pace with the demand for ever more sophisticated fabrics.

Swift drove the car through the main entrance, passing into the mill yard beneath an arched, freshly painted iron sign which proclaimed 'Samuel Parker Mills 1806' in gleaming bronze letters. The building was substantial, made of huge blocks of dressed stone which had originally been a pale parchment colour, then blackened with smoke and soot and recently sandblasted to a creamy butter yellow.

'This is the first Yorkshire mill I've been in,' Pete said, stepping lightly over the polished cobbles of the yard and looking upwards to where the now defunct mill chimney towered above them, resting on its massive bed of concrete. 'I've been reading up on the history of mills,' he said, squinting towards to the chimney's square top. 'And, ee by gum, those old mill masters were certainly mighty fond of their erections!'

They entered a side door and climbed a long flight of steps, conscious of the faint but steady vibrations of moving machinery coming from the body of the mill. At the top of the steps there was a sign to the directors' and administrative offices. In the waiting-room there were samples of Parker Mills's current projects and various textile magazines for the edification of visitors. The room was lined from top to bottom in seasoned pannelled oak.

Clive Parker's office was empty. They knocked at the door of his personal secretary's room. She rose to meet them, a glossy, stylish woman in her late thirties. Her greeting was cordial but guarded. Her automatic, 'Can I help you?' faded into silence as Swift showed his identification. 'We've come to speak to Mr Clive Parker,' he told her.

'He's in a meeting with the sales team,' she said. 'It should be finished in about half an hour.'

'Would you please get him for us,' Swift said. 'Now.'

She hesitated. 'I don't think I can disturb him.'

'Then if you'll take us to the meeting room, we will,' Swift told her.

'Ah.' She was quick now to understand the gravity of their visit and hurried away. The three officers followed at a distance.

'Maybe we should institute a policy of making appointments to arrest people,' Pete said, *sotto voce.* 'Apprehension and caution offered at the time and place of your choice, to suit your busy lifestyle.'

Sue smiled. 'Stop it, Pete. This is serious.'

'I know,' he said. 'I always get whimsical when things are really serious.'

Within moments, Clive Parker was walking purposefully from the conference-room, his wolfish features stern and remote, his eyes seeking out each officer in turn. The secretary followed him, closing the door behind her and blocking out the curious faces of the several occupants around the oval conference-table. As Swift stepped forward, she melted away into her office, a model of discretion.

'Say your piece, Chief Inspector,' Parker said, having an instantaneous grasp on the situation, and maintaining an iron self-possession. 'As I'm assuming I don't have any choice, I'm perfectly prepared to come along with you. But you're making a terrible mistake.' As they passed the door of his secretary's office, he spoke in commanding tones. 'Call my lawyer, will you, Suzanne. Tell him I've been arrested. Wrongfully. And that I'd appreciate his early advice.'

'Very well, sir.'

Sue and Pete exchanged a glance as Parker strode past them to fall in line with Swift.

'You've got to hand it to him,' Pete murmured in her ear. 'The guy's got balls.'

* * *

As Clive Parker was admitted into custody, so Jamie was given notice of his own imminent release. Clive Parker requested that two people be informed of his arrest: his son and his daughter. 'They will inform my wife,' he said. His manner was very much that of the grandee. Swift wondered at what point his carefully cultivated carapace would crack.

His solicitor, Hugh Worthing, arrived within the half hour, a grim-faced man in his forties, as bulky as Parker was racehorse fit. But, like his client, he had an air of unassailable confidence, a man who knew how to work on people's weaknesses so that even the most assured could be persuaded to doubt themselves.

Swift asked Sue to work with him in the initial interview. She knew better than to make protests once he had made a decision. She simply prayed that she could fulfil his expectations and ride it out as regards her wariness of Clive Parker. The nature of his complaint, the criticisms of harassment and professional incompetence made her wince whenever she thought of them. She prayed also to be spared from any of the queasy episodes she had been experiencing over the recent weeks of her pregnancy.

Swift went through possible lines of questioning with her, offering one or two options bearing in mind the possible advice Worthing might offer. All the time he was talking she was wondering how convinced he was of Clive Parker's guilt. She had noticed over the year she had worked with him that on occasions he could be surprisingly secretive. Maybe not as a deliberate ploy, maybe simply because at times he was unwilling to create unnecessary confusion by setting certain hares running. She wanted to ask him outright, but there was something about his manner which stopped her. She had the feeling this was one of the times when he was firmly holding the reins and the best way to support him was to listen hard and respond to every twitch on the leather.

During the course of their discussion Pete took a phone call from the forensic lab. The examination of Josie's phone and her ring revealed that they had both been wiped clean. There were no prints or traces of DNA on either item. Pete swore softly to himself, wondering if the continuing lack of hard evidence was finally going to lead to the collapse of this investigation. But when he passed on the news to Swift, the chief inspector merely gave an enigmatic smile, as though the news was neither surprising nor troublesome.

★ ★ ★

Jamie collected his belongings at the desk and signed the release forms. Sergeant Joyce Rugg then took him into the privacy of a small interview room and gave him the news of his father's arrest. He stared at her in dumb disbelief. 'Dad!' he whispered, his face crumpling in bewilderment and hurt. 'They think Dad killed Josie?' He bowed his head and was unable to speak for a time. Joyce Rugg became concerned.

'Is there someone you would like me to contact to come and fetch you?' she asked.

'To take you home?'

Jamie raised his head. He thought of his mother and then his sister. He had always been fond of his sister, but somehow, everything to do with his family now seemed distorted and tainted. He said, 'I'd like you to contact Louise Rushworth.'

★   ★   ★

Swift started the interview with Clive Parker by requesting some simple statements of fact. Where had Parker been at the time Josie was murdered. With whom?

His solicitor listened, po-faced, yet with an unmistakable air of lofty contempt.

Parker said, 'As you will appreciate in my capacity as the bridegroom's father I made sure to keep circulating between the main reception rooms on the ground floor of the hotel, ensuring that all was going well.'

'Where were you at around eight-thirty?' Sue followed up.

Parker gave her a long stare. 'I was in the bar with some friends of ours from New England. I left them probably ten minutes or so later and then I went out into the garden for a breath of air.' His gaze was still trained on Sue, forceful and challenging. 'On my own, Sergeant Sallis. I needed a short spell of peace and quiet.'

Hugh Worthing leaned towards Parker and murmured in his ear, a glance of warning on his face.

'It's all right, Hugh,' Parker told him. 'I've nothing to fear in being open about the truth.'

'Did you join your wife?' Swift asked.

'No. I told you, I wanted a few moments on my own.'

'Your wife was also in the garden,' Sue said in a clear, level voice.

There was a small beating pause. 'I walked around the south aspect of the hotel,' Parker said. 'However there were one or two groups of people standing on the west lawns just beyond the main entrance. Cassandra was no doubt with one of those gatherings.'

'How long were you alone in the garden?' Swift asked.

'There's no need to answer that,' Worthing said sharply.

Parker put up a courteous hand to acknowledge the advice, which he then ignored. 'About fifteen minutes. I was interested in looking at the rose garden. There's quite a good variety of bushes, and clearly they had been carefully watered to keep blooming in this drought.' He paused, with an air of making a careful search through his memory in order to give flawlessly accurate information. 'I then went back into the hotel, by which time it was coming up for nine o'clock. Adrian Gowland, the best man, was in the reception area having a smoke, and we had a word. I recall that we commented on how well things were going. He went back to the bar, and I was about to go into the ballroom when a rather wild looking young man came along. I didn't know him, and assumed he was a friend of the Haygarths. He was in rather a state and had probably had too much to drink. I asked him if he was with anyone, and he muttered something incoherent. I thought the best thing to do was encourage him to leave. Which he did.' He laid his hands on the table. They were steady as a rock. 'And, as I realize that in police investigations the timing of events is crucial, I can tell you that the time was then around nine-fifteen.'

Swift and Sue exchanged glances. Parker's estimate of his time of departure into the garden and re-entry into the hotel checked with the videotape.

'So between eight-forty and nine o'clock, you were on your own,' Swift commented. 'Can anyone vouch for your presence in the rose garden during that time?'

'It's possible,' Parker responded. 'But not that I know of.'

'So you would have had time to go up to the bridal suite via the back entrance, to have a confrontation with Josie and then drown her in the bath,' Sue stated quietly. 'You would have had time to get back the way you had come and to be in the reception area at nine o'clock. And you would certainly have been anxious to get rid of the 'wild looking young man' who could well have seen you in or near the room where the killing took place.'

Worthing was now becoming very restive. Parker gave an exaggerated sigh. 'Yes, Sergeant Sallis, indeed I would have had time to leave the garden, to go up to the bridal suite and commit the terrible crime you are accusing me of. But I did not.'

There was something about his impregnable assurance and his exaggerated verbosity which aroused Sue's contempt. He was not charismatic at all, she thought, he was an egotistical, domineering windbag. She arranged her features into cool impartiality.

Parker turned his gaze away from Sue and addressed Swift. 'You're making rather a pig's ear of this, aren't you, Chief Inspector? First you arrest my son, which was obviously a blunder, and one which I'm assuming you have now put right by releasing him. And then you arrest me, which is a similarly ill-thought-out mistake. Who will be next, I wonder?'

Swift placed the plastic bags containing Josie's phone and wedding ring on the table. 'These were found in your desk drawer. They belonged to Josie. Can you tell me how they got there?'

A spasm of sensation rippled across Parker's face. The look which flashed between him and his solicitor had an electric quality. 'I have no idea,' Parker said quietly.

'You hid them there, didn't you?' Sue said. 'You took the phone from the bridal suite because you thought it might contain information which would be damaging to Jamie and your family.'

Parker's mien of patient disdain was back in place. He fixed an icy gaze on Sue. 'No, I did not take this phone from the bridal suite. I was never in the bridal suite at any time. There was no reason for me to have any interest in either the phone or the ring.'

'Josie had taken the ring off, hadn't she?' Sue insisted. 'It was lying next to the phone, discarded and rejected. Just as Josie had already rejected Jamie and was planning to go off with someone else.'

'You are not making any sense, Sergeant Sallis,' Parker said scathingly. 'Your suggestions are no more than grotesque fantasies and your phraseology is somewhat confused.'

Swift laid the bagged airline tickets and the estate agent's letter found by Melanie on the table. 'These documents indicate that Josie was planning to go away with your son-in-law Piers Redmond. They were going to start a new life together in Barcelona. We have Redmond's confirmation that this was true.'

As he was speaking, a nerve began to twitch beneath Parker's eye. His mouth opened slightly and for a moment he was at a loss to speak as he stared at the documents before him and absorbed the astounding information. 'Piers,' he hissed. 'Piers *fucking* Redmond!' His eyes flashed hatred. He put a hand over his heart and began to take long deep breaths as if attempting to ward off a panic attack. The emotional temperature in the room had soared.

Worthing instantly stepped in and requested a break in which to confer with his client. 'I think my client might require a cessation of any further procedures today on medical grounds,' he said, but Parker threw up a hand to banish all thoughts of a sick dispensation.

Sue spoke into the tape then switched it off. She and Swift left the room. Sue leaned against the wall in the corridor. 'That was high octane stuff,' she said.

'Are you all right?' Swift asked.

'Yes. I'm fine. But Parker really gets to me. I'm sorry.'

'It didn't show,' Swift said. 'Unlike his ignorance of the Josie/Piers arrangement which was written all over him.'

'Yeah. The pompous, patronizing twat.'

'Yes. But a truthful twat, as far as his remarks to us were concerned.'

'Mmm.'

'And he had a point about our recent arrests,' Swift added ruefully. 'We got it wrong. So now, we've got to get it right.'

'What next?'

'I want you to stay here. Pete should be back from the Moorlands, so you and him can team up to question Parker further when he's had a breather. Find out what he knows or suspects regarding Josie's death in the light of the findings about Josie and Piers. I doubt if he'll say much. And Worthing will be much more insistent on shutting him up, now we've produced some evidence.'

'Right. And where are you going, sir?'

'I'm going to the Moorlands. And then I'm going to see Jamie Parker. And after that — well, it depends on what I turn up.'

★   ★   ★

John Ford regarded Swift with an expression of weary resignation.

'I quite understand that you need to make another inspection of the grounds and the building and I don't suppose I've any choice but to offer you a free rein, but we do have another wedding booked in for three o'clock and some of the bride's family and guests are already here.'

'I don't intend to cause a riot,' Swift said, with a faint smile.

'I've had to make a complete rearrangement of the bedrooms to create an alternative suite to the one now referred to by the staff as the 'Bride in the bath suite',' Ford said with a touch of sourness. 'And you might be interested to know that our lunchtime snacks in the bar have suddenly become immensely popular. People have been coming in droves. And their visits to the cloakrooms always seem to take them up to the first floor for a quick tour of the bedroom corridors, presumably in the hope of a glimpse of the scene of the crime. But, of course, none of the brides booked in for future weddings want to use *that* room. Naturally if you need the key for the suite, Chief Inspector, you're only too welcome to it.'

332

Swift put on a sympathetic expression, accepted the key Ford offered and walked out into the gardens. Parker's account of his sojourn in the garden had interested him. He made for the rose gardens first and then headed back past the entrance and around the northern aspect of the hotel. The extension housing the conference suite took up around half of the north side, projecting a few feet from the original Victorian building. The windows extended almost to ground level. The Venetian blinds were closed, as Piers had indicated, but as Pete had reported from his earlier visit, one of the blinds had a bent slat, and it was perfectly possible by putting your eyes on a level with that slat to see into the conference room. Anyone could have seen Piers and Josie together from that viewpoint, with far less likelihood of being seen than taking a peek through the door opening from the entrance foyer. Swift looked on the ground for signs of footprints, but because of the extensive drought and the downpour the evening before there was very little useful to be seen. He would alert the forensic team, but doubted they would come up with anything.

Moving on, he walked around to the back of the building which faced west. There were two back entrances: a large double door leading to the kitchen area and a smaller door which opened directly on to the back corridor Saul Williams had described. Taking the first stairway he came to, he found himself at the far end of the corridor housing the bridal suite where Josie had died. He let himself in and made a quick reappraisal of the two rooms in the light of his steadily developing theory of what had happened on the night of Josie's death.

Satisfied that his current knowledge of the hotel's inner and outer geography was sufficient for his needs, he drove to Jamie's flat. Louise Rushworth opened the door. 'What is it, Chief Inspector? We've only just arrived back from your place.'

'I'd like to speak to Jamie,' he said, stepping forward so that Louise had little choice but to move to allow him to pass.

Jamie was standing in the doorway of the sitting-room clutching a steaming mug and a digestive biscuit. 'What's happened?' he asked, his face white with strain. 'You haven't charged Dad, have you?'

'No. We're still questioning him.'

'So why are you here? You've only just released Jamie.' Louise went to stand beside her client, shaking back her Titian hair and looking decidedly foxy.

Swift addressed Jamie. 'I'd like you to

come with me to the Moorlands Hotel. I think it might help us to get to the truth of what happened to Josie.'

Louise opened her mouth to protest. And then she looked at Jamie and saw a glimmer of determination in his eyes. She let him speak for himself.

'Yes, if you think it will help, I'll go,' he said. 'I'd like Louise to come too.'

'That's fine,' Swift said, not at all averse to taking a legal witness along on this particular project.

Predictably John Ford appeared none too happy to see Swift again. On seeing Jamie following on, his unease deepened. He threw Swift a look of anguished appeal. *Please, no more dramas. I have a wedding party about to arrive.*

Swift led Jamie and Louise to the ballroom. 'I know this is painful, Jamie, but I want you to take yourself back to last Saturday evening. You'd finished the wedding breakfast, you'd been talking to friends and dancing with Josie. You were having a great time.'

Jamie looked around him at the vast unpeopled room. There were no windows to the outside: the only source of light was from the entrance lobby so that the room was dim and full of shadows.

'This place looks dead now,' he said, sadly.

'That evening it was full of life and people laughing and dancing.'

Swift left a pause, respecting Jamie's reawakened grief. 'Now, around eight-thirty you noticed that you couldn't see Josie so you went to find her. I want you to show us all the places where you looked.'

Jamie took them back into the foyer and down the corridor to the bar. From there they went through to the dining-room, a huge salon with windows to the east and south. 'This is where we were married,' Jamie said. 'They put all the chairs in rows and the table under the window was like an altar. Full of flowers.'

'Where did you have the wedding breakfast?' Louise asked.

'In here,' Jamie said. 'The staff set up the tables while we were having the photos taken and everyone was milling around and drinking champagne.'

Swift said, 'But at around eight-thirty Josie wasn't in here?'

'No. She wasn't in here or the bar, so I went to the cloak-rooms and asked some of the women guests coming out of the Ladies if she was there. One of them said she was, so I hung about waiting for a bit. I realized the person had been mistaken so I went back to the bar and the ballroom and then I went into the garden.' He glanced from Louise to Swift. 'Do you want me to show you?'

'Do you remember the route you took?' Louise asked.

'It's quite simple,' Jamie said, walking ahead. 'The rooms here all link with each other.' He led them back to the entrance. Beyond the glass doors flowers were being unloaded from a van parked beside the entry steps, huge cardboard boxes fragrant with roses and lilies. Jamie watched as they were carried inside, then walked down the steps and stared into the front garden.

'God! He looks so desolate,' Louise muttered.

'Yes. But his memory seems to be functioning well.'

Louise said, 'I've been giving some thought to what might happen if you were to charge Jamie. And it seems to me that one of the unexplained factors here is why no one has come forward to state that they saw Jamie here on the ground floor of the hotel, or in some place other than the bridal suite around the time Josie was killed.'

'Yes, you have a point. On the other hand, if Jamie was becoming increasingly anxious whilst he searched for Josie, was moving quickly and not engaging with anyone, then it's possible his presence wouldn't have been remarked on or remembered. After all there had been a lot of alcohol consumed, people were excited and tired and generally not at their most vigilant.'

'Hmm,' Louise said. 'Even so.'

'We've had a man on the job for the past three days asking questions which might possibly have thrown up a witness to speak for Jamie, but so far nothing useful has emerged. But then, to date, we've only been able to contact a proportion of the guests, probably around half of them.'

'If you do bring a charge against him,' Louise warned, 'I shall do my utmost to find a witness to vouch for him.'

'That's exactly what I would do in your place,' Swift said.

'After all you've got very little else to build a case the CPS will want to run with. They'll be thinking of all the holes a clever defence would make in such a fragile edifice.'

Swift did not disagree.

'I'm not sure what this exercise is about,' Louise said, 'but I hope it's going to produce something useful.'

She and Swift joined Jamie as he stood looking out onto the lawns to the front of the hotel. 'There were one or two groups of people around here, chatting and getting a bit of air.'

'Can you remember who?'

'There were some of my parents' friends I haven't seen for years. And Janice who works at my mother's shop. Then some of Josie's parents' friends a bit further down. I don't know their names. Melanie would be able to tell you.'

'Were your mother or father with either of these groups?'

Jamie's face twitched. 'I don't think so. No. I was getting a bit panic-stricken by then, wondering where Josie could have gone. I went back into the hotel.'

'Did you look in the rose garden, or around the side of the hotel which the extension looks on to?' Swift asked.

'No. There didn't seem to be anyone round there. And it had suddenly dawned on me that Josie might have gone up to the suite. She'd been having a bit of a problem keeping her dress hooked up at the back when she was dancing. It had some special fastening arrangement, and I thought she might have gone up there to try and sort it out. Or maybe she just wanted a bit of peace and quiet. I suddenly really wanted to see her . . . ' He blinked hard.

Louise threw Swift a look of appeal.

'Which way did you go?' Swift asked Jamie.

'Up the main stairway.'

'Not the lift?' Swift asked.

'No. It's quicker just to run up on foot.'

He led the way through the foyer, and went up the broad stairs with an energy Swift hadn't seen in him before. When they got to the door of the suite he stopped dead.

'Are you all right, Jamie?' Louise asked.

He nodded. He looked at the door which Swift had earlier unlocked but left open. He depressed the handle and gave the door a slight push. It swung open, stopping when it connected with a rubber door stop let into the carpet just a few inches from the base of the wall.

'Did the door swing open like that?' Swift asked.

'More or less.'

'Did it swing as far?'

'Maybe not quite as far.'

'What happened next?'

Jamie's expression stilled. Swift and Louise waited.

Swift took some typed sheets from his pocket and unfolded them. 'In your evidence to Sue Sallis, it's at this point where your memory went blank,' Swift said. 'But in your hypnosis session you recalled a number of things. You recalled that you couldn't see anyone else in the room.'

'Yes, that's right,' Jamie said.

Swift consulted the transcript of the sound recorded on the videotape. 'You said there was a strong scent — bath essence. You said you felt something 'really, really bad'.'

Jamie flinched. He put his hands up and clenched the fingers tight. 'I don't want go on with this,' he protested. 'I don't want to go into the bathroom. I just can't do it.'

'Fair enough,' Swift said evenly. 'Let's just go back over what happened when you first came into the room. This scent you mention. You refer to it again later on in the session at the point you were trying to think of ways of resuscitating Josie. You were not sure what to do. You thought you should bang her chest and try to breathe air into her mouth.' Again he consulted the transcript. ' "Breathe, breathe. Breathe life back into her. There's this sweet, sweet smell. It's making me sick. God, I'm going to throw up'.'

Jamie sat down on the bed, his shoulders hunched. 'Yes, I remember. I felt the bile rising up in my gullet.'

Swift continued his account, speaking in a calm, clear voice. 'When I first read the transcript I'd assumed that the smell you referred to when you first came into the room was of bath essence. But later on when I watched the video I began to think that the smell you first referred to was a different one from the bath essence.' He paused. 'That's right, isn't it?'

Jamie moved his head, making a fleeting indication of assent.

'That first smell you were aware of was a fragrance which you recognized, wasn't it?'

There was another silent assent.

'A fragrance used by only one person you know.'

Jamie let out a trembling sigh.

'You knew that person, but you didn't see them,' Swift continued, 'because they were standing behind the entry door to the suite. But in some way, either conscious, or unconscious, you registered that presence and you knew the identity of the person who was deliberately remaining concealed behind the opened door.'

Jamie said nothing.

Swift turned to Louise who was looking on with perplexed concern. He moved to the door of the suite, and then stood against the wall at the side of the door, his feet close to the rubber door stop. 'Would you come and stand here in my place,' he instructed her, 'with your back flat against the wall.'

She hesitated for a moment and then did as he asked.

'I want you to watch me,' Swift told Jamie. He left the room, closed the door and immediately re-opened it. The door swung open obscuring Louise from Swift as he came back into the room and stood looking towards the bathroom.

Jamie looked on.

'Can you see Louise?' Swift asked him.

Jamie shook his head.

'Is where I am standing now roughly the same place you were stood before you went into the bathroom?' Swift asked Jamie.

A small affirmative sound came from his throat.

'And I can't see her either. So clearly it was possible that when you came into the suite that evening someone could have been hiding behind the door without your seeing them?'

Another accepting grunt.

'After a few moments you went into the bathroom and found Josie in the bath. You were horrified by what you saw and you froze. And then you let the water out of the bath, pulled Josie on to a towel on the floor and tried to revive her. And all the time you were doing that you were still aware of this sweet smell. It made you feel sick. You retched once or twice, we can hear it on the soundtrack of the videotape. But you weren't sick. You went very still and quiet, not knowing what you should do next.'

'Yes,' Jamie offered spontaneously, his face

twisted with revulsion.

'You had two terrible traumas to deal with, didn't you, Jamie?' Swift said with low intensity. 'The death of your bride, Josie, and the knowledge that she had probably been killed. And during those dreadful moments, which you subsequently blocked out of your memory, the inescapable truth of who had killed her was beginning to fix itself in your mind.'

Jamie stared at him with dumb pleading.

'Do you know the name of the sweet perfume you could smell?' Swift asked him.

'It's called 'Janey'.' His voice was dull with despair.

'It's an exclusive fragrance made under licence to the designer Janey Morrell, is that correct?'

'Yes.'

'And it's only available at the few outlets who stock the Janey Morrell label?'

'Yes.'

'I believe that Janey Morrell designs are stocked at a well-known fashion shop in Ilkley?'

'Yes.' His voice had sunk to little more than a faint vibration.

Swift's voice was low and urgent. 'Jamie, it's my belief that there was only one person wearing that particular fragrance at the wedding. Who was it?'

'No! Don't! Don't make me say it,' Jamie moaned.

Swift spoke with quiet regret. 'I put it to you that it was your mother, Cassandra Parker.'

Jamie's spine curved into a bow. He sat with his head drooping, his arms hanging loosely between his legs.

14

Swift sat in his car at the high point of Ilkley Moor, looking down on the rooftops of the town and across the sweep of the valley. The clouds were plump cushions of dazzling white riding high in the sky. The rain of the evening before had not been a herald of a change in the weather, merely a tantalizing token of relief for the parched fields and the dried grassy flanks of the dales.

He was aware of his reluctance to confront Cassandra Parker and thus begin the inevitably long-drawn-out battle which might or might not result in gaining an account of the killing of her daughter-in-law.

She had been silent and unresisting at her arrest, accepting her fate in the manner of a latter-day queen receiving the news of her death sentence whilst still occupied with affairs of state. As he had entered her shop, to the audio and visual accompaniment of his uniformed escort drawing up outside, she had instantly registered his presence and courteously excused herself from the customer she was talking with. Whilst her assistant looked on in dismay she had listened without protest as he arrested her on suspicion of the murder of Josephine Emily Parker. Her untroubled acquiesence in being taken away to the station for questioning under caution had been tantamount to a confession of guilt. But silence and a yielding demeanour were not sufficient evidence on which to bring a charge of murder.

Somewhere, not far from where he sat, Jamie Parker would be sifting through the events of the evening of his marriage, struggling to get to grips with the image of his mother killing his bride and at the same time to banish that grotesque picture from his thoughts for ever. And, as if the young man had not had enough to endure, now he must play the role of talebearer of his mother's guilt and also prepare himself to act as key witness for the prosecution if she came to trial.

His thoughts drifted away to Naomi and the need to talk to her about the news Geoff had given him. Suddenly restless for action, he straightened up in his seat and fired the engine. It leapt into life, ticking over with a low soft whine. As he pulled at the wheel he was conscious of a keen sense of mourning for this world which would never be freed from ugliness and evil, and a simultaneous yearning for those who had already made their escape and left it.

'Where is he?' Sue asked Pete and Geoff.

'He'll be lurking in some back-of-beyond spot contemplating the wickedness of this cruel world,' Geoff said.

Sue was worried. 'Do you think he's OK? He's been keeping himself going by sheer will power these past few days. Most people would still be on a sicky, coddling themselves after a bout of this wretched flu. My dad had it and he was knocked out for a couple of weeks.'

'He lives for the job,' Geoff said. 'So just watch it, young lady, and make sure you hold on to a life beyond the curdled minds of criminals and the stale smell of villainy that hangs around this place.'

'Hey, Sarge, it's not that bad,' Pete said.

'Give yourself another twenty years and come back and tell me that again.' Geoff advised. 'So what's the reckoning on the angle our chief is going to take with Mrs Cassandra Parker — wife, mother, business-woman and murderess?'

'He's got to get a confession from her,' Sue said.

'What about Jamie's evidence?' Pete asked. 'That seems fairly clear. And the solicitor was there to witness what was said.'

Sue made a grunt of dissent. 'Jamie didn't actually state that it was his mother who murdered Josie. He agreed that someone wearing the same perfume as his mother uses was behind the door just after Josie was murdered, and he didn't disagree when the boss led him to the point of accepting that she was the killer. But he didn't give a verbal statement to confirm it. And maybe he never will. Would you want to stand up in court and shop your own mother, even if you did think she was an evil bitch?'

'I would if she'd bumped off my best girl,' Pete said.

Sue frowned in concentration. 'The evidence simply isn't strong enough. If we take this case to the CPS, what are their barristers going to say? They'll say it's all very well and good except for the fact that any defence silk worth their salt will drive a tank through a case built on the evidence available.'

'What about the phone and the ring?' Pete asked.

'No prints. Nothing to connect her with them.'

'Except they were in hubby's desk drawer,' said Pete, putting his hands behind his head and tipping his chair back. 'Which probably tells us she hates his guts and wanted to frame him.' He pulled his face into a grimace of gloom. 'But, let's face it, that's not much use to us.'

'Somebody *must* have seen her going up to the bridal suite,' Sue said, glancing at Geoff.

Geoff held up his hands in surrender. 'Don't look at me, love. I'm doin' me best, sifting steadily through the bodies.'

'Well now we've got our man, maybe you could up a gear from steady to urgent,' Sue said with a touch of acid.

The two men glanced at each other. 'Ooh,' Pete's lips framed silently.

*   *   *

'I am not guilty,' Cassandra Parker intoned for the benefit of Swift, her solicitor and the tape-recorder. They were the only words she had used since entering the interview-room.

Swift recognized that mechanical repetition of innocence interspersed with silence was probably the best card she could play. In so doing she ran no risk of exposing her inner thoughts and whatever conflicts stirred her conscience, nor of allowing herself to be tripped up by clever questioning or hectoring. He guessed that her lawyer, a slick young man in a highly expensive suit, had apprised her of the important principle of keeping your cards close to your chest and never helping

350

the other side unless you had to.

'What was your relationship with Josie Parker?' Swift asked.

Silence. Cassandra stared at a point somewhere behind Swift's head, wearing a martyred expression.

'Did you like her?'

Her silvery irises flickered. 'Yes. I did.'

Was this a breakthrough? Swift wondered. He presented Cassandra with the phone and the ring. She looked at them, her face stripped of emotion. 'Have you seen these before?' he asked.

'I believe the ring is the one Jamie gave to Josie when they were married. He showed it to me when he bought it. I can't say about the phone. They're all much of a muchness, aren't they?'

'I put it to you that you took the phone and the ring at the time you confronted Josie. At the time you killed her.' Swift knew he was wasting his time.

She shook her head. 'You can 'put it to me' until the cows come home, as my mother used to say.'

'And that you hid it in your husband's desk to divert attention from yourself?'

She returned his hard stare.

'Or maybe to get back at him for some wrong he has done you?'

A light kindled and then died in her eyes.

Swift showed her the incriminating airline tickets and the rental agreement. He was met with stony passivity and silence.

'You're showing no surprise or dismay, Mrs Parker. Which tells me you already knew all about this. Which then tells me that you had every motive to be angry with Josie for betraying both your son and your daughter and destroying your family.'

She stared at him, her eyes like stones.

He confronted her with the whole scenario. Of how she had been standing in the garden talking with friends when she saw Josie come into the entrance foyer and enter the conference-room. Of seeing Piers repeat the same sequence of actions. Of moving from one group of guests to another and then drifting off and making her way around the north side of the building and gaining a view of Piers and Josie through the broken slats of one of the blinds. Of thinking things through and then following Josie to the bridal suite to demand an explanation. Of losing her temper when Josie refused to deny the affair, and maybe mocked Cassandra's distress.

'May I remind you that my client has a signed witness statement to say she was in the garden at the time Josie was killed,' the solictor pointed out. 'From a Mrs Janice Scott.'

Swift had only minutes before being informed of this remarkably felicitous alibi written and signed by Mrs Scott just the day before, most likely shortly after he left *Arabella*. 'Witnesses sometimes lie,' he said, addressing his remark to Cassandra. 'Especially when their future employment depends on the person who asked them to do so.'

'Janice Scott is a very honest person,' Cassandra said. 'She's worked for me for over ten years.'

'If she's so honest, then hopefully she won't go so far as to lie in court under oath,' Swift said acidly. He leaned forwards towards her. 'You lost control, didn't you, Cassandra? You couldn't bear it that Josie made light of her embrace with Piers Redmond. You couldn't bear it that she had it in her power to destroy your daughter's marriage. Because Diana is the person you are most concerned about, isn't she? You would do anything to protect her happiness. Even commit murder.'

At the mention of Diana, Cassandra flinched, and then maintained a self-righteous silence.

'You lost control,' Swift repeated. 'You experienced a moment of such intense hatred you were provoked to kill. You reached for

Josie's ankles and pulled her under the water until she stopped struggling. Until she was dead. On an impulse you picked up her mobile phone and her ring which were lying on the edge of the bath. And when you heard footsteps approaching the suite you hid behind the door. You waited until your son Jamie was occupied in trying to resuscitate Josie, and then you slipped away.' He broke off drawing in a breath. 'I have an intimation from Jamie to indicate your presence at the crime scene at the time of Josie's death.'

Cassandra froze. Her pupils dilated and shivered, then hardened into glassy contempt. 'I am not guilty,' she said.

★ ★ ★

'We'll have to release her,' Swift told the team, flinging himself in the chair behind his desk. 'Even though in my book she's as guilty as George Joseph Smith.'

'Can't we lean on the woman who provided the alibi, get her to retract?' Pete demanded.

'We can try,' Swift said. 'I doubt if it will do any good. Janice Scott has been well schooled and got her account off pat. She probably even believes it by now. What would she have to gain from going against her previous evidence?'

'The pursuit of truth and justice?' Sue suggested with heavy irony.

Pete rubbed at the hair on his forehead. 'There must be some forensics: a hair, a print somewhere.'

'She was wearing a turban,' Sue said, recalling Cassandra's plumed wedding head-gear. 'And carrying long buckskin gloves which she could have used to wrap the phone and the ring in when she took them. Or she simply wiped them clean before she put them in her husband's desk.'

'We could get forensics to go over the crime scene yet again,' Swift said. 'Maybe do the entire house over. We could have the floors up, crawl all over each priceless piece of antiquity. It'll cost a fortune, and we won't find anything. Because what is there to find?'

A gloomy silence fell.

'This all hinges on Diana,' Swift said intently. 'Or rather Cassandra's feelings for her daughter, in preference over her son. Think about it — why didn't Cassandra come forward to save Jamie when we arrested him?'

'Maybe she would have come forward if we'd charged him,' Pete suggested.

'Maybe. But in my view Cassandra's mind was always focusing on Diana, and how to ensure that the issue about Josie and Piers's plans never came to light.'

Pete snorted. 'Some hope of that! It was bound to come out, whatever.'

'I agree. But Cassandra wasn't thinking logically. The murder had been done as an impulsive act of fury. As Cassandra remarked to me a day or two ago, 'I'm a tigress where my children are concerned'. Except this particular tigress was only roused on behalf of her daughter. Having killed for her and demolished the enemy, Cassandra was now desperately engaged in trying to cover her tracks and thus obscure the reason behind the killing. But I don't believe she's all that bright in regard to thinking matters through. I don't think it's occurred to her that if she pleads not guilty and goes to trial all the dirty linen will have a very thorough washing in public.'

Pete's eyes gleamed. 'So — we get her to confess with a promise that the Piers/Josie thing will be kept well under wraps.'

'Which she will not believe,' Swift said. 'In fact the minute we say 'Trust us', she'll do exactly the opposite. Wouldn't you?'

'She won't confess,' Sue said baldly. 'Not at the prospect of being sent straight into custody. Can you imagine it? No bone china and silver candelabra at supper time. And she'd have to do her own nails.'

Forty-eight hours after her arrest, there being no further evidence come to light, Cassandra Parker's lawyer had demanded that she be released and allowed to return home on her own recognizance and with no restrictions.

Swift left the station in the mid afternoon with the prospect of taking the rest of the day off. He found Naomi at home with a group of friends. They were sitting in the garden drinking lager and looking celebratory and festive. They made him feel like an albatross. He went into the kitchen and dug in the fridge for a beer. He loosened his tie, sprang the clip on the beer can and allowed himself a moment of pure and morose frustration. And then he drank the can at almost one go.

Naomi came in, light and lovely in sawn-off denim shorts and a clingy lemon top which showed her midriff. 'Hi!' She stood very close to him. 'Yet another bad day at the office?'

'You could say that.'

She cocked her head on one side and appraised him. 'What's up?'

'You've been seen,' he said, 'seeing a married man, whose wife is dying of cancer.'

Her look was one of sweet tolerance — her mother's death had made her grow up fast. 'Yes,' she said. 'He's the schools' art advisor for the county. He asked my 'A' level group if we'd like to do an original work to auction for charity. I think I told you at the time, Dad,' she said with an arch look, 'but you probably had your mind on other things.'

He gave a regretful nod of acknowledgement.

'We made a communal sculpture on the theme of courage in the face of death. It fetched over a thousand pounds at auction. Proceeds going to his wife's favourite charity. It's been fantastic fun for all of us. And not just in the pub!'

Swift closed his eyes in shame. 'And I'm a bloody detective.'

'Yeah, Dad.' She gave him a gentle dig in the ribs. 'But not with your nearest and dearest. Thank God.'

★   ★   ★

Early the next morning the body of a woman was found in her car parked beside the Cow and Calf rocks on Ilkley Moor. On the passenger seat were an empty bottle of paracetamol and a half empty bottle of Laphroaig.

In Swift's morning post there was a letter with a local postmark, posted the day before at 7.30 p.m. It was handwritten in a shaky, sprawling script. There was no address or date.

For the attention of Chief Inspector Swift

Dear Sir,
I hereby confess to the murder of Josie Haygarth, and I will put my signature at the end of this letter so that this document is binding and legal.

I know what I am going to do is cowardly and selfish, but I can't live with what I have done and that Jamie should know of it. It is like a big black weight pressing down on me. I know my death will specially hurt Diana and I hope she will still think of me with love when you give her this letter to read. She is the best daughter I could ever have wished for. I killed Josie because I wanted to save my family. I was angry and wicked and cruel, but at the time I believed I was doing the right thing and I told myself I was not guilty of a crime, even though I had taken a life.

Please ask Diana and Jamie and Josie's family to forgive me. (Clive will no doubt take comfort from his latest lady friend.)

Yours faithfully
Marjorie (known as Cassandra) Parker.

Swift sat at his desk staring at the letter. Sue came to stand beside him. 'The dead woman on Ilkley Moor is confirmed as Cassandra Parker,' she said. 'She'd left identification details in the car's locker with a request that Diana Redmond be informed. Diana's going to the mortuary now to make a formal identification.'

Swift didn't say anything for a moment. He handed Sue the letter. She read it through carefully and then handed it back. 'Poor deluded woman. Will you show this to Diana, sir?'

'I think I should, don't you?'

'Yes.'

He folded the letter and put it back in the envelope. 'So our case is concluded. We know the identity of our killer and we have a signed confession. We should be pleased. Despite all the mess and the meaningless waste of life.'

'It is a result — of sorts,' Sue said gently.

'Yes, indeed.' He looked up at his sergeant. 'How is the baby doing, Sue?'

She smiled and put her hand over her stomach. 'Fine. A new life beginning, isn't that amazing?'

'Yes, it is,' he said, getting to his feet and picking up the letter. 'It's the best thing we've got.'